FALL OF ANGELS

BOOK THREE

BY

KEARY TAYLOR

First Paperback Edition: November 2011

Taylor, Keary, 1987-
Vindicated (Fall of Angels) : a novel / by Keary Taylor. – 1st ed.

Summary: Time is ticking for Alex and Jessica must find a way to save him before he's
pulled back into the world of the dead. But saving Alex will require asking help from
Cole and returning to the place Alex saved her from.

ISBN 978-1467909471

CHAPTER ONE

The world fell still as I watched the feather drop to the deck. It spun in a perfect circle just once before landing on the wooden surface.

There should be nothing in this world more innocent looking than a feather.

But in that single feather I remembered everything that was wrong with my life. There were so many panic-filled, sleepless nights. Endless nightmares that plagued me every time I slept. The dark eyes that bore into mine before I was branded. Realizing who Cole Emerson truly was and what he wanted from me. The snapping sound of Alex's neck giving under Cole's hand and the way Alex's dead body cooled in my arms. I remembered looking into Cole's cold black eyes, framed with swollen black veins, before he returned to the afterlife. And knowing the same thing was going to happen to Alex.

And I remembered the first time I had shown Alex my scars, the way he leaned in and pressed his lips to my brand. There was the first time he told me he loved me. There were so many nights in my bed, my body wrapped up against his. Every touch, every kiss, every *I love you* flashed through my head.

All the things that were right in my world and everything that was wrong with it was summed up in that single feather as it settled on the deck.

In the world of angels, nothing is ever simple.

But the feeling inside of me was simple, it was real. My love for the man on one knee in front of me was real. This moment was real.

The sun created a glow around Alex's body as it continued to rise, barely breaking over the tree tops. He was radiant, perfect in every sense of the word.

"Yes," I whispered.

The smile that spread on Alex's face made one break on my own as he stood, reaching into his pocket. My eyes fixed on the small black box he pulled out, its surface covered in lint, large patches of the velvet completely rubbed off.

He lightly took my hand in his, his eyes watching my face the whole time. He paused for just a moment, an endless flood of memories washing through his eyes. All the hurt and all the joy we had experienced together was there. Alex's eyes seemed to glow though as a small smile spread on his lips again and he slid the ring I had been waiting the last six months for onto my finger.

"We may not have forever," Alex said as I looked up into his face. "But we've got to make this enough to last forever."

I bit my lower lip as I pressed my forehead to his, closing my eyes and breathing his scent in. Even through my eyelids, the entire world seemed to glow, just like everything inside of me was. "I love you, Alex."

"You know I love you," he said quietly.

"I do."

I felt it before I saw it, the smile that cracked on Alex's face. "I can't wait to hear you say those two words in a white dress." I couldn't help but let a small laugh escape my lips. "I've imagined it about a thousand times." As I opened my eyes to look at him, Alex's face grew more serious. "I hope you know that I've wanted this for... *so* long," he said, his voice full of longing and a hint of pain.

"I know you have," I breathed, squeezing his hand in mine. "It just wasn't the right time until now."

Alex's hand came to my cheek, his grey eyes burning into mine. "Thank you for understanding. I know nothing about these past few months has been easy for you."

"You appreciate something more when it was hard to get," I said with a small smile.

"Who said that?" Alex asked, a playful grin on his own now.

I chuckled and shrugged my shoulders as Alex's hand dropped from my face. "I have no idea. I may have just made it up."

Alex chuckled as well. "How about some breakfast?"

"French toast sounds great this morning," I said. "And it's Amber's favorite."

3

"French toast it is then," Alex said as he pressed a kiss to my forehead and headed back inside.

I watched him as he walked back into the house, the sunlight reflecting blindingly off the metallic surface of Alex's wings. As soon as he was out of view, I nudged the feather that had fallen from his wings toward the edge of the deck. Not realizing I was holding my breath, I pushed it over the edge, watching as the breeze picked it up and carried it out over the surface of the lake.

I saw it land in the water, the luminosity of it becoming saturated and dulled by the water. With a hard swallow, I turned my back to it and walked inside.

This was the first of how many lost feathers?

Amber staggered out of her room, her eyes squinted and her hair in a wild mess around her face. "Whatcha' making?" she asked with a croak.

"Your favorite," Alex answered as he started cracking eggs into a dish.

"See, this is why I put up with all your crazy angel crap," she said as she tried to run a hand through her tangled hair, and settled on a barstool. "You feed me."

Alex just chuckled as he pulled the milk out of the fridge. "Why don't you see if Caroline is awake yet, Jessica?"

"Sure," I said as I headed toward the stairs. I hoped he couldn't hear the way my heart quickened. There was something about Caroline that terrified me.

I knocked on the door to Alex's old bedroom and listened for a reply. From within I faintly heard a stifled cry and what sounded like scratching. "Caroline?" I called softly. "Can I come in?" When I didn't hear an answer, I pushed the door open.

She sat on what was my old double sized bed, rocking back and forth, a picture sitting in her lap. Tears slowly made their way down her scarred face. She was scratching at the skin on her left arm so furiously there was blood under her fingernails and more dripping down her arm.

"Caroline!" I said as I jumped across the room. I pulled her hand away from her bleeding arm, kneeling next to the bed. "Caroline, look at what you're doing."

She barely even glanced down at her arm before she looked back at the picture. She gave a sad sigh. A small smile spread on my lips as I looked down at the photo. It was a picture of Alex holding a basketball, wearing a red uniform and a huge grin. He was probably about sixteen.

"It was better that I wasn't in his life," her scratchy voice came out. "He's such a good man. He wouldn't have turned out that way if I'd been around."

"Maybe you wouldn't have turned out this way if you'd been around," I said as I continued to look at the picture.

Caroline chuckled as she looked up at me, her yellowed and dull looking eyes settling on mine. "You've got spunk, kid. You fight for what you want."

5

"I do now," I said quietly. Cole's words echoed through my head. *What are you willing to do to save him?* As I ushered Caroline up the stairs I knew the answer to that question.

Anything.

"Are you alright, Caroline?" Alex asked in alarm. I opened the coat closet and pulled the first-aid kit down from the top shelf.

"It's nothing," she said as she shook her head and sat down at the dining table.

I walked into the kitchen, wetting a few paper towels in the sink.

"How long until they notice?" Alex asked with a sly grin as he leaned into my side, his eyes glancing at the heavy ring on my finger.

I just smiled and walked over to the table without answering his question. Sliding a chair right next to her, I set to cleaning Caroline's arm off.

"Whoa, there," she suddenly said, grabbing my wrist. "What do we have here?"

"Apparently ten seconds," I said to Alex with a chuckle. He laughed too as he flipped more of the French toast.

"What?" Amber asked, her voice still groggy. At the same time the front door opened and in walked Rod.

"That's quite the rock," Caroline said, a slightly gross looking smile creeping on her cracked lips as she met my eyes. "Our boy did good."

6

"What?" both Amber and Rod said at the same time.

"He did it?" Amber asked, her voice hitching in excitement and awakness.

"Finally," Rod said as he rolled his eyes, a smile spreading on his face.

Alex walked to my side, wrapping an arm around my waist. "Yeah, yeah, we all know I took too long."

"*Way* too long," I teased as I pressed a kiss to his cheek.

"When did this happen?" Amber asked as she bounded over, jerking my hand toward her. "Why haven't you told me yet?"

"Relax," I chuckled. "It just happened less than ten minutes ago."

"I'm sorry," she suddenly blushed slightly. "Mornings don't make me very nice. Congratulations Jess." She pulled me into a hug.

"Still bleeding over here," Caroline said in her scratchy voice.

Amber and I both laughed and I sat back down to finish cleaning Caroline's self-inflicted wound.

There were so many things that weren't right in my small world. There was the never ending angel situation. My future mother-in-law obviously wasn't doing very well in getting clean. I couldn't help but think of Emily, how Cormack was now gone for good. She had said that everything would be alright earlier that day.

And in that moment, with everyone eating breakfast happily and talking over one another, I almost believed her. In that moment, I was happy.

"Sal?" I called as I walked through the front door later that day. There were piles in every corner, things strewn out on the counter, dishes piled in the sink. I could tell the housekeeper had not been by in a while. "Sal?"

I found her in her office, curled up in a big plush chair that was in the corner. Her knees were tucked up under her chin, her arms wrapped tightly around her legs. She looked anxious.

"Is everything okay, Sal?" I asked, my eyebrows furrowing together.

"I had a bad dream last night," she said as she stared vacantly at a spot on the wall.

"Do you want to talk about it?" I asked as I squatted next to the chair. I was careful not to touch her. She still didn't like physical contact.

"Roger was there," she said in a quivering voice. "His breath smelled so bad. He was hitting me again."

"Oh, Sal," I said as I felt my stomach sink. Sal's ex-husband was now serving a life-sentence for nearly killing Sal when he was drunk. Sal was the way she was because of Roger. "I'm so sorry. He's gone now though, remember? He can't hurt you anymore. They locked him away."

She squeezed her eyes closed, taking in a long breath. "I don't want to see him anymore."

"Have you been having other dreams about him?"

She nodded her head. "He was scary."

"Yes, he was," I said as I stood. "I have a surprise for you," I smiled as I said it, attempting to change the subject.

"Is it a new book?" she asked, her tone instantly lifting.

I shook my head, holding my hand out to her. Sal's face looked confused at first. Her eyes trailed from my shoulder, down my arms, and then finally resting on my finger.

"You're getting married?" she asked in an excited tone. I just nodded. "It's beautiful! And it matches your bracelet!"

I let my eyes take in the ring again. It was set with a marquee diamond, fixed in a wide band made of intricately carved vines, small diamonds set in the lacy pattern. I'd never seen anything like it. And it did match the bracelet Alex had given me on Valentine's, just days after we had met.

"When?" she asked as she let go of my hand.

"We haven't picked a date yet, but soon," I said, the smile on my face bitter sweet.

The cell phone that Alex had gotten me the day after we got back from England suddenly vibrated. I flipped it open, a text from Rita asking if I could come in for Austin that afternoon. The shift started in just over an hour.

"I have to go Sal," I said as I slid the phone back into my denim shorts. "I wanted to let you know though."

"Thank you," she said with a smile. Just as I was about to walk out the door she called "Jessica?" I stopped, looking back at her. "Don't let them take him."

My blood suddenly chilled. "What did you say?"

"Hmm?" she asked, her eyes starting to glaze over.

"You said 'them'," I said quietly.

"Them who?" she asked, quietly, her eyes fixing on a place on the wall.

"Never mind," I said as I shook my head. Sal was in a different place now. "I'll see you later."

I went and changed, telling Alex that I was filling in for Austin. We made plans to go out that night, to try and work some details out. I agreed absentmindedly, heading out to my GTO and climbed inside.

Don't let them take him.

I knew they were already trying to take Alex. I had seen what had happened to Cole. His entire frame started collapsing in on him, like he was being sucked away from the inside out. Cole had said how the dead couldn't stay long in the land of the living. Cormack had told me how difficult it was to stay here.

I had seen the brief moments when Alex would close his eyes, how his knuckles would turn white as he held onto the edge of the counter. How something in his countenance seemed to quake and shiver.

Alex could be pulled back at any moment.

And somehow I had to stop it.

But I had no idea how I was going to keep the inevitable from happening.

CHAPTER TWO

The sky started to gray over as I spent my day inside the bookstore. There was little to do as it was a Tuesday afternoon and the sky threatened to open at any moment. The hours slowly ticked by until closing, the only excitement of the day was showing Rita the ring and hearing her congratulations.

I tried not to think that there was the real possibility of telling her I was a widow so soon after the actual wedding.

After my shift ended, rain started to drizzle as I pulled into the parking lot of the restaurant. Alex's black truck was already dotted with drops. I stepped inside the door, my eyes immediately finding him. He would be hard to miss. Everyone in the entrance was staring at him. Ignoring them, he gave me his dazzling smile and indicated to the hostess that we were ready to be seated.

"I always feel so weird going out like this," I chuckled as I sat across from Alex, picking up the menu the woman had set in front of me. "You don't eat at all and I only eat when you make me."

"Forgive me for pretending to be normal," he gave me a half smile. He was doing a better job than me at pretending half the restaurant wasn't staring.

"It feels like I can hardly even remember what that is anymore," I said with a sigh. "Normal." Alex reached across the table and took my hand in his. As I looked into his gray eyes, I felt my throat tighten. They were just one more reminder that he wasn't supposed to be here anymore.

"What made you change your mind?" I asked quietly. "You were so determined before."

He gave me one more small smile before letting go of my hand and leaning back in his chair. "It was Caroline actually. We talked while you were with Cole. And I just kept thinking about how it would have been better if she had been a part of my life, even if it was just for a little while. A little while would have been better than nothing at all.

"I'm ready to move on, Jessica," he said as his eyes burned with intensity. "I'm sorry it has taken me so long."

"I understood your reasoning," I said as my eyes dropped to the surface of the table. Alex's hand was suddenly under my chin, lifting it until I looked at him again.

"Moving on?" he breathed, so much weight behind his voice.

"Moving on," I said, pushing the knot from my stomach. We both sat back as our waitress introduced herself and brought water. I ordered a bowl of soup and a salad, Alex ordered the most expensive steak on the menu.

"You money waster," I teased him as soon as the waitress was gone.

"Hey, it sounded good," he said in mock defense. "If I can't eat it I can at least look at it, right?"

I just chuckled and shook my head. "If you like torturing yourself, I guess."

We were quite for a moment, Alex studying my face. "Don't get mad when I bring this up, okay?" Alex said, his eyes softening.

"What?"

"I know how things were between you and your parents but we need to tell them about the engagement. In person. Especially your mom."

My eyes dropped to the table, my hand rubbing the brand on the back of my neck without thinking about it. "I don't know if that is a good idea."

"She's your mother, Jessica," he said in a low voice. "I know she hurt you in the past but it's time to let that past go. You haven't talked to her in how long?"

"Five years," I answered quietly, recalling the day I overheard her talking to the mental institution, the day she decided to have me committed.

"I want to meet her. I can't be married to someone and never meet my own mother-in-law."

"Alex, she…"

"We're moving on, remember?" he cut me off.

"Moving on," I said quietly. If Alex could forgive his mother, who had abandoned him completely for his entire life, couldn't I forgive the woman who had raised me? She had been there for me, for everything else in my life. She'd just been trying to help me.

And really, who could blame her for the things she had done? I had thought I was crazy myself at times.

"Okay," I answered, looking Alex in the eye. "We'll go out to Ucon."

"Really?" he asked excitedly.

"We're moving on with life," I said, my insides all twisted up. "I have a few days off next week. I'll call my dad tonight and let him know we're coming."

"I can't wait," he said, giving me a sly smile. I just glared at him. "Hey, maybe it won't be as bad as you think it will be."

"I think it will be exactly as bad as I think it will be," I said sarcastically. "Anyway, we should probably talk to Amber and Rod about going out with us. Dad still hasn't met him and I don't think he was too happy with Amber for waiting so long to tell him she was already engaged."

"Not a bad idea," Alex said as he dug his cell phone out of his pocket. "I'll ask him about it right now."

I pulled my own out, and clumsily set to texting Amber.

I heard the clatter, the sound of someone tripping over a purse set on the floor, the sound of dishes flying off of their tray.

And the next second I felt the searing pain of the steak knife embedding itself into the fleshy space where my shoulder connected to the rest of my body.

It happened so fast, I didn't have time to react. Alex leapt across the table, pulling me into his arms, a look of horror filling his face. Just as I felt his body tense to flee before anyone could even see what had happened, I shook my head, grabbing the handle of the knife and yanked it out.

I barely contained the scream that threatened to rip from my body. Instead, I pushed Alex away, breathing out "Sit back down."

Confusion crossed his face but the next moment he was back in his seat, across the table from me.

A total of less than two seconds had probably passed.

My entire front was covered in the scalding hot soup as the waitress landed on her hands and knees, her feet still tangled in the straps of the purse. A dozen pairs of eyes turned in our direction as the room fell silent. I realized then that the knife was still clenched in my right hand. I hoped no one noticed as I dropped it into my lap.

"Oh my…" the waitress started to apologize as she scrambled to get to her feet. "I am so, so sorry! Are you alright?!"

I looked across the table to Alex, who stared wide-eyed at the already disappeared cut in my exposed flesh.

"I'm…" I struggled for words. "I'm fine. I think we're going to go though. I kind of need to change."

16

Alex stood before she could even respond, grabbed my hand and was hauling me toward the front door. I glanced back just once, meeting the eyes of nearly every person in the restaurant.

Alex opened the passenger door to the truck, and picking me up around the waist, not so gently sat me on the seat before closing the door. He stalked around the front, shaking his head as his brow furrowed. He pulled the driver's door open and slid in next to me.

He turned those gray eyes on me, his stare not quite cold, but definitely not lovingly.

"What. Happened. In there?" he said slowly but deliberately.

I struggled with what to say, my mind racing over everything.

I had never told Alex about how Cole had tested his theory. The theory that I was stuck, that I was neither fully dead, nor fully alive. That I could never move on to the afterlife. The afterlife Alex was soon going to be pulled into.

"You'd better say something Jessica, because I'm freaking out over here if you haven't noticed!"

"Okay, okay!" I half shouted, closing my eyes for just a moment to collect myself. "You know there's something different about me, more different than before you... died. You've seen how I can do things I shouldn't be able to. When Cole and I talked, he told me some things. What you saw back there, that's just the beginning of it."

And then I told him. The full story of what had happened that week I spent with Cole in his abandoned, ruined mansion.

I told him how I hadn't changed at all since he had died. I hadn't aged one second. Alex had already seen some of the evidence of my apparent indestructability. I'd survived the car crash with Austin, I'd survived Cole's own knife, in a much deadlier place.

I confirmed what Alex had already suspected. That I was already eighty percent the same as he was: an angel.

But I couldn't bring myself to tell him about the never moving on part. Admitting that I couldn't die was more than I could handle.

As I finished, I leaned back in the seat, my eyes never leaving Alex's face. He sat there silent for what felt like a very long time.

"Okay," he said quietly.

"Okay?" I finally breathed. I hadn't realized that I had been holding my breath.

"Okay," he said, nodding his head. He reached across the middle seat and took my hand in his. "Let's move on."

I just smiled. "Well, if you're really okay, I think I'm going to get off your seat before I ruin it with all the gunk on me."

Alex cracked a smile, his eyes slightly glazed-over looking. His mind was obviously still on all the secrets I had just spilled.

"Are you going to be okay to drive home?" I asked doubtfully.

"Yeah," he answered, shaking his head. His eyes snapped to my face, his expression clearing. "Yeah, I'll see you at home in a minute."

"'K," I chuckled, pressing a kiss to his cheek before hopping down from the truck.

I didn't think to check my phone for Amber's reply to my text until I got back to the house and found it empty. She had replied "*if I have to*" to my suggestion to return to Idaho and with another text that she and Rod were going apartment hunting that night and that they'd be back pretty late.

After changing into clean clothes, I settled into the swing on the lower back deck and held the phone in my slightly shaking hands. Slowly, pushing each button very deliberately, I dialed my dad's cell phone number.

"Hello?" he answered after only two very short feeling rings.

"Hi," I said simply, my mind suddenly blanking.

"Who's this?" he asked.

"It's me, Dad, Jessica."

"Hey kid!" he replied excitedly. I couldn't help but smile. "I didn't recognize this number."

"Yeah, it's my new cell phone."

"Is everything okay?" he asked. "You don't exactly call often."

19

"I'm sorry, I know I promised I would call more. I was just wondering if you were busy next weekend?"

"Why? What's up?" his voice was hesitant.

"Um, Alex and I were kind of thinking about coming out there."

There was silence for nearly thirty seconds. "Dad? You still there?"

"Yeah, I'm here. Of course," he recovered. "I'd love to see you again. But, Jess, are you sure about this? I mean, your mom's going to be here."

"I know," I said quietly. A faint breeze picked up off the water sending goosebumps flashing across my skin. "Like you said, she's still my mom, and I hope I'm still her daughter. I think it's time to move on."

My dad was quiet again for a moment and even through the phone I could sense the emotion he was feeling. I felt the back of my own throat tighten. "Yeah, it is," my dad said with a scratchy voice.

"Let Mom know, will you? I don't want this to be a total shocker to her when I show up at the house."

"Okay."

"Oh yeah, I think we're bringing Amber and Rod with us."

"Wow, it's like Christmas came in September!" he chuckled. "Getting both of my girls back home."

"I'll see you soon, 'k, Dad?"

"Alright, I love you kid."

"Love you too, Dad."

Just as I hung up the phone, the door to my apartment opened and Alex stepped out. He stood there in the warm late summer air in just a pair of basketball shorts, his flawless skin glowing in the moonlight.

There was nothing quite like the sight of Alex shirtless.

"How'd it go?" he asked quietly through the dim light.

"Fine," I said as I patted the space next to me. "Dad's expecting us. I told him to give my mom fair warning."

Alex chuckled as he sank into the space next to me. I leaned into him, he wrapped his arm around my shoulders, and I closed my eyes and breathed his familiar scent in.

"How about October third?" he said quietly as he rested his cheek on the top of my head.

"October third?" I asked, unsure of what he was talking about.

"The wedding. How about October third?"

My heart picked up in pace, butterflies suddenly filling my stomach. "That's like, three weeks away." Alex nodded. "Why that day?"

"It was my grandparent's anniversary," Alex said as he laced his fingers with mine. "I've never seen two people more in love than them. It must be a lucky day."

"We don't need luck," I said quietly. "I love you more than anything. It will be perfect. However much time we have."

Alex didn't say anything, just pressed a kiss to the top of my head.

"Amber is going to be ticked we're getting married before her," I chuckled. I was trying to play it cool but inside I was jumping up and down clapping my hands in excitement.

Just then I heard the sound of tires pulling into the driveway. "Speak of the devil," I said. A few moments later we heard the sound of the front door opening and closing.

"Jessica?" I heard Amber call from inside.

"Out here!" I shouted just loud enough for her to hear me.

A few moments later Rod and Amber walked out onto the lower deck, hand in hand. Rod's dark features were nearly lost in the diminished light.

"We found it!" Amber said excitedly. She was practically bouncing up and down. Rod just smiled and shook his head at her. "We found the perfect apartment. It's right on Chuckanut Drive and it look out right over the ocean. It's amazing, Jessica! You have to see it!"

"Did you already submit an application for it?" Alex asked.

"We've already got keys, man," Rod said with his own smile as he held them up, jangling them in the air.

"I'm moving in tomorrow after we go furniture shopping!" Now she really was jumping up and down.

"You're moving out?" I asked, my voice sounding downfallen. "Already?"

She nodded. "And Rod will be moving in after the wedding. He still has a few months left on his contract in his old apartment anyway."

"Congratulations," I said as I smiled up at her.

"I know! I've never had my own apartment before! And you two will finally have the house back to yourselves," she said with a wink.

I glanced at Alex with a smile as he squeezed my shoulder and looked down at me.

"So," Rod said as he dragged two other chairs over towards us. They both sat. "Have you love birds set a date yet?"

"October third," Alex said, meeting Amber's eyes. Her eyes narrowed and Alex hurried on. "It was my grandparents' anniversary." Her eyes softened just a bit.

"Wow, and I thought we were going fast!" she laughed. "That's like three weeks away, right?"

"Yep," Alex said at the same time that I nodded.

"Well, congrats again you guys," Rod said as he took Amber's hand in his. "You two deserve it."

CHAPTER THREE

I woke the next morning and felt the still warm sheets next to me. As I glanced around the room, I saw Alex standing by the window, his hands braced against its frame.

I sat there watching him for a while. His wings were out, trailing down to the ground, the light reflecting off of them where it came through the slats of the blinds. His entire frame trembled slightly, all of the muscles in his body taught and strained. His breathing came in slow, labored draws.

Careful not to make any sounds, I slid off the bed and walked up behind him. I gently placed a hand on his arm. His eyes jumped to my face, a gasp filling his throat. He turned slightly, grabbing my forearms. His fingers gripped me so tightly my skin started turning white. His eyes squeezed closed, his breath continuing to come with labored effort.

"Stay with me, Alex," I said quietly, squeezing his forearms. "Concentrate on me. You aren't leaving me. Not now, not ever."

"I…" he gasped. He squeezed me harder. "I'm… not… leaving."

Very slowly, his body stopped shaking, his grip loosened. And then he collapsed to his hands and knees, half taking me down with him. I kneeled next to him, laying my hand on his back, fighting back the fear that wanted to consume me.

"It's getting stronger, isn't it?" I asked.

Alex only nodded.

"We're going to figure this out," I faked calm. "I'm not going to let them take you from me."

Alex didn't say anything, just nodded as he pulled himself to his feet. I stood as well, meeting his eyes, everything in me suddenly wishing they were still blue.

"Jessica?" Amber's voice floated down the stairs.

"Coming," I called back. I held Alex's eyes for another long moment before stepping out the door.

Somehow I had to figure out how to stop this. But how did you stop a dead man from joining the afterlife? It was going to take more than simply loving Alex to save him.

"I think I've got all my stuff packed," Amber said as I reached the top of the stairs. "Rod is coming over to help me load everything up."

"Wow, that was fast," I said as I raised my eyebrows at her.

Amber suddenly looked uncomfortable, her eyes flicking to the stairs.

"What?" I asked.

She looked to the stairs again. "It's just, well, Caroline kind of scares me. She's just..."

"Is that why you're so eager to leave?" I asked, feeling my stomach sicken.

"Well, it's part of it I guess. I just, don't really trust having her in the house," she said, twisting her fingers around each other. I could tell she felt bad for telling me this. And the thing was that I couldn't blame her for feeling that way. Caroline made me uneasy too.

"It's just until she can get clean and then we will help her find her own place, help her find a job."

Amber nodded, a sad little smile twisting in the corner of her lips. "I hope so. It's really sad she was never a part of Alex's life. He's such a nice guy."

"Yeah," I agreed, a pang in my chest forming. "Yeah, it's too bad she missed out."

The door opened and in walked Emily and Rod.

"Okay, he had better be lying about there being a ring on your finger," Emily said as she stopped in the entryway, crossing her arms over her chest. "Or you're in some serious trouble."

I just chuckled and held up my hand, wiggling my fingers. "I guess I'm in trouble," I said sheepishly.

"Oh my gosh!" she squealed as she bounded across the room to me, throwing her arms around my shoulders. "Congratulations!"

"So... you're not mad?" I asked as I hugged her back.

26

"Well, maybe a little, but whatever," she said as she took a step away from me, taking my hand in hers and inspecting the ring. "Dang girl. Spoiled much?" She chuckled and stepped away from me, resting her hands on her hips. "At least now you won't go back to being all moppy."

"Thanks for reminding me of that," I rolled my eyes at her. I watched as Amber and Rod started carrying boxes outside.

"And I'm going to be your maid of honor, right?" she said, wiggling her eyebrows at me.

I just chuckled and shook my head, "Is there a chance you won't murder me if I didn't ask you to be?"

I didn't think about what I was saying until it was too late. Emily's face blanched, her eyes growing big. I instantly felt terrible, wishing I could take back my words.

Emily's eyes narrowed and she shook her head at me. "You," she said as a smile slow formed on her face. "Not funny."

"Sorry," I said with a chuckle as I followed her into the kitchen. "Of course you're going to be my maid of honor." She grabbed an orange from off the counter and started peeling it. Amber called a quick good-bye and then she and Rod were gone.

"Anyway, I just wanted to let you know that I saw Alex's mom creeping around a pretty shady part of Bellingham last night. I was on my way back from the homeless shelter when I saw her. I thought you should know, what with trying to get her clean and whatnot."

"Serious?" I said with a downfallen sigh. "Crap."

"Lots of crap," she said as she bit into a juicy slice.

"Hey, Jessica," Alex said from the stairs. His face looked all too serious. "Can I talk to you for a second?"

I glanced back at Emily. "Go for it, I've got to get going actually. I just thought you should know."

"'K, thanks for telling me," I said as I walked her to the door. As I watched her go, I was amazed at how cheery she was considering it had been just over twenty-four hours since Cormack had gone back to the afterlife. She had taken his advice to heart though. She was already setting up volunteer work to try and redeem herself.

"What's wrong?" I asked as I turned back to face Alex.

He held up a long and quite disgusting looking needle with a piece of toilet paper. "I found this in Caroline's bedroom. I heard her leave the house around midnight last night."

"That's the reason Emily came over. She said she saw her last night in a part of town she shouldn't have been in."

Alex's face fell, his shoulders slumping. "I'm so sorry," I said as I put my arms around him.

"I was stupid for thinking I could get her to clean up on my own," he said as he laid his cheek on the top of my head. "I should have just checked her into rehab the second we got home."

"You've been doing the best you can. And it's not too late. We could still try and get her some help."

"As long as we can find her," Alex said as he stepped away from me. I then noticed he had changed into his work clothes. He sighed again as he grabbed his truck keys from off the hook by the door. "Well, I've got to go to the rental house. All the trim is supposed to be delivered in about an hour."

"Okay," I said as I laid a hand on his arm and pressed a quick kiss to his lips. "Are you okay? You seem really down. Especially considering you just got engaged."

He gave a half smile, his eyes still sad. "I just want everything to be perfect. This just isn't how I had hoped everything would happen."

"As long as there's you and there's me, it is perfect," I said as I held his eyes. "That's the only part that matters."

"You're right," he said, pressing a kiss to my lips again. "That's all that matters. I'll call you in a bit, okay?"

"Alright, have fun," I chuckled and closed the door after him.

I found one of the dozens of bridal magazines Amber had left behind and took it out with me onto the upper back deck. Still in my pajamas, I settled onto one of the reclining chairs. I had flipped through a dozen pages before I noticed him. A man with shoulder length hair, perfect complexion, and dark eyes, watching me.

And he was standing on Cole's back deck.

My heart leapt into my throat and I nearly fell off my chair as I sat up straighter. But by the time I righted myself and looked back again, the man was gone.

Cole's house had sat empty and untouched since he had killed Alex. It had never been sold or placed on the market. There shouldn't be anyone creeping around it.

I'd changed into some denim shorts, pulled on shoes, and was walking down the street in less than sixty seconds. My palms felt sweaty and my stomach was in knots. My heart threatened to hammer out of my chest as I stood in front of Cole's front door. Pressing my lips into a tight line, I knocked three times.

I wasn't sure if I was relieved or not when no one came to the door. Very quietly, I turned the doorknob and cracked the door open. "Hello?" I called.

When no one replied, I stepped inside. The house smelled stale, abandoned for too long. After checking the main floor, I determined there was no one inside. I found the deck clear too.

Maybe I was seeing things.

But the feeling of fear and dread settled into my stomach, a feeling I was far too familiar with. I closed the door behind me, trying to shake it, and walked to Sal's house. I found her lying in her bed, her sheet pulled around her head.

"Are you alright?" I asked as I sat on the bed next to her.

She just shook her head. "I'm tired. I didn't sleep last night. I didn't want to see Roger."

"Oh, Sal," I said, my heart aching. "I'm so sorry. Is there anything I can do to help?"

She just shook her head.

"Do you want me to make an appointment with your doctor? Maybe she could help."

Sal shook her head again. I sat there silently, unsure of what to do or say. "Sal," I said cautiously. "You haven't seen a new neighbor have you?"

"No, just Alex's scary mom."

I chuckled, feeling the shift in Sal's mood. "I'm hungry," she pronounced, climbing out of her bed suddenly. I followed her up the stairs into her kitchen. She proceeded to pull out the makings for a BLT.

"Do you want one?" Sal offered.

"That's okay," I refused politely. "I've got some errands I have to do. Do you want me to get you anything at the store?"

"Umm, some socks, and a jar of honey."

"Alright," I said as I walked to the door. "I'll see you tomorrow, Sal."

The knot in my stomach wouldn't release as I closed her door behind me and started back home. I couldn't help but look over my shoulder.

X

Blackness wrapped around me like the coldest blanket that ever existed. I groped around me, searching for a surface to orient myself, but there was nothing. Wherever I was, it felt empty and void of anything.

Jessica, a voice whispered through the dark.

I whipped my head around, my eyes searching wildly for the source of the voice.

Jessica.

"Who's there?" I demanded.

They're watching you.

That time the voice was unmistakable.

"Cole?"

They know something's wrong. Four times now they should have had you before them and yet they haven't.

"What are you talking about?" My heart was hammering in my chest. My eyes searched wildly through the dark, seeking Cole's familiar face.

Don't let them see for themselves what has happened to you, Cole's butter smooth voice said through the dark. I suddenly sensed a presence next to me in the dark. *It is the only advantage you have against them to save him.*

"To save Alex?" I repeated quietly.

You must be more careful. They will try to take everything from you.

"What am I supposed to do?" I asked, panic rising in my throat, threatening to claw me from the inside out. "How do I stop them from taking Alex?"

The air suddenly seemed to be shifting, growing warmer by the second. The ground beneath me started to vibrate.

"Cole?" I said, my voice panicked. "How do I stop them?!"

They are watching you.

CHAPTER FIVE

"Cole!" I gasped, sitting straight up in my bed.

"Whoa!" Alex jumped next to me in the bed. "Jessica, it's just me. Cole's gone, remember?"

I placed a hand over my eyes, trying to catch my breath. My heart was still racing. I forced my breathing to slow.

"You want to talk about it?" Alex asked, placing a hand on my arm.

I let my hand drop to my lap, blinking my eyes hard to try and clear the sleep from my head. "No," I lied. I shook my head. "It was just..."

"A nightmare," he said quietly. "It's okay. You've seen enough in your life to still have them every once in a while."

"Sorry," I whispered, resting my chin on my shoulder, not quite looking him in the eye. For some reason I didn't want to tell Alex what I had just dreamt about.

"Don't apologize," he said as he leaned forward and kissed my forehead.

I gave him a sheepish smile, slumping back against my pillow. "Still no traces of your mom?"

Alex shook his head, his lips tightening. "No, and I looked everywhere I could think yesterday. She doesn't seem to want to be found."

The house felt oddly silent as I extended my senses. I then remembered that Amber was gone. "So…" I dragged out the word. "We have the house to ourselves again?"

A crooked smile worked its way onto Alex's face as he looked down at me. He shifted his body on top of mine, his lips greeting mine. I traced my hands down his back, enjoying every rise and fall of his frame, my fingers brushing against his raised scars.

One of Alex's hands slipped behind my back, nearly lifting me off the bed as he pulled me closer to him. His lips trailed down to my throat, his other hand working its way down my stomach, and then slipping down my thigh.

"Three weeks and you're *mine*," he said in a rough voice against my skin.

"I'm yours already," I sighed, my eyes closed.

"*All* mine," he said quietly as his lips moved further down my chest.

"Hey, now," I said as I fought everything my body was telling me. "We've made it this long. Let's not blow this streak just weeks from the big day."

Alex let out a growl, pressing his lips one more time to the skin at the edge of the neckline of my tank top. "*Soon*," he growled.

"Finally," I said in mock exasperation.

"Hey, now," he repeated, raising an eyebrow at me as he propped himself up on his forearms. I just chuckled. "So," he moved on. "I've got an idea."

"Oh, yeah?"

"Uh huh," he nodded, a smile starting to spread again. "Now that we have the house to ourselves, and we're going to be inhabiting it as a married couple soon, I thought maybe it was time to act like real grown-ups and move into the master bedroom."

I glanced around my current bedroom, memories attached to every corner of it. The basement apartment had been a solace for me. When my life was at one of its lowest points, I had felt protected within these walls.

"Moving on?" I said quietly as I lifted my head from the pillow and pressed a kiss to Alex's lips.

"Moving on," he repeated, giving me a soft smile.

"And if Caroline ever comes back, she could use the apartment," I said as Alex rolled off of me and stood. I couldn't help but smile as I took in his half naked form.

"*If* Caroline ever comes back, she's going straight to rehab," he said in an exasperated tone.

I actually felt excited as we started moving things around, clearing out the few things Amber had left behind, switching the mattresses, boxing up my things and carrying them up. I had been waiting to move on with Alex for so long, and now it was finally happening. I had the ring, and even though we had been living together since basically the first day we met, it actually felt like we were making the *choice* to do so.

As Alex started taking all of my clothes out of my dresser he held something up against him, a smirk crossing his lips. "What do we have here?"

"That," I said as I snatched the black lace out of his hands, my face blushing instantly. "Is for the honeymoon." Butterflies filled my stomach.

"And this one?" he said as he pulled another red item out of the drawer.

"Okay, I think it's time I took over the dresser!" I said as I walked over and pushed him away from it, grabbing the red lace from his hand.

"You haven't been shopping since I proposed," he teased as he leaned against the doorframe with his arms crossed over his chest. "Were you preparing for something else? You dirty, dirty girl."

"Out!" I yelled with a laugh, chucking a pair of underwear at him.

"And now she's throwing panties at me," he said in mock shock, dodging the blue fabric. "Where does she draw the line?"

I just shook my head as he winked at me and grabbed a box off of the floor, and headed upstairs with it.

Well that was embarrassing.

"So where *do* you want to go on the honeymoon?" Alex asked, already walking back into the apartment.

"I guess I hadn't really thought about that part," I blurted before I even thought about it.

Alex just chuckled as he stood in the doorway. "And what part were you thinking about?"

"Shut up," I just chuckled as I finished emptying the dresser.

"I'm just saying," he shrugged his shoulders. "Anyway, we should probably book something soon considering that we're only a few weeks away."

"Wow," I said with a sigh as I leaned against the now empty dresser. "There's so much to do. I still have to get a dress, we've got to get a cake. All that stuff."

"Whatever you want," he said as he crossed the room and pulled me into his arms. I closed my eyes as I leaned into him, his familiar scent filling my senses. "I'll make it happen for you."

"I just want it simple I think," I said quietly. "Nothing fancy. Just us, Sal, Emily, Amber and Rod. Rita and Austin. Caroline if we can find her."

"And your parents."

"And my parents," I said with a sigh.

"You'll survive, I promise."

I swallowed hard, knowing that I could survive *anything* physically. "Let's just finish moving stuff. I'll deal with that when we get there."

It took surprisingly little time to move all of my things into the master bedroom considering that I had lived in this house for over two years now. It felt so strange to see all my things in the large bedroom, my personal things spread about the master bathroom. I felt so grown up all the sudden. Like I had a real life.

The next two days passed in a blur. Alex and I booked tickets to Costa Rica and a little house right on the beach for a full week. Alex decided he wanted to brave the wedding cake on his own. I couldn't complain, no one would do a better job.

I told Austin the news, and to my surprise he didn't get worked up about it. He had been happy for me. It was nice to see that he was losing interest in me.

Sal continued to get little sleep and I could only hope that she would not decline while I was gone to visit my parents. I let Emily know what to expect while she was taking care of her.

No sign of Caroline was found and I felt both angry and sorry as we packed to leave for Ucon. It was so unfair of her to leave Alex again, after everything he had done for her. She was just going to keep sinking deeper and deeper until she was gone. Until she stood before Cole.

With not a cloud in the sky, the four of us threw our bags into the back of Alex's truck and loaded in. Considering the fact that Alex no longer required sleep, he and I had decided to make the trip overnight. With no major airports close to Ucon it was easiest to drive.

I still wasn't looking forward to the thirteen hour drive. It only prolonged my dread.

"Have you talked to mom or dad since I told him we were coming?" I asked Amber as Alex pulled out of the driveway.

"No," she said with a sigh. "I think he's still pretty mad I didn't tell him sooner about the engagement."

"Sorry, babe," Rod said. "Guess I should have thought about it for two seconds and asked permission first or something."

"It's not too late," I said as I glanced over at Alex and raised my eyebrows at him.

He chuckled. "Okay, I got the hint. We'll do it together, Rod. He won't be able to shoot the both of us. I'm pretty sure I'm faster than you so you can be my shield when he pulls out the gun."

"Thanks, man. You're a great friend." The cab broke out into laughter. It felt good to finally laugh.

The sun started to set behind the trees as we drove south on I-5, casting the sky in a summer orange.

"I was thinking we could go dress shopping with Mom, maybe," Amber said quietly. "What do you think, Jess?"

"You're serious?" I asked, turning in my seat to look at her. I saw from her face that she was.

"Moving on, remember?" Alex said so quietly only my ears could pick up on his words.

I didn't say anything for a moment, looking at Amber's face blankly. "We'll see how things go."

"I'm thinking a big ball gown," Amber start to rattle on. I gave a few nods and *uh-huh's* to let her know I was half-listening as she continued to ramble. She was talking but I wasn't hearing her. All I could think about was the tone of my mother's voice as she told me over and over that the nightmares weren't real, that I needed to get over this phase.

My insides felt hollow.

As we neared one in the morning, Amber laid her head in Rod's lap, who had crashed not long after she started talking about wedding stuff, and fell asleep herself. I sighed as the truck became quiet, scooting to sit closer to Alex, and leaned my head on his shoulder.

"How you doing?" he asked quietly, placing his hand on my knee and giving it a squeeze.

"I'm kind of freaking out, but okay, I guess," I said.

"I'm really proud of you for doing this, you know. I know this isn't easy for you."

"It's not. She said some really terrible things to me. I wanted her to believe me but she didn't."

"Did..." he trailed off for a moment as he formed his thoughts. "Did she ever see your scars?"

I shook my head. "I don't think so. I was really young when it all started but I was obsessive about keeping them covered up."

"Maybe you should have shown them to her."

"Maybe," I whispered.

I barely saw the glint of the headlights on its eye before it jumped in front of the truck. A doe bounded across the road, pausing right in front of us. Alex slammed on the breaks, the truck skidding to a stop as the deer jumped into the brush on the other side of the freeway and into the open country.

As I watched it prance away, I saw him, long blond hair blowing as he stared back at me with dark eyes. Watching me from the side of the road.

"Alex," I whispered. As I blinked, he was gone.

"I saw him," Alex said in a low voice, his eyes staring at the place the man had been standing.

"He's..." I trailed off. Somehow Amber and Rod were both still asleep.

"One of us," Alex said quietly as he started the truck forward again.

I fought back the shaking that started in my hands. Cole's words flooded back to me.

They are watching you.

"Alex, I have something to tell you," I barely whispered.

"What?"

"You remember a few days ago, when I had the nightmare about Cole?" He nodded. "Cole was talking to me. I don't think it was just some dream. He said 'they are watching you'."

"Who's 'they'?"

"I think... I think it might be the council," I said with a shaky voice.

"Why you? What would they want from you?"

"I don't know," I lied. Cole's other words came back to me. *They know something's wrong. Four times now they should have had you before them and yet they haven't.* They were realizing their mistake.

"Is this about Cole?" Alex asked, his voice suddenly terrified sounding.

I shook my head. "I don't think so. They have Cole back."

I felt Alex's form relax slightly, a breath crossing his lips. "Maybe I can try and talk to him, see what he wants."

"Somehow I don't think that would be a good idea," I breathed. "They're already trying to take you back. Don't get any closer to them than you have to."

"I won't let them take me before the wedding, I promise," he said as he laced his fingers with mine and pressed a kiss to the back of my hand. "And I won't let them do anything to you either."

"I know," I said quietly. But something in me sensed that it was *me* who was going to have to start protecting *him*.

Sometime around three in the morning I finally fell asleep, slumped against Alex's side. By the time I woke up at seven, I found we were at a gas station and Alex said we were only just over an hour away. I also found a text from my dad, asking when we were going to be getting in.

Not long, I texted him back. *Please make sure you're home when we get there.*

I already am, he replied. *Relax. Things will be okay.*

Then why did I have the sickening feeling in my gut that they weren't?

Rod and Amber came back out of the store, gas station food piling out of a plastic bag. We all loaded back into the truck and got back on the highway.

"I got some Twinkies just for you, Alex," Rod said with a proud smile as he handed a handful up to Alex. I tried to hide the smile that cracked on my face as I suppressed a chuckle.

"Thanks for looking out for me," Alex said as he grabbed them.

"What about you, Jess?" Amber said as she peered into the contents of the bag. "We got doughnuts, soda, Twizzlers, and some Pop Tarts."

"We're eating healthy today!" I proclaimed, a slightly too fake sounding laugh bubbling out. "I guess I'll take some Dr. Pepper if you've got any."

Amber chuckled. "How did I guess that's what you'd want?" she said as she handed it up. "Hey, are you feeling okay? You're looking kinda' pasty. Well, pastier than usual."

"I'm fine," I lied as I swallowed hard. I didn't miss the way Alex's eyes flickered to my face. He knew better. He could probably hear the way my heart was racing.

As the miles flew by, my palms started sweating and I felt slightly light headed. "Breathe," Alex whispered. "Do you need me to pull over for a bit?"

I shook my head. It started spinning as the small towns started becoming familiar. I fought back bile as we passed the trucking yard, thought I might pass out as the familiar fields came into view. I was fighting a fully-fledged panic attack as we turned at the one convenience store in town and passed what was my grandmother's house before she passed away.

And then there it was, the female voice from the GPS announcing that we had arrived at our destination.

The same red brick walls greeted me, my mother's familiar flower beds bursting with color. The same lopsided apple tree stood in the corner of the yard, permanently injured by my soccer ball at the age of six. Everything about my childhood home looked exactly the same.

The front door opened as we came to a stop. Alex stepped out of the truck at the same time my dad came down the step. My hands shook so violently I couldn't get the door open at first.

"It's going to be okay, Jessica," Amber said quietly from the back, placing a hand on my shoulder. I just shook my head. My ears were ringing.

Alex walked around the front of the truck and opened the door for me, saving me from my fumbling. His gray eyes met mine and I tried to draw courage from them as I looked at him. My hands shook all the more as I slid my engagement ring off and tucked it into my pocket.

"Just until we talk to them," I said quietly. Alex just nodded and offered me his hand, and helped me down.

Then I finally saw her, my mother, standing on the small porch.

There was no moment of perfect reunion, of the two of us running into each other's arms and hugging, tears running down our faces. Instead, there was a long awkward moment of our eyes locking on each other, neither of us saying anything.

Dad crossed the yard, a bright smile on his face. He pulled me into his arms, giving me a tight squeeze.

"I've missed you, kid," he said. "She's probably just as nervous about this as you are," he added quietly.

"I doubt that," I let out a quivering breath.

"Alex," my dad said as he took a step away from me. He went to hold out his hand to shake Alex's, then seemed to change his mind and pulled him into a hug instead. "Good to see you."

"It's good to see you too, Dennis," Alex said as he met my eyes over Dad's shoulder. He gave me a small smile, bolstering my courage.

While Amber started the awkward introductions of my dad and Rod, my eyes found my mom again. She stared in much the same way everyone else did, like they couldn't quite comprehend the unnatural look of me. She finally gave me a small smile, took a step down off the porch, and started across the lawn.

My mom had always been a beautiful woman. Her hair was the same deep brown as mine but her curls were always perfectly tamed. Her eyes were wide and hazel like mine as well. But she had the perfectly shaped nose, perfect lips. I knew Amber would age gracefully over time for the fact that she could be my mother's clone.

"Jessica," she said in a soft voice as she stopped just a few paces away from me. She looked slightly bewildered as she took my face in, now that she was closer.

"Mom," I answered. I attempted a small half smile and gathering my courage, closed the space between us and wrapped my arms around her. I must have caught her off guard, considering the awkward way she put her arms around me. I tried not to shudder as her hands came to rest on my raised wings.

"It's good to see you."

I swallowed hard, fighting back my racing heart. "Yeah, it's… it's good to see you too."

She stepped away from me, giving a small smile, and turned to Alex who hung hesitantly back.

"You must be Alex," she said, hesitating for a moment as she took Alex's glorious being in, and finally holding out her hand.

"And you must be Claire," Alex said with his signature smile. He accepted my mother's hand.

My mind started fading out then, knowing I didn't have to pay attention to all the introductions. I'd survived the initial reunion, despite my doubts. Maybe I could handle the rest of the weekend.

All the gas station junk food had been unneeded, Dad had cooked one of his so called "famous" breakfasts. Piles of not quite cooked enough hash browns, scrambled eggs, the fattiest bacon he could find on the shelf at the store, and orange juice from frozen concentrate. At a time when I ate more than once every three days, this was my favorite breakfast.

We each helped ourselves to a plate, Rod and Dad's piled to the point of being overflowing. At my suggestion, we headed out to the back patio to eat. Alex could make his helpings disappear easier outdoors.

"So my youngest daughter is getting married," my dad said around a mouthful of food. "And my oldest has been living with her boyfriend since the day she met him."

"Our girls have gotten all grown up," my mom said in attempt to appear more casual. I didn't miss the sweat on her brow, and it wasn't due to the temperature.

"Hey, I'm about ninety-percent sure Jessica's still a virgin," Amber piped in, raising an eyebrow.

"And I'm about one-hundred-percent sure Alex is still one too," Rod picked up.

"Thanks for that Rod," Alex chuckled, looking down at the table in embarrassment and shook his head.

"Wow, Amber," I said as I set my fork down, and placed my face in my hands, elbows resting on the table.

"Too much information," my dad said as he squirmed. "But good job, Jessica." He patted my knee under the table.

"I can see Amber hasn't changed much these last few months," Mom shook her head, a half smile on her face.

"I'm still me," Amber said, flashing a bright smile and batting her eyes. The whole table chuckled.

The rest of the meal passed in a slightly awkward state. Thank goodness for Amber and her blabbing on and on about wedding stuff. No one else got the chance to say much. With the food cleared, Dad helped us carry in our bags.

"If the lot of you can behave yourselves," my dad said as we walked down the hall. "You're welcome to stay in your rooms. If you can't, there's the couch in the living room or the floor for you boys."

Alex and Rod both chuckled. "We promise to be on our best behavior, Mr. Bailey."

Amber and I's rooms were right next to each other. As Dad walked away to let us get settled in, I paused at the door. Just one more place that didn't have good memories.

"You're doing great," Alex whispered from behind as he shifted our bags around. "You'll survive this too."

And so I pushed the door open.

I could tell they hadn't left my room a museum to my memory. It was obvious this was meant to be a guest bedroom now. My old twin sized bed had been replaced with a queen, the walls changed from my former turquoise to a more neutral cream. But several of my pictures still hung on the wall, a reflection of the girl I didn't think I was any longer.

We stepped inside and Alex set the bags down on the floor at the foot of the bed. I closed the door behind me, leaning against it, reminding myself to breathe again.

"Hey," Alex said as he walked to me and wrapped his arms around my waist. "You made it."

"Yeah," I breathed as I leaned my head against his chest. "I did."

"So how long are we going to wait to tell your parents we aren't just a horny couple living together anymore?" Alex asked, using his natural ability to lift the mood.

I chuckled. "As long as it takes you to go and ask Dad's permission."

"I'll be right back then," he said in a low voice as he pressed a quick kiss to my lips.

"You're going to do it right now?" I asked, surprised.

"Why wait?"

"I thought you and Rod were going to do it together?" I asked as I raised an eyebrow at him.

"Rod can handle himself," Alex said before pressing one more quick kiss to my forehead and stepping outside.

It felt as if my insides were filled with butterflies. This was real. It was really happening.

After digging in my bag, I found a change of fresh clothes and made my way to the bathroom. As I passed Amber's room I heard her giggling and what sounded like it might be Rod growling. I just shook my head and smiled as I hurried to the bathroom.

Starting the hot water, I stripped down and turned my back to the mirror.

My flesh was so raised after the whole Cole incident that I had to be careful with what I wore. Something too thin and it wasn't difficult to see a pattern or flashes of metallic light in the sun.

It hadn't been easy keeping the scars hidden from my mom as a child. I became obsessed with keeping them covered up. I remembered having fights with her as I refused to wear certain shirts she had just bought me. Eventually as I grew to be an early teenager I think she came to appreciate what she assumed was modesty.

I attempted to pull a brush through my mane after I dried off from the shower and pulled on a pair of denim shorts and a sea green t-shirt. Staring in the mirror, I told myself I couldn't stay in the bathroom for the remainder of the trip. As if on cue, Amber started knocking on the door.

"Come on, Jess," she called. "You've been in there forever. There's a line forming out here."

Collecting my dirty clothes, I opened the door and stepped out.

"You okay?" she whispered as I met her eyes.

"Yeah," I said. She pulled me into her arms for a quick hug, gave me a small half smile and then went in the bathroom. As I put my clothes back in our room, I heard Alex and my dad laughing about something. Cautiously, I poked my head around the corner, half looking into the dining room and caught Alex's eye. He smiled at me and nodded. I stepped in the room, realizing my mother was sitting at the dining table too.

"So, did you have a nice conversation?" I said in attempt to divert the awkwardness that was trying to claw me to death from the inside.

A crack formed on my mother's lips. She stood and walked over to me, wrapping her arms around my shoulders.

"Congratulations, sweetie," she said. Her voice actually felt warm. "I'm so happy for you."

I reached into my pocket and pulled out the ring. "So I guess it's okay if I put this back on?"

Alex and my dad chuckled. My mom released me and pulled my hand into hers as I slipped it on.

"It's gorgeous," she fussed as she examined it. "And look, it matches your bracelet."

"He did pretty good," I said as I met Alex's eyes.

"I'll say," Mom said, pulling me into another quick hug. "So when's the date?" She stepped away and went to sit by my dad at the table again.

"October third," I said, my stomach filling with more butterflies as I said it.

"That's like, less than three weeks away now isn't it?" my mom said in shock, her eyes growing big and blinking rapidly.

I just nodded. "Neither of us wanted to wait long," Alex chimed in. I walked to his side and sat in the chair beside him. He took my hand in his, rubbing soothing circles into the back of mine.

"Good for you," my dad said, his eyes slightly narrowed as if he was thinking about something serious. My dad didn't know what Alex was now but he did know that there was a whole lot more to the angel thing than he once thought. I wondered if he suspected what the truth was behind the gun-shot wedding.

"Where are you having the ceremony?" my mom asked. Her voice was slightly tight sounding.

"We haven't picked an official venue yet," Alex answered, looking down at me. We really hadn't talked about it at all yet. There hadn't been much time.

"It will be in Washington though," I said quietly, meeting my parent's eyes. I felt relieved when they both just nodded.

"I'll have my secretary clear my schedule for a few days around then," Dad said, winking at me. I just smiled back at him.

Just then, Amber and Rod walked into the room, Amber's hair still dripping slightly from the shower.

"I thought we were doing this thing together, man," Rod said in mock hurt as he narrowed his eyes.

"Time to grow up," Alex teased. "You're on your own with this thing."

Rod just shook his head. "That hurts, Alex. That really hurts."

The room erupted in laughter. It felt good to relieve some of the tension.

"So, Mr. Bailey," Rod said as everyone quieted. "I really love this daughter of yours and I plan on being around until she gets sick of me and even after she gets sick of me. Can I have your permission to marry her?"

My dad stretched out his hand to Rod. "Welcome to the family," he said as they clasped hands.

Out of the corner of my eye I saw a flash of movement through the glass back doors. But as soon as I looked, it was gone.

"Did you see that?" I barely breathed, only Alex's ears keen enough to pick up on my words.

"I saw something," he said back.

"Jessica?"

I realized then that everyone in the room was looking at me expectantly. I must have missed a question.

"Sorry," I said, trying to snap my attention back into the room. "What did you say?"

"I suggested we throw an engagement party tomorrow for you and Amber. You two could invite all your friends out."

I hoped my face didn't fall at his suggestion. I didn't have any friends here. "Sure dad, that sounds great."

CHAPTER SIX

Four hours later, I sat in the back seat of my mother's car, listening as she and Amber talked non-stop about wedding-related things. I felt overwhelmed as I half listened to everything that was involved. Dresses, cakes, decorations, flowers, invitations. It all made my stomach knot. I didn't have the energy to join in the discussion. I just stared out the window, watching the familiar scenery flash by.

There were only two wedding dress shops in Idaho Falls. As I stepped inside, the area smelling of brand new fabric and French vanilla candles, I took in the rows and rows of white, billowy fabric, the mannequin's, the veils, and the shoes. And then I realized my grave mistake in agreeing to this outing. Nearly every dress was sleeveless; nearly everything would leave my scars exposed.

A plump, friendly woman greeted us as we entered and in a whirlwind, set to guiding us through the racks of white dresses.

"Are you feeling alright?" Mom asked as we followed the woman. "You're awfully pale."

I shook my head. "I'm feeling kind of queasy actually. Maybe I'll just help Amber and watch?"

She gave me a concerned look, almost like she didn't quite believe me, and then slowly nodded. "Alright."

We browsed through racks and racks of dresses. The sales woman talked about different types of material, different waistlines, different beading and embellishments. It all started to sound like gibberish to me. Everything Amber pulled to try on was a huge ball gown with ornate tops and a hefty price tag. It was a good thing Rod's pockets went deep because I knew my parent's didn't run that deep.

I ran my fingers over the fabric as we I waited for Amber to try the next dress on. A small bit of sadness settled into the pit of my stomach. I had no idea what kind of dress I wanted. I hadn't allowed myself to think about it. And there was nearly nothing I could wear that wouldn't scream the truth of my life to everyone in attendance.

Then I saw the off-white colored lace, the sweet-heart neckline, the bronze sash, sitting at the end of the rack, pushed up against the wall. I traced my fingers along the eyelets, the waves of fabric that brushed the floor. I ran my finger along the ridge of the totally strapless-ness of the neckline.

It was perfect.

But I could never wear it.

"What do you think?" Amber said from behind me, pulling me out of my haze of self-pity. I gave her a small smile, watching as she turned in a full circle.

"You look beautiful."

Amber tried on dress after dress. And in between each of them, while the lady who worked the shop helped Amber get dressed, my mother and I sat in awkward silence.

We may not have been fighting but the wounds of the past weren't getting healed today.

As I suspected, we walked out of the shop without anything, Amber as indecisive as ever. I felt a hollow spot in my stomach again as I eyed the lacy dress one more time before we left.

X

"So you made it through the day," Alex whispered as we crawled into bed that night.

"Somehow," I said as I nestled up against him. "I'm completely exhausted though."

"How was the dress shopping?" he asked as he ran his fingers along my upper arm. My skin flashed with goosebumps.

I sighed, feeling my stomach clench up again. "I didn't even try anything on. Nothing would have covered the scars."

He was quiet for a moment, considering what I had said. "Maybe you shouldn't cover them up. They're a part of you and everyone that is coming should be able to accept that."

I shook my head. "No way. That would be a disaster."

He didn't reply, just dipped his head, pressing his lips to my bare shoulder. He worked his way down my arm, his hands coming to the hem of my tank top and lifting it, exposing my stomach. His lips trailed to my bellybutton, his hands slipping down my thigh.

"So I have an idea," he breathed against my skin.

"I have a few ideas right now myself," I sighed as I ran a hand through his short sandy hair.

He chuckled. "When we get back home," he said as he spread his kisses to my sides, lingering for a moment, then returning to center. "We should stay in separate bedrooms until the wedding."

"Why?" I asked, my nose scrunching up.

"One," he said as he worked his way higher. "Because if we have many more nights like this we aren't going to make it to the wedding."

He was right there.

"And two, it will make it all the better come the wedding night."

I considered it, while hormones rushed through my body. "This is a really bad, good idea."

He laughed again, sliding up my body until his lips met mine. "Agreed."

A knock at the door sent my heart into my throat and Alex to the other side of the bed in a fraction of a second. A moment later my dad poked his head inside. "Just wanted to say good-night."

"Night, Dad," I said as I pressed my lips in a tight line, trying to hold a half-scream, half-laugh back.

"Good-night, Dennis," Alex said, his voice perfectly calm.

My dad looked at us a second longer, and then a sly smile crossed his lips before he closed the door. Two seconds later we heard another knock and the sound of springs squeaking as Amber and Rod jumped apart.

I couldn't hold my laugh back as I heard my dad awkwardly tell Amber and Rod good-night.

"Oh my gosh. I can't believe I almost got walked in on by my dad," I laughed quietly. "I *never* thought that would happen."

"I kinda' like getting you into trouble," Alex said as he stared up at the ceiling, reaching over and pulling at the waistband of my shorts with one finger, snapping it against my skin.

"Yeah, I don't think sleeping in the same bed is going to be an option much longer," I breathed as I rested my arms above my head. "You don't even sleep anymore. What are you going to do all night?"

"Good question," he said, his voice filled with wondering.

Even as he spoke, I felt edges of my consciousness starting to blur, sleep already pulling me under.

I had dreams that night of chasing Cole through the forest surrounding Lake Samish, begging him to stop, begging him to tell me how to save Alex. But as soon as I thought I was gaining ground on him, he would slip out of sight.

I woke with a hollow feeling in my stomach.

The day was a whirlwind of activity. Amber spent the majority of it on the phone, calling half of the population of Idaho Falls, Ucon, and the surrounding area that was between the ages of seventeen and twenty-one. Alex and I were sent out to get food for the party that night.

"I think we've got to try and talk to him," Alex said as we walked through the aisles of the grocery store. We'd been discussing what we had seen yesterday, both agreeing it must have been the mystery angel.

"I don't want you going anywhere near him," I said as I placed three bags of chips in the cart. "If I get the chance, I'll try and talk to him."

"That really doesn't seem like a good idea either. Angels have been trying to take you your whole life, what makes you think this one isn't trying to do the same thing?"

I had to pause and think about it for a bit. Angels *had* been trying to take me for a long time. This one kept showing up, just as Cole had reminded me of how they should have received me by now but hadn't.

"They won't take me," I said as I shook my head. "You made a trade."

"I still don't think it's a good idea," Alex said, his shoulders tight, his hands gripping the cart a little too tightly.

"Who knows, maybe we won't see him again."

"Somehow I doubt that," Alex sighed. "We've see how persistent residents of the afterlife can be."

I tried to place the man's face, to match it to a council member but the only one I could recall was Cole.

Why couldn't the afterlife just leave me alone?

X

The party was worse than I had expected. There had to be nearly one hundred people there, considering the population of Ucon was only eleven-hundred, it was a lot. The backyard was packed, people gathering around the food table, stuffing their faces full. I hung back against the wall of the house, Alex by my side, chatting with some guy. I was pretty sure I had gone to high school with his older brother.

I saw all the looks that kept coming in my direction, and in Alex's. I saw the way the male eyes lingered on my skin, on the shape of my legs. I saw the way they licked their lips, heard the way their heartbeats quickened. Amber's friends were practically drooling over Alex.

"Is that really Amber's sister?"

"I thought she was in an institution or something."

"Isn't she that girl who ran away in high school?"

"Dude, she has a ring on her finger, this is a freaking engagement party. You can't just go ask her out."

The talk was flying.

My palms were sweating as I tried not to meet anyone's eyes. I didn't want to keep being reminded of how everyone from this town thought I was an insane insomniac. It had been bad enough facing my mother, it was so much worse to have to be facing the entire town.

"I'm going to go get some more ice," I said to Alex. He met my eyes for a minute, his own sad and apologetic looking. He knew how hard this was for me.

I stepped in the quiet house, walking into the front living room where no one could see me through the back glass doors. I leaned against the wall, tipping my head back, and letting out a slow breath.

You can do this, I told myself. *You just have to make it until tomorrow night and it will be all over.*

Feeling my insides start to calm, I opened my eyes.

He was there again. Standing in the middle of the road, just watching me through the window.

I reacted without thinking. I crossed to the front door in one too-fast movement and yanked the door open.

"Hey," I called as I jumped down the front step. The man started walking down the street, right on the yellow line. "Hey," I said again as I crossed the lawn, quickening my pace to catch up with him.

62

He didn't look back at me, just continued to head west down the road.

"What do you want from me?" I demanded as I followed him. "Why are you following me?" He still remained silent. "I know what you are and I know where you've come from. You're not supposed to be here. So *why* are you *here*?"

The sun sank in the horizon, washing the earth in brilliant golden tones. Just before it sank below the top of the buildings, I was blinded for a short moment. I held my hand up to block the light, squinting to make out the man's form.

But he was already gone.

My breathing was coming in gasping breaths, my hands shaking. Not from fear, but from anger.

Why couldn't the afterlife just leave me alone already?

Shouts rose from the direction of my parents backyard and before I could even think, I was jogging back. As I rounded the corner, I saw Rod's fist connect with another boy's jaw. Rod's nose was already bleeding, covering his lips and teeth with red. The other guy just growled as he was knocked to the ground, swinging back at Rod as they hit the ground.

Alex shoved his way through the crowd, grabbing Rod by the back of his shirt and pulling him off of the other guy. Holding the two apart as they continued to try and swing at each other, Alex turned hard eyes on the other guy. "You seriously need to leave now." Even though he didn't raise his voice, it was filled with enough power to make anyone shake.

Giving Rod and Alex looks that would kill if they could, he spit red liquid on the ground. Wiping at his mouth with his bare arm, he shoved Alex's hand away and walked around the other corner of the house without looking back once.

Everyone stood in a circle for a silent moment, shock at seeing an actual fight break out in the middle of a party.

"Let's move on people," Dad said, waving everyone away from Rod and Alex. Erupting into conversations, they disbursed.

"What was *that* all about?" I asked, turning my focus to Amber who was fussing over Rod as he cradled his hand.

"That," she said as she grabbed a napkin and some ice cubes from the table. "Was Todd."

"Your ex who beat the crap out of you?" I asked, my insides flaring instantly.

Amber nodded. "He showed up a few minutes ago, calling me a deserting whore. He tried grabbing me."

"He seriously *shouldn't* have done that," Rod said through clenched teeth. "You should have just let me at him, Alex. Guys like that need to learn a lesson or two from someone who can stand up to them."

"And if I hadn't stepped in you'd be spending the night in a jail cell," Alex piped up, his voice sounding on edge. I saw the way his entire frame was shaking.

The afterlife was calling.

"Cool it!" Alex barked, his tone just a little too harsh.

Amber and Rod ducked inside to take care of his hand and bleeding nose, their expressions slightly startled at Alex's outburst.

"His temper is really going to get him in trouble someday," Alex said. He squeezed his eyes closed, taking a deep breath.

"I saw him again," I said quietly, changing the subject. I softly put my hand on his quaking arm. "I followed him.

"You did?" Alex's eyes flashed open. "And?"

"And nothing," I said, watching as Alex's frame stopped quivering. "I asked him what he wanted but he didn't say anything. And then he literally disappeared into the sunset."

"Creeper," Alex said under his breath. I couldn't help but chuckle. Alex cracked a smile too.

CHAPTER SEVEN

Alex paced in the living room, talking out his cell phone to the police about Caroline. Things didn't sound good.

I forced the orange juice down as I half listened to him, setting my glass in the sink. I stared out the window over the kitchen sink, not really seeing anything. I hadn't slept at all the night before, just stared up at the ceiling, lying next to a silent Alex.

I was feeling desperate. Why couldn't I think of a way to save him? Alex had saved me, now why couldn't I do the same thing?

"Jessica?" I heard my mom's hesitant voice from behind me. "Could we talk for a while?"

I felt my stomach drop out and I suddenly wished I hadn't drunk the juice. "Sure," I managed to squeak out.

I'd known this conversation was going to come sometime during this trip but I'd started hoping that maybe we were both going to chicken out of it. Apparently my mom was braver than I was.

I followed her into the office, settling into one of the swivel chairs. She closed the door behind us and sat as well.

We just stared at each other for a while, both unsure of what to say after all this time.

"You're so grown up now," she said with a small smile on her lips. It didn't quite look real. "You're not a girl anymore. You've become a woman."

I just nodded, my lips tight.

"Tell me about your life now," she attempted to keep her voice up, trying to sound engaged and excited. "What have you been up to?"

"Um," I struggled to talk around the lump in my throat. "Well, I've been in Washington for a few years now, as I'm sure dad's told you. I've made a few friends. I go to a yoga class a few days a week. The instructor is my best friend. I work in a book store. I really like my boss."

"A book store?" she said with a smile. "You did always love to read at nights."

I swallowed hard as the subject we were both dancing around was hinted upon. "Yeah, I really like the job. I've been there a few months now."

"Tell me about how you met Alex," she said as she tucked a leg up under her.

I felt a smile crack on my lips. "Well, I was care taking what was then his grandparent's house. It was the middle of the night and I heard the door upstairs open. I thought someone was breaking in," I chuckled, recalling the fear that leapt through me. "I grabbed a baseball bat and nearly clobbered him in the stairway." Mom started laughing. "I thought he was a burglar."

"That must have scared the tar out of you," she chuckled, covering her mouth.

"Yeah," I said, my eyes falling to the floor between us. "And then he told me the house was his, that his grandparents had died and left everything to him. Things were a little awkward for a bit."

"Isn't life crazy sometimes?" Mom sighed, shaking her head slowly.

"It sure is," I said quietly, twisting my fingers around each other.

There was a moment of quiet before she spoke again. "I'm glad to see you so happy, Jessica. At least you seem to be."

"I am," I said as I met her eyes.

"I just wish we could have gotten you the help you needed sooner."

My insides hollowed out as she finally said it.

"Did you start seeing a psychologist after you left?" she asked, her voice sounding so innocent and caring.

And every fight we had had, every plead, every scream slammed into me again. It took everything I had in me to not bolt for the door.

"I didn't need a psychologist, Mom," I said, my voice quivering. I closed my eyes, fighting back the sting behind my eyes. I wouldn't cry, I would *not* let her see me cry. Again. "I needed you to believe me."

"Oh sweetie," she said in a sweet tone. My eyes opened to see her concerned expression. It turned my insides hot. "I believed you believed it all. But you seem to have moved on."

"I didn't just move on," I said, my voice escalating. "Things changed, but I never moved on! I couldn't move on."

"Calm down sweetie," Mom said, her eyes growing wide and hard.

"No, Mom," I practically yelled. "I will not calm down! I was stuck in hell and you wanted to pretend none of it existed!"

"That's because it didn't, Jessica," she said, her tone rising too. The frustration I knew too well flooded back into her eyes.

"It was real, Mom!" I practically yelled. As I said the words, I grabbed the hem of my shirt and lifted it over my head as I stood. Wearing only my bra, I turned my back to her, the morning light coming from the window reflecting a metallic glint. "Do these look made up to you?"

I heard her gasp as she took the wings in. With one hand, I gathered my hair in one hand and pulled it away from my neck, exposing my brand. "It was real," I half whispered.

Something that sounded like a sob escaped my mother's chest and as I looked back at her, I saw tears glistening in her eyes.

"Why would you do that to yourself sweetie?" she asked quietly. "You're such a beautiful young woman."

"You think..." I stuttered. "You think I would do something like this to myself?!"

I couldn't take it anymore. I crossed to the door, walked out, and slammed the door behind me. Amber and Rod had poked their heads out of their door, their eyes widening as they took in my nearly topless form. Rod got his first glance at my scars.

"You okay?" Amber asked quietly.

"Do I look like I'm okay?" I said sharply as I yanked my shirt back down over my head. Without waiting for her to reply, I stalked down the hall toward the back door. Yanking it open, I stepped outside, leaving the door knob bent into the shape of my hand. I was too furious to care.

I found Dad and Alex sitting on the back deck, both their eyes widening as they saw me.

"Jessica, I..." my dad started.

"She's just so..." I started raging as I paced back and forth. "I even showed them to her and she still didn't believe me!"

"Jessica, your mother..."

"Don't defend her, Dad," I said coldly as I turned my eyes on him. "Just don't."

I didn't wait for either of them to say anymore as I started across the back lawn. There was an opening in the fence that let out into the back alleyway that led to a park that hadn't gotten much use in the last decade. Walking over to the swing set, I flopped down and slowly pushed myself back and forth, the rusty chains creaking above me.

I was glad when Alex didn't follow after me. I just wanted to be alone for a while.

I knew people judged me for leaving my family behind. They thought I had abandoned them, that I was a reckless runaway. But how was I supposed to live with a person who thought I was insane? Who wouldn't show the slightest bit of support in the terror that filled my life?

I needed a mother to hold me while I cried, someone I could just be afraid with.

But she wasn't that kind of mother to me.

Things felt so out of control right now. I was like I had been strapped to a rocket that was hurtling through life. I couldn't get a grasp on everything that was happening. Maybe it was more like I had been strapped to missile. I needed to figure out how to diffuse it and fast, or everything was going to blow up. And then that would be the end.

Trying not to think about my mother, I turned everything else over and over in my head. Alex was being pulled back. He didn't have long. I had seen what happened to Cole, the way he started falling apart and slowly faded away.

If they can't claim you, what are you willing to do to save him?

I was *willing* to do anything. But I just didn't know what I *could* do.

And now the council was watching me. Cole had said to hide what had happened to me. That it was the only advantage that I had against them.

How was I going to use my supposed immortality against them? How was that supposed to help me? It wasn't like I could give my life for Alex. He was already dead, traded his life for mine.

The countdown was on but I didn't know how many numbers were still left on the clock until this thing exploded and it was all over.

Because if Alex was taken back for forever, that would be the end.

Exhaustion washed over me as the minutes rolled by as I sat on that swing. The answers weren't going to come to me that day.

I had probably been sitting on that swing for almost an hour when my phone suddenly started vibrating. As I pulled it out I found two text messages.

You need to get home, like now! Amber's said.

I think you should come back right now, Dad's read.

Great. What was going on?

I crossed the park, made my way back down the grass-filled alley, and crossed back to the house. As I walked inside, I found Amber and Rod sitting very stony faced on

72

the living room couch, looking on edge. Alex stood in the hallway, his arms crossed over his chest, his expression very serious. My dad was at the end of the hall, knocking on his bedroom door.

"Claire?" he called. "Are you okay?"

I just heard a muffled cry from inside.

"What's going on?" I demanded. All of their eyes turned to me.

"Alex went to talk to Mom after you left," Amber said, her face sullen. The way her eyes were so big, I knew there was more to it than she was going to say in front of Rod and my dad.

I looked over at Alex, my eyes questioning. He just shook his head, sending the message of *talk later* with his eyes.

"Claire?" Dad knocked again.

"Just…" my mom struggled to talk. "Just give me a little bit. I'm… okay."

My dad glanced back at the rest of us, his brow furrowed. He glared at Alex for a second then looked over at me. I must have looked pathetic enough for him not to yell at Alex for doing whatever he had done to her.

"I'll be out in the garage," he said as he turned and started back down the hall. "Come and get me if she comes out."

As soon as my dad was out of the house Amber and Rod turned confused eyes on Alex. "Dude," Rod said, his eyes narrowing. "What did you *say* to her?"

73

I looked back at Alex, dying to know the same thing.

"I just went to talk to her," he started. "I said that maybe she should be a little more supportive of her daughter."

"And that made her scream like that?" Rod asked doubtfully. "I thought you must have suddenly turned into a vampire or something the way she screamed and tore out of that room."

My stomach sank as I started putting the pieces together.

"Mom will be fine," I said in a small voice. Taking Alex's hand in mine, I half dragged him out the front door. Closing it behind us, I walked him to the middle of the yard so we wouldn't be overheard.

"What did you do?" I demanded, my eyes burning as I looked at him.

"Like I said, I told her that maybe she should be a little more supportive of you and consider that the things you told her about were true," Alex said, his voice not even defensive.

"And?"

"And... her reaction wasn't what I was hoping for. It was just like you said it was, only *I* was hearing it from her myself," Alex's face was sad looking. "And so..."

"And so what?" I demanded when he paused.

"I showed them to her," Alex said quietly.

"Them?" I said through clenched teeth. "You showed her your *wings*?"

Alex just nodded. "She can't really doubt anymore." He fought back a small smile.

I just stared at him for a minute. I didn't know what to say. This was something I had never seen coming.

She finally knew the truth. My mom might not have understood it fully, but she had to know that I wasn't crazy anymore. She had seen it with her own eyes.

"Thank you," I said quietly, relief flooding through my body. I wrapped my arms around his waist and rested my head on his chest. Everything inside of me felt ready to collapse. I was so tired.

"You're welcome," he said as he laid his cheek on the top of my head.

I sighed, breathing in the summer air. "I'm ready to go home."

"Me too," Alex said quietly.

The next few hours were tense and awkward as we waited for my mom to come out of her room. To pretend I wasn't freaking out inside, I called Emily to check on Sal. She said Sal wasn't looking too good and Emily didn't think she'd slept at all since I'd left. I made a note to call her doctor as soon as we got back.

With little else we could do, we started packing our things back up, the mood somber and quiet. Alex and Rod hauled our things back out to the truck. Amber and Rod both had to be back to work the next day, we couldn't stay another night to make sure Mom would be okay.

Just as the boys stepped back inside, the door to my parent's room cracked open.

"Are you guys leaving?" Mom asked quietly as she stepped out.

"In just a few minutes," I answered. In a way I kind of felt sorry for her. I couldn't even imagine the shock of seeing what she had seen, having never believed this was real.

"Well, I wanted to say good-bye then," she said as she walked into the living room. My dad walked back in from the garage then, his face looking relieved to see her.

Amber rushed forward, wrapping her arms tight around my mom's shoulders. "We'll see you soon."

"Yeah," Mom whispered back. "Congratulations again. I'm really happy for you."

She hugged Rod next, and to my surprise, hesitantly hugged Alex. I didn't miss the fear in her eyes though.

She looked at me with a mix of emotions in her eyes. I tried to smile as I looked back, unsure if I succeeded or not. I wrapped my arms around her loosely.

"I'm..." she started to say, her entire frame trembling. But she couldn't seem to make herself say it.

"Bye, mom," I said quietly. "I'll see you in two and a half weeks?"

She just nodded as we stepped away from each other. She still looked at me with fear in her eyes. Like I was more of a freak now than I had ever been.

Wrapping up the good-byes, the four of us headed outside and loaded into the truck.

"Well, your dad didn't shoot us," Rod said as Alex pulled onto the street. "I guess that makes this weekend a success."

I gave a half smile as everyone else laughed. I wasn't sure if I would call this weekend a success or not.

Just as we were getting back into Idaho Falls a light went off in my head. "Hey get off on this exit," I said. I then gave him a few more directions. As we pulled into the parking lot I saw a smile creep onto Alex's face. "Um, I'm kind of going to have to borrow your card. If that's okay?"

"Of course," he said with a smile as he pulled out his wallet. I glanced back at Amber and saw her beaming face. I bounded back into the store by myself.

Less than fifteen minutes later we were rolling back down the freeway.

CHAPTER EIGHT

I collapsed into my bed thirteen hours later. In less than two minutes I was asleep.

And then Emily showed up.

"How long ago did she crash?" I faintly heard her say just outside the door to my new room.

"About three hours ago," Alex answered. I heard him rummaging around in the kitchen. I wondered if he was cooking for Emily.

"Dang," she said. "Well, I guess I'll let her sleep them. We all know she doesn't get enough of that."

"I'm up," I called in a throaty still-asleep voice.

The door opened and in came a yoga-clad Emily. I suddenly felt bad for missing so many of her classes lately.

"So," she said as she planted herself in my bed. "How did the trip go?"

"Alex showed my mom his wings," I said as I rubbed my palm against one of my eyes.

"You did *what*?" she called toward the door.

"I showed her my wings," he said as mundanely as if he were repeating something about the weather.

"I heard that the first time," she said as she rolled her eyes. "And why was that a good idea?"

"Let's just say not all of the trip went so well," I said as I rolled onto my side, propping myself up on an elbow.

"I'm sorry, babe," Emily said with a small sideways smile. "Was everything else okay though?"

"Uh, sure," I lied, thinking of the council member who was following me, of the fight that broke out at the engagement party.

"Well," Emily drew out the word, her face forming one of her brilliant smiles. "Today was my first day at the University."

"Oh yeah! How'd it go?"

"It was so amazing! I actually felt legit, and I'm getting paid some real money! And I'm finally done at that crappy coffee shop."

"That's great," I beamed at her. But I saw the way her smile didn't quite meet her eyes, saw the bags under them. Cormack leaving was harder on her than she was letting on.

"Then I'm actually going back down to the homeless shelter in a few hours," she said, her face falling just slightly. "I'm volunteering at a few different places. Gotta' tip the scales back in my favor."

I wasn't sure what to say as the conversation turned to Emily's judgment. I put a hand on her knee, giving it a small squeeze. "You're a good person, Emily."

"Who's done a very bad thing in her past," she said quietly as her eyes fell to the comforter under us.

"You can do it," I encouraged.

She suddenly flashed me another smile, unfolding her legs as she got up. "Well, if you're really awake you should get out here and see what Alex is working on."

Furrowing my brow, I climbed out of the bed and walked out the door and into the kitchen.

Alex had two cakes before him, one three-tiered and square shaped, the other six-tiered and rounded. He was kneading a big white ball of what I assumed was fondant icing. The round cake was already flawlessly covered.

"So which one do you like?" Alex asked as he started rolling out the icing.

"Uh," I struggled. "You're making full-on preliminary cakes?"

"Well," he said as he started covering the square one. "To be honest, I've never made a wedding cake before. I wanted to make sure I could do it."

"You had doubts?" Emily said as she rolled her eyes.

"Hey," he defended as he glanced up at her. "I'm not perfect at everything."

"Yeah, right," Emily and I both said at the same time. Everyone erupted into laughter.

"So, have you picked your colors yet?" Emily asked as she turned her eyes on me.

"Yeah, I need to know how to proceed after you pick one of the cakes," Alex piped in as he put the finishing touches on the fondant.

"And we need to get dresses figured out," Emily said.

"Geeze, I've only been home a few hours," I said in mock defense.

"And your wedding is in only eighteen days," Emily said seriously as she raised her eyebrows at me.

"Whoa, you're right," I breathed as it all hit me. "What do you think Alex? Colors?"

"Sorry," he said as he chuckled. "This one is totally up to you. I'm a guy, remember?"

I chuckled and rolled my eyes at him. "Fine, I'll look through some of Amber's bridal magazines and see what I like."

"Then we can go shopping?" Emily asked hopefully as she pressed her palms together.

"Then we can go shopping," I smiled at her.

"Yay!" she cheered like a high school girl. I wondered if her overly cheerfulness was a cover for how she was really feeling inside. "Well, I've got to get going but I will be back tomorrow morning to give you a hand with this stuff."

"'K, see you later," I called as she walked out the door.

"So, which one?" Alex asked as he wiped his hand on that silly white and pink checkered apron. It was a relic of his grandmothers.

I considered for a moment. "I like the square one. The round one is just going to be ten times more cake than we are ever going to need."

"It's a wedding," he smiled. "We're supposed to go over the top with everything."

"Yeah, and what are we supposed to do with *these* cakes?" I teased him.

Alex's brow furrowed. He hadn't thought of that part. And then with perfect skill and balance, he picked the both of them up and headed toward the door. "Wanna' get that for me?"

I chuckled as I opened it and he bounded to Emily's car before she pulled away.

The homeless would get to enjoy two undecorated mock wedding cakes.

Alex came back inside and started cleaning up the remains of his cake experiment.

"No word about Caroline, right?" I asked as I settled onto one of the barstools.

Alex shook his head. "I did go file a missing person's report about two hours ago. They didn't seem too eager to help find a drug-addicted woman though."

"She's still a person."

Alex nodded. "A person who isn't wanting to be found. Honestly I'm not planning on her showing up for the wedding."

"She'll be there," I said, feigning confidence.

Alex looked up at me, giving a sad half-smile. "I was thinking we should go look at wedding locations today. We'll be lucky if anything is available."

"I've got the rest of the day off," I smiled. "I'm working the next six day straight to make up for all the work I've missed so I guess today's our only chance."

X

Over the course of the next seven days Alex and I found our perfect venue, I finally settled on the colors of rosewood red and bronze, worked more hours in a row than I had ever worked before, and finally managed to drag Sal into her doctor's office.

It hadn't been a smooth experience and would have been impossible if not for Alex helping to keep her calm with his angelic talents. She left the office with a prescription for sleeping pills and an anti-anxiety medication. Sal said she would refuse them, that she didn't want their drugs.

Was I a bad person for slipping them into her food every day? Sal was finally looking rested and finally seemed to relax. I didn't feel too terrible.

Emily, Amber, and I went dress shopping. I was grateful for Alex's deep pockets as they both picked out matching dresses, found shoes and jewelry. And together we picked out my bouquet.

It was starting to feel like my time at work was my only down time. I could quietly stock the shelves, letting Rita handle the cash register. Work was busier while Austin took it easy and let his casted arm heal up. Life felt slower within the walls of the bookstore. It felt like everything inside made sense, like my impossible world was just another story from one of the books on the shelves.

But things were far from perfect. As I left work late one night, the silent council member had been standing across the street, just watching. And literally with the blink of an eye, he was gone again.

I didn't like sleeping by myself at nights. I hadn't done it for months and months now. I had gotten used to curling up into Alex's body in the middle of the night, stealing his warmth, of the sound of his breathing. Now the sheets on the other side of the bed were always cold.

But I knew what would happen if we stayed in the same bed before the wedding.

On a morning when Alex was at the house finishing up the rest of his remodels and showing it to a potential renter, I sat on the floor of the master bedroom, my folder of drawings spread out before me. Next to them lay the leather bound book of names.

The names of the dead I had stood trial for.

My eyes trailed over the images, taking in the details I had captured with pencil. The council's chairs, my holding cell, Cole's shadowed brand. I picked up one of the drawings, looking at it more closely.

It was rougher than most of the other ones, as if I had drawn it in a hurry. It was a picture of me, about to fall off the catwalk, a pair of beautiful wings sprouting from my back. One set of angels was trying to pull me up into never ending bliss, another set were trying to drag me down to the fiery depths with them.

It may have been the council who sentenced a person to heaven or hell but it was their minions that took them there.

I opened my leather book, my eyes trailing over the names.

Lisa Donovan.

Ted Meyer.

Gabriel Sanchez.

Kimberly Seely.

So many names. I had experienced trial for hundreds and hundreds of people.

Why had they gotten out of it?

I felt like there should have been an answer here. There was something I was missing.

What are you willing to do to save him?

What could I do? How could I fight against beings that weren't even in my world?

If they can't claim you...

I'd seen the proof that I couldn't die at this point. As Cole had said, four times now I should have died, and yet I had not stood before the council. But the thought that the council could not claim me seemed too impossible.

I wasn't sure how this was supposed to help me.

My phone vibrated on the floor next to me and I opened it to a text from Emily.

Where are you?

"Crap," I said under my breath as I scooped the pages back into their folder and stashed it and my name book back in the darkest part of my closet.

It felt like it took me forever to get to the restaurant. Emily seemed pretty annoyed that I had completely forgotten about her. I gave her an apologetic smile as we sat in our booth.

"I'm so sorry," I started after we ordered. I tried to ignore the way the waiter stared open-mouthed. "I got... distracted."

"It's fine," she said with a sigh as she twisted her napkin between her hands. "I just... I'm having kind of a crappy day."

"Want to talk about it?" I asked, watching as the napkin shredded between her hands.

"It's just hard, you know? I meet this totally amazing guy. He's perfect. And then he's gone. I mean, I know I didn't really know him, and he was dead, but still."

"It doesn't seem fair."

"No, it isn't," Emily said as she leaned back in her seat, rubbing her eyes. "It royally sucks."

Our drinks were brought with our salads at the same time. I tried not to meet the waiter's eyes. He was borderline creepy.

"I'm really sorry," I said, unsure of what to say when he finally left. It seemed that when angels were involved there were no happy endings.

"You know, I look at you and Alex and there's not a doubt in my mind that its love between the two of you. Anyone can see it. But I don't... I don't really think that's what me and Cormack had."

"What do you think you had?" I asked cautiously. Emily had blown up at me once about her jealousy before. And then run straight to Cole to console herself.

"I don't know," she said quietly, shaking her head as her eyes stared at the blank space passed my left shoulder. "A connection, I guess? As simple as it sounds I guess that's what it was."

I leaned forward, resting my forearms on the table. "I think... maybe you just needed someone. Do you think anyone else could have given you the hope and drive that Cormack did?"

Emily met my eyes, not answering for a long moment. "No," she answered simply.

"Then I think that it's okay if you didn't actually love Cormack. He affected you. You needed him for a time and I think he needed you."

A small tug of a smile worked its way to Emily's lips. Her eyes reddened slightly.

"Cormack didn't have to be the end for you, Emily," I said as I took her hand in mine. "There's still someone out there for you."

Emily chuckled, a smile spreading on her face. She wiped at her cheeks, brushing away the few tears that broke free. "Good going, Jess," she teased. "You made me cry."

I chuckled with her, sitting back in my seat. "Sorry. You okay?"

She rolled her head in a circle, stretching the muscles in her neck, closed her eyes for a moment, and took a deep breath. "It's okay. I'm okay. You're right. It's time to let life move on."

I could only give her a small supportive smile as she plastered a bright, fake one onto her face.

"So, you've got his ring size?" Emily asked, changing the conversation as she forked a big bite into her mouth.

I nodded. "I just got paid yesterday, so we're good to go."

Emily's eyes suddenly narrowed at a spot over my shoulder. "Someone's watching you," she whispered.

I whipped my head around, my heart leaping into my throat. I only caught a glimpse of dark eyes and sandy colored hair before he was gone.

"Do you know who that was?" Emily asked, her eyes looking back to the place where the man had disappeared.

"I didn't see anyone," I only half lied.

Emily shook her head, looking back down at her food. "Sorry, I didn't sleep very well last night. Maybe I'm just seeing things."

I knew she wasn't.

We finished eating and headed for the jewelers store. I felt overwhelmed as soon as we walked through the doors. Emily's eyes lit up as she scanned the glass cases.

"Welcome ladies," a man with a very feminine voice greeted us with a brilliant smile. "Is there something I can help you find today? A little something special for yourselves?" he asked with a wink.

"She's ring shopping," Emily spoke up when I hesitated. "She just got engaged and the wedding is less than two weeks away."

"Ooo," he drug out, giving me a mischievous look. "Shotgun wedding huh?"

I just nodded, giving a small smile. "October third."

"Wonderful!" he said as he clapped his hands together, flashing a brilliant smile. His teeth were just a little too white. "Well we have a wonderful selection of men's wedding bands. Right this way ladies!"

CHAPTER NINE

I said good-bye to Emily as she headed toward the University and I started back down the highway to the bookstore.

There was something inside of me that felt wrong as I drove down the road. It was the feeling of the calm before a lightning storm.

And then the traffic started to slow down. I leaned out my window, trying to get a glance at what was going on ahead of all the cars.

I could see a gray SUV plowed into the side of a restaurant, its front end totally embedded into the glass window. A mangled blue sedan was sitting on its side, halfway on the curb, halfway on the road.

People started jumping out of their cars as traffic came to a stand-still. I stepped out, looking back down the road, searching for signs of flashing lights. There were none.

"Call 911," people started shouting as everyone gathered around the horrendous wreck. I slowly walked over, looking for signs of life inside the vehicles. People ran in and out of the restaurant, a woman with small shards of glass stuck in her face came stumbling out to the curb. My stomach lurched.

It wasn't until I came within ten feet of the building that I smelled it.

A propane leak.

"Clear out!" I shouted before I could even think about the words. I shoved my way into the building. "There's a propane leak! Get out of here!"

The entire inside of the building was littered with glass, people still trying to help those who had been injured by the crash. They all paused and looked at me for a moment.

"You've got to get out of here!" I yelled again. "This place could blow any second!"

They finally jump to life and people started racing through the front door.

The smell of propane was getting stronger.

With everyone cleared out of the building, I ran back outside. Others were clearing people out, shouts about the propane leak erupting all around. I watched as a man clambered out of the blue car, his entire frame shaking, but otherwise looking alright.

"Who was in the gray SUV?" I asked to no one in particular. People started looking around as they continued to clear out of the vicinity.

I looked back at the SUV, the propane smell growing stronger by the second.

Running faster than I should have, I yanked the door open, nearly tearing it off the frame. Inside was a woman and who I assumed was her teenage daughter. Both were unconscious, blood dripping from various wounds.

I unbuckled the teenage girl first, being careful not to injure her further. Gathering her up in my arms, I stumbled back toward the retreating crowd. Picking out a man who looked strong, I handed the girl off.

"You," I said pointing to a girl who looked my age who stood close by. "Call 911 and stay with her until help comes."

I didn't wait for either of them to respond before I ran back to the SUV. The driver's side door was forced closed, half of the SUV stuck in the brick wall of the building. Checking to make sure no one could see what I was doing, I yanked harder, bending the door around the brick.

The woman rested with her head against the steering wheel, the airbag deflated in her lap. There were many gashes in her forehead, a long, dripping one in her right arm. The entire frame of the car had been twisted and the center consul of the vehicle was pressed into the seatbelt. After yanking hard enough, the entire unit snapped and the woman slumped into my arms.

Just as I started to carry her away, I saw a match being tossed toward the car.

The entire SUV and most of my body was consumed in flames. Glass sprayed all around me as the rest of the window and the store exploded.

I'd never screamed like I did as the flames licked at my body. I knew, even before I dropped her to the ground, that the woman I was trying to save was gone. I watched as her hair burned away, her flesh blackened.

I landed on the rough cement on my hands and knees before collapsing onto my face.

That's when I felt him. Standing in the crowd right before me.

In a movement that was too fast for any bystanders to see, I leapt up and grabbed the man around his waist.

The next instant later I was standing on the narrow stone catwalk.

In the afterlife.

I was shoved to the ground as the man I held onto pushed me away. I looked up at him with fear pulsing in my body. His black eyes looked down at me, his wings raised and menacing.

"Jessica?" I heard the horrified voice call from behind me. I whipped my head around to see a small gathering of angels on the spiral staircase that lined the cylinder. And there he was.

Cole.

"You will not escape judgment much longer," the blond man before me half growled, half hissed, reaching down to grab me.

At the same time, I heard the beat of powerful wings. The next moment, strong arms wrapped around my chest from behind and I was being pulled upward.

"What are you doing here?" Cole hissed into my ear. "You can't be here."

"I grabbed him," I answered in a shaky voice as Cole hauled me upward another thirty feet before setting me on a section of the staircase. As I dropped to my feet, Cole whipped around, lashing out his arm, just as the other angel had ascended, blood in his eyes. As Cole's arm connected with the other man's face, he went sailing across the cylinder, crashing with force into the stone walls.

"Why did you bring her here?" Cole bellowed, his entire countenance seeming to grow with power and force as he leapt across the cylinder. His hand met the other angel's throat, and Cole pinned him against the wall.

The man clawed at Cole's hand, his eyes wide with fear. "I didn't mean to. She grabbed me. She must have been pulled back with me."

"Why were you near her?" Cole hissed.

The other man's eyes narrowed, becoming cold. "You know why."

Cole slammed his head against the wall, an angry growl clawing out of his chest. Gripping tighter around his neck, Cole literally hurtled him down into the fiery depths below.

I hadn't realized I had been holding my breath until Cole turned back to me. He beat his wings again, coming to stand before me on the stairway.

"You shouldn't be here," Cole said simply as his eyes traced my face.

94

I could only shake my head.

"I told you not to let them know what has happened," his eyes narrowed.

"I didn't mean to," I struggled to talk. My eyes flashed back to the fiery space below us. "I don't know what happened."

"You're not supposed to be able to come back here," he half whispered, looking around. There were only three other angels in the whole cylinder that I could see, the ones Cole had been speaking with. They watched us intently. "Things are happening, you should not be here."

"Then get me out," I said as I met his black eyes.

Cole looked at me for a long moment. Slowly he raised his hand, tracing his fingers lightly against my cheek. His skin didn't burn and decay now. The rules of the afterlife were different than the rules of the world of the living.

"I've missed you," he breathed.

I closed my eyes as my skin tingled, my stomach did a little quiver. "I need your help."

"Come see me when you're closest to death. Wish it, and it will happen."

Before I could ask him what he meant, he pushed me off the staircase and I plunged toward the fiery depths.

I sat straight up with a gasp, spreading my hands out in front of me to catch my fall. But I was sitting on the sidewalk, my clothes tattered and shredded. There was a crowd gathered around me, fear and concern in their eyes. I could hear sirens wailing in the background. Not ten feet from me I made out the form of a body covered with a kid's blanket. The woman's feet poked out the end of it.

"You should probably lie back down until the medic's get here," a woman said as she placed a hand on my shoulder warily. I looked up at her, blinking hard, trying to get my brain and body functioning at the same time.

I shook my head as I shifted my weight forward, pulling myself to my feet. "No, I have to…" I stuttered, my body swaying slightly. My clothes were charred and still smoking slightly. Something in my stomach twisted. "I have to go."

And before anyone could stop me, I took off into the crowd back to my car.

My hands shook as I worked my way out of the traffic jam. I fought to keep my eyes focused on the road as everything inside of me felt like it was shifting and solidifying. I fought to force every breath in and out.

Something felt wrong.

Something wanted to go back.

I pulled into the parking lot of the bookstore, a full forty minutes late for my shift. Thankful for the black yoga pants and extra work shirt I had in the back of my GTO, I changed in the car, put my singed hair in a loose braid, careful to make sure my brand was still covered, and wiped the blackness from my face and arms.

I still looked like I'd taken a visit to hell.

"I'm so sorry I'm late," I started apologizing to Rita as I walked through the door. "There was this huge..."

"Did you hear about the accident?" Rita asked me absent mindedly as she turned up the radio. "Just down the street from here. There was a woman killed. A building exploded!"

"Yeah, it sounds like it was terrible," I swallowed a hard lump. If I'd been just a few moments faster I would have been able to save her.

The image of the match being thrown toward the car flashed across my vision.

The angel who had been watching me had thrown it. He'd been trying to kill me.

They know something's wrong.

"Those poor people," Rita said quietly as she leaned against the counter. "Nine people taken to the hospital."

I nodded, even though I only half heard what she had said.

"Bystanders reported that a man stepped in front of the SUV, which swerved to avoid him, hitting a blue sedan in the process," the news caster said. *"The sedan rolled into the curb and the SUV collided with Garry's Deli..."*

I zoned the rest of the report out. He'd caused the accident. He'd just been waiting for me.

And an innocent life had been lost in his quest to expose me.

"I'm going to go stock the shelves," I said quietly, my stomach feeling queasy. "Has Austin come in to help you at the counter?"

"He's not coming in," she replied as she shuffled something around behind the counter. "His youngest sister was admitted into the hospital last night. The family is staying with her."

"Is she okay?"

"She's been waiting for a kidney transplant for a few years now," Rita said with a sigh. "None of the family is a match and things have taken a turn for the worse."

I felt my stomach twist all the more. "I hope they find a match for her soon."

"Me too. That poor girl has gone through so much."

As I worked in the back room I couldn't help but feel once again like I was strapped to a missile. Everything was going to blow up at any moment. The danger we were all in had just been taken to a whole new level.

The day passed painfully slow. But eventually my shift ended and as I walked out to my car in the evening light, I couldn't help but feel paranoid. I was constantly glancing over my shoulder, my eyes scanning for a pair of black ones looking at me from the shadows.

Sliding into my car, I carefully worked my way to the freeway.

I had to stop this. They had killed an innocent woman.

Somehow this whole crazy angel crap had to stop.

When I arrived back at home there was a note on the kitchen counter from Alex, saying he had gone out with Rod for some "guy time". I actually felt relieved. I had too many things going on in my head, things I wasn't sure if I wanted or could talk to Alex about.

Sal was already asleep when I went to check on her. I checked her pill bottle and discovered she'd taken one of the sleeping pills on her own.

I took a shower, watching as the burnt parts of my hair broke off and slipped down the drain. I scrubbed my skin until I couldn't smell the smoke anymore. Pulling on some pajamas, I started pacing the living room.

There were a few things Cole had said that I couldn't stop thinking about. He seemed genuinely concerned when he said "things are happening, you should not be here". I'd never seen Cole act concerned. And something just felt weird about the cylinder as I visited. The hushed tones the other angels used as they talked to Cole, the demanding tone the other angel used, the one who had accidently taken me back with him.

But it was his last few words that I couldn't understand the most. "Come see me when you're closest to death. Wish it, and it will happen."

What did that mean? When was I closest to death? Did that mean I had to try and cause my death that apparently couldn't happen? Did I have to wish death upon myself in order to see Cole and ask for his help?

I had so many questions these days but never any answers.

CHAPTER TEN

The next four days flashed by in snapshots. There was wedding planning. There was work. There was wondering what Cole was talking about.

And there was the constant glancing over my shoulder.

I couldn't tell Alex what was wrong. Something big was going to happen. Something was coming, or maybe I was running blindly towards it. But I didn't know if it was going to be a good or a bad thing. Until I knew what I was doing I had to keep Alex in the dark. I had to keep him safe.

I could see the fear in Alex's eyes with each passing day. The way his hands would quiver as he stood with them braced on the countertop told me just how hard the afterlife was trying to pull him back. His breath would catch in his throat, his eyes would squeeze shut.

And something felt different in me. There was something inside of me that felt like it was constantly shifting. Like the parts of me that were still alive were battling with the parts of me that had changed into something else.

A part of me wanted to go back.

Alone in the bookstore, I sank to my knees as my breath caught in my throat. Black spots filled my vision as my brain tried to focus. It felt like all of my insides were trying to break free or disappear, I couldn't make my brain function enough to be sure.

As I flopped forward, catching myself on my palms before I collapsed on my face, I looked up. Trying to focus on something, anything to keep me where I was supposed to be, I searched the bookshelves before me, on the books on the very bottom shelf.

Then I saw it. A title long dusty and forgotten about.

Death, Sleep, and the Traveler by John Hawkes.

The world suddenly solidified and my entire being came into focus.

I didn't even pull the book off the shelf to see what it was about as I stood. I had my answer.

Come see me when you're closest to death, Cole had said.

It was so simple.

I counted backward from twenty as I lay on my bed alone that night. My palms were sweaty and my nerves threatened to eat me up from the inside out.

Closing my eyes I went over it again in my head, already feeling the buzz of sleep the two pills I had taken were starting to give me.

I couldn't die. I was stuck.

But the body slows down when it sleeps. The heart slows, the blood slows, the brain slows.

Sleep was as close to death as I could get.

I'm coming, Cole, I thought to myself as my brain started to blur.

The space around me was dark, the kind of black that swallows everything whole. I felt around me but reached nothing but air.

"Cole?" I said cautiously.

No answer came.

I felt panic and anger surge in my system as I felt around again in the dark. I didn't have time to wait. Cole had told me to come and here I was.

So where was he?

"Cole!" I shouted.

And suddenly I felt a presence behind me, felt the air become warmer on the back of my neck.

"You figured it out," his honey smooth voice filled the darkness.

"You could have been a bit more specific," I tried to sound confident.

"We were being watched," Cole said as I sensed him walk around me. "I had to be careful."

"Where are we?" I asked, hugging my arms around me.

"In an in between place," he said quietly as he came to stand before me. "Not quite the world of the living, not quite the world of the dead."

"Like Limbo?"

"I suppose it has been called that before."

"Are we alone?"

"For now," Cole said. "You never know when a proxy will send a soul here to wait."

"What do you mean?" I asked. Proxy. That was what I had been.

"Where do you think the people you stood trial for went while you experienced their judgment?"

I didn't answer. I had honestly never considered that before.

"In being granted your life back for a period of time, you traded experiencing death over and over again, just not your own. The people you stood trial for died at the same moment you fell asleep. And they came here as you stood their trial. They waited, until the final judgment was made and you returned to the world of the living."

"That hardly seems fair punishment for wanting to live," I said in a cold voice.

I sensed Cole shrug. "Life is a precious gift to be given. It comes with a heavy price."

"It's not right."

"Those people you stood trial for owe you a great debt. They never had to experience their actual judgment."

104

I just shook my head, fighting back the knots that were forming in my stomach.

"I need help, Cole," I started, feeing the panic rising in my blood again. It was time to move on to the reason I had come. "I don't know how to fight the council. I'm being followed. A woman was killed because of him, because of all of this. What is going on?"

"I told you before that they know something is wrong. Five times now you should have died, should have been ready for your own judgment, and yet you are still walking among the living, still have a heart that beats, albeit it differently than most, in your chest.

"They want to know why, and there are some that are not happy about your condition. Like Jeremiah."

"The one who's been following me?"

"Yes."

I heard Cole sigh, heard him rub his hands together. "Things are changing in my world, Jessica. The afterlife is in chaos. The council changes. Every few centuries it shifts. Members are replaced, new ones are established.

"The man who has been following you is the man who held my position while I pursued you. My place had to be filled and Jeremiah was... promoted, if you will. And then I returned and was reinstated to my leadership of the condemned. He wasn't happy about my return. He set the change into motion. He wants my position back when the shift happens. He believes if he brings you back, if he can figure out what has happened to you, that he can gain it. I believe he is also trying to provoke me into acting, into doing something that will make me lose my position."

"He tried to kill me, Cole," I breathed. "He caused an explosion. I lost some hair but I wasn't injured. Another person was *killed*."

"He's a branded angel, Jessica," Cole said as he took a step closer to me in the dark. "We will stop at nothing to get what we want."

"I have to stop this," I said as my jaw tightened. "This must end."

The air started to warm around me. The ground at my feet started to shift. I was waking up.

"You're running out of time," Cole said through the blackness.

"Cole!" I shouted as everything pulsed and throbbed. I reached out for him but only found air.

CHAPTER ELEVEN

I woke to blinding light, streaming through the massive window that overlooked the lake. My mind was racing as I blinked the sleep from my eyes, going over everything I had just learned.

There was a knock at the door and a moment later Alex stepped inside. He wore a red t-shirt and a pair of white basketball shorts. I couldn't help but grin as he crossed the room to me. Red was always my favorite color on him.

"Good morning sleeping beauty," he breathed as he crawled over the foot of the bed, sliding up my body.

"Morning," I said as my lips met his.

"You look really amazing when you sleep, did you know that?" he asked as he brushed the back of his hand against my cheek.

"You watch me sleep?" I asked as I raised my eyebrows at him. "Doesn't that seem just a bit creepy to you?"

He chuckled. "Just occasionally. There's not exactly a lot to do around here at night."

"Just a few more days and there will be plenty to do at night," I teased.

"Six days," he growled, biting at the neckline of my tank top playfully.

"I can't wait to see what Costa Rica is like," I said as I ran my hands through Alex's sandy blond hair. "You've practically traveled the world and the only place I've ever been to was Cole's decaying mansion."

"Sandy beaches," he said as he kissed my throat. "Warm waters," he moved to the space just below my ear. "And three-hundred yards of ocean front all to ourselves."

"Sounds like paradise," I said as I closed my eyes, picturing the scene Alex was painting for me.

He kissed me softly on the lips, a slow lingering one. I looked up into his gray eyes as he hovered over me.

"I love you," I said softly, wrapping my arms around his waist. "I wouldn't still be here if it wasn't for you. I owe you everything."

"You're worth it," he said with a half-smile. "I don't regret anything these past few months."

My phone suddenly vibrated on the nightstand and I reached over to grab it. It was a text from Rita, asking where I was.

"Crap!" I half shouted as I practically pushed Alex off of me and bounded to the closet. "I didn't realize what time it was! I never sleep in this late!"

"Are you still covering for Austin?" Alex asked from the bed.

"Yeah," I called as I pulled on the first pair of clean pants I came across. "His sister's gotten really bad I guess. No one dares leave her side."

Pulling on a shirt, I raced for the bathroom next, trying in vain to tame my hair. It seemed pretty pointless, the curls were going to do whatever they wanted to do.

Just as I was about to run out the door, I stopped short. "Emily," I said, steadying us both as I practically ran into her. As she met my eyes, I realized hers were red and swollen, trails the tears had made on her cheeks still evident.

"Can I just... hang out with you today?" she said, her voice quivering as she wiped at another tear that had broken loose.

"Hey," I said as I pulled her into my arms. "What's the matter?"

"I just..." she took in a shaking breath. "It all just kind of hit me again today. Cormack being gone, all the work I have to do to reverse what I've done."

I felt my heart sink. I couldn't even imagine what Emily was going through. It was hard enough when Alex wouldn't ask me to marry him, but at least I still had him. Cormack was gone. For good.

"Well, I have to work today," I said as I rubbed circles into her back. "But you can go in with me. If nothing else maybe you can find a good book to read to distract yourself."

Emily stepped away, nodding as she wiped another tear away. "Thanks," she said, giving me a half-smile.

We climbed into my GTO and I made my way to the freeway. Emily rested her forehead against the window and closed her eyes.

"I don't even have a date for your wedding," she said in a small voice.

"Trust me," I said as I merged my way into the basically non-existent traffic. "You don't need one. There's literally only going to be you, Sal, my parents, maybe Caroline, Rod and Amber, and Rita and Austin. It's not exactly an extensive guest list."

"I'm really happy for you, you know," Emily said. "You and Alex are perfect together."

"Thanks," I said as I reached over and gave her hand a quick squeeze.

We got to the bookstore, Emily set to browsing the shelves, and I started helping Rita out with the three customers at the counter. She always panicked when there were more than a few people in the building.

The day died out after the first hour and by eleven, there wasn't a soul around besides, Rita, Emily, and myself. So I practically jumped when the bell at the front door chimed.

"Austin," I said as he walked up to the counter. "How is everything?"

He put his elbows on the counter, letting his face settle into his hands. He looked dead tired. "Not so good. She's declining pretty rapidly."

Rita came walking out of her office, a white envelope in hand. "Here you go honey," she said as she handed it to Austin across the counter. "I put a little bonus in there too."

"You didn't have to do that, Aunt Rita," he said as she came around the counter and hugged him.

"I know," she said as she patted him on the back. "But I know these aren't easy times for you or your family financially."

I noticed Emily then, standing quietly at the end of the counter, holding a book in her hands. She watched with concern in her eyes as Austin wiped a stray tear from his eye.

"Is everything okay?" she asked quietly.

Austin practically jumped when he heard her and looked embarrassed to have her see him crying. "Uh," he stuttered. "It's Emily, right?"

She just nodded.

"Um, it's just my sister," he started to explain, even though he really didn't have to. "She's been waiting for a new kidney for a long time now, but she isn't up high enough on the donor list. She's not doing so good."

"I'm so sorry," she said, her eyes sad looking. "That's terrible. How old is she?"

"Seven," his voice cracked as he spoke. He took a deep breath as he wiped his eyes again. "I'd better get back to the hospital. Mom hasn't slept in a few days. I'm going to see if I can get her to go home for a bit."

Rita just nodded, a sad look on her face.

"Good luck," was all I could say, wishing there was something that I could do.

Austin walked back outside. I noticed Emily's eyes following him when she suddenly said, "I'll be back in just a minute." With that, she dashed out the door.

I didn't mean to spy, but I couldn't help but be curious while I watched through the glass as Emily caught up with Austin. She talked to him with rapid words I couldn't make out. Austin's brow furrowed for a bit, he asked something that looked like "why?" and Emily started talking rapidly again. When she was finished, he just looked at her for a long moment, like he was evaluating what she had said. And then he suddenly hugged her. When he stepped away he pulled a pen out of his pocket. Searching for a scrap of paper, Emily finally offered her hand. Austin started writing something down, hugged her again when he finished, then got in his car and left.

Emily was beaming when she walked back into the bookstore. I hadn't seen her look that happy since before Cormack was gone.

"What was that all about?" I questioned, making sure Rita was out of earshot.

"I'm just going to go visit Austin's sister in a little bit," she said as she sat down at the counter. "Austin is going to go put his check in the bank and then swing back by and pick me up."

"Why?" I asked, looking at her doubtfully. Somehow I sensed she wasn't telling me the full story.

"Because she's a sad little girl who could use all the support she can get," Emily said innocently.

I looked at her doubtfully for a moment longer.

"Oh yeah," she suddenly spoke up. Reaching for the book she had been holding earlier, she slid it down the counter. "I wanted to buy this book."

"Vampires?" I said skeptically as I raised an eyebrow at her.

"Hey," she said defensively. "At least it's not angels."

CHAPTER TWELVE

My shift ended and I drove home through the dark. The air felt still and cold as I parked the GTO in the driveway and walked up to the front door. The door creaked as I opened it, startling me in the dead quiet of the evening.

And then I saw Alex, sprawled out on the living room floor. His t-shirt was shredded to pieces around him, his wings spread out around him. He clutched at his bare chest, his eyes wide and staring up at the ceiling.

"Alex!" I screamed as I dropped my things and fell to his side. "Alex!"

"Jessica," he barely managed to breathe. He took a gasping breath. He squeezed my hand so tightly it actually hurt.

I stared horrified at his body. It seemed to quiver, to shake and re-solidify. "Alex, stay with me!"

Reaching for a place inside of me, to a place that was dead and gone, a place that was more angel than human, I made a plea. *If you can hear me Cole, don't you dare let them take him from me.*

"Don't you dare," I hissed aloud through clenched teeth. Alex was too out of it to even realize I said anything. Lifting my eyes, I said a little louder "Don't you *dare* take him. I will not let you take him from me again!"

Shifting my body, I straddled Alex's chest with my legs, careful not to put any pressure on his already struggling to breathe chest. Placing my hands on the sides of his face, I forced his eyes to meet mine.

"Alex," I said clearly and calmly. "You promised me that you wouldn't let them take you before the wedding. We're only days away. Don't you dare break your promise to me."

"I'm..." he struggled as his eyes started to lose focus. "I'm... trying."

"Try harder," I said, hating how my words were sounding. "I need you Alex. You are all that I have. I cannot lose you. I am going to figure this out. I will get you out of this. I just need a little more time."

Alex met my eyes again, his own looking confused. His breath caught in his throat and he suddenly made a choking sound. Alex's eyes rolled into the back of his head.

"Alex!" I screamed. "Don't do this! Don't let them take you!"

His body started to quake all the more.

It was then that I noticed how his skin looked just the tiniest bit tighter on his body. His veins seemed to stand out just a fraction more.

I swore under my breath.

"Hang on just a few minutes longer, Alex," I said in a panicked voice. Gripping one of his hands tightly in mine, I lay next to him on the ground.

It was the hardest thing I had ever had to do, to force my body to relax. I concentrated on making my heart slow, on making my thoughts clear and relax.

I closed my eyes and pictured the afterlife. The stone cylinder, the council's chairs, the stairway that surrounded.

It didn't take long for everything to blur and feel hazy.

When I opened my eyes I was there.

Not just in the Limbo blackness I had spoken to Cole in.

This was the afterlife I had visited every night, the afterlife Jeremiah had accidently taken me back to.

I was seated on the spiral staircase, alone. Just slightly below me, across the cylinder, the council talked hurriedly, in angry voices.

"We agreed to give more time," a woman with blue eyes said defensively. "A few months is not more time."

"A few months is plenty of time," a black-eyed man hissed. "It is more than he should have been granted."

"It was very generous," a white-bearded, blue-eyed man said, his expression downfallen.

I wanted to shout to Cole who sat with the rest of them, to somehow get his attention. But what would happen if the full council knew I was here, an undead, non-proxy?

Cole, I thought with everything I had. *Cole, I'm here.*

116

And as simple as that, Cole's eyes shifted to the walls. In just a fraction of a moment his eyes found mine.

Please, I mouthed, shaking my head. *Not yet.*

Cole held my eyes for a moment longer, his expression looking as if he were debating how to resolve this.

"Enough!" he bellowed, snapping his attention back to the council. "More time was granted. A week or two longer will not hurt anything. We all know what his fate will be anyway."

Jeremiah glared at Cole. "Soft," he hissed quietly with a cold stare.

Coiling his arm, Cole landed a hard blow to the side of the other angels head, knocking him from his seat. An angry cry ripped from Jeremiah's chest as he simply gave a powerful beat of his wings, hovering in the air before his seat.

"Calm yourself, my brother," the leader of the exalted said, his eyes narrowing. "As you've said, another week cannot hurt anything. We will reevaluate then as to what the boy's fate shall be."

Cole's eyes glanced up at me again, giving me the smallest of nods.

I felt my insides relax just slightly. I nodded back to Cole. Taking a hard swallow, I looked down into the depths below me, and silently jumped.

A gasp escaped my throat as my eyes slid open, seeing the darkened ceiling above me. Half a second later, Alex sat upright, a terrifying sounding gasp coming out of his own lips. His eyes searched around him, confused.

"What happened?" he asked his voice sounding frantic. His expression still confused he climbed to his feet, pulling me to mine.

"You were... having a hard time," I struggled to come up with an answer.

"Why were you on the floor with me?" he asked, his eyes looking doubtful.

"I'd been holding your hand, telling you to hold on, and I fell asleep." It wasn't entirely a lie.

He looked at me for a long moment, evaluating what I had said. His expression finally softened and he closed the gap between us, pulling me into his arms.

"I'm sorry," he whispered into my neck. "It's getting almost impossible to fight it off."

"I know," I said quietly, my mind reeling. "You'll make it to the wedding though."

It took a moment, but Alex finally nodded in agreement. He then took a deep breath and started toward the kitchen. "I need to cook something. What sounds good tonight? I'm assuming you aren't tired after your nap."

"How about Thai?" I suggested. I wasn't hungry in the least. But Thai was the first thing Alex had ever cooked for me.

Truthfully I did want to sleep. I needed to talk to Cole again.

"My specialty," Alex smiled as he started digging through cupboards. Less keen eyes would have missed the shaken way Alex moved, anyone else wouldn't have smelled the fear that was clouding about him. Alex was terrified.

I gave him a smile back and took a seat at the bar to watch the man who would be my husband in a few days make me dinner at midnight.

CHAPTER THIRTEEN

"Sal?" I called the following evening after I got off work. Closing the door behind me, I checked for what kind of order the house was in. Perfectly clean. The housekeepers had been by earlier that day. "Sal?" I called again. Hearing shuffling below me, I descended the stairs and stopped short in the doorway to her office.

There were pictures strewn everywhere, dozens if not more than a hundred of them. All of them featuring a smiling, younger, saner looking Sal. And a man I could only assume was her ex-husband.

"Sal?" I asked as I continued to stand in the doorway. "What happened?"

Sal was seated in her office chair, her feet propped up on the desk, a book in hand. "Hmm?" she mumbled, her eyes never lifting from the page.

"Are you okay?" I asked as I dropped to my hands and knees and started gathering up the pictures. I felt slightly horrified when I realized there was a large red X over Roger's face in every single picture.

"I'm fine," she answered casually as she continued to read. "This is a really good book."

"I'm glad you're enjoying it," I answered distractedly. I looked at a handful of pictures. There was one of them together on some beach with palm trees around them. Another of them wearing heavy coats and snow all around. Several taken on the back deck of the house here on Lake Samish. In at least half of the pictures I saw Roger had a drink in his hand.

Sal didn't say another word as I continued to pick up endless pictures, all depicting a perfectly happy couple. But I noticed the bruises she had tried to cover with clothing and make-up. He had ruined Sal's life.

Dumping them all in a box, I shoved them to the very back of Sal's closet. I debated with myself on whether it was better to simply throw them into the trash. For some reason I felt guilty for considering it.

"How have you been sleeping?" I asked her as I came back into the office.

"Good," she answered without looking up at me. "Roger has only come to see me once this week."

"You're still seeing him?" I asked, concern growing in my stomach.

Sal nodded. "He was standing in my shower when I went to go to the bathroom earlier. I screamed and he went away."

121

My brow furrowed as I leaned against the desk. I wasn't sure if this was just another of Sal's more out of it moments or something to be concerned about.

She suddenly snapped the book closed, causing me to jump violently. "Are you nervous?" she asked as she laid the book down on the desk and leaned toward me on her elbows.

"Nervous?" I asked, still distracted by my thoughts.

"About the wedding, silly!" she chuckled.

"Oh, yeah," I said, putting on a smile for her. It wasn't easy. "I guess a little."

"You shouldn't be," Sal said as she smiled. "You and Alex are meant to be together."

"I know," I replied. I couldn't tell her that the reason I was nervous was because I knew that once the wedding was over, we might only have a few more days. If I didn't figure this thing out fast I might be a widow who hadn't even been married for a whole month.

"Emily dropped my dress off earlier this morning," Sal beamed as she jumped to her feet and ran into her room. I followed her and flipped the light on. She came out of her closet a moment later carrying a bronze colored dress similar to Emily's rosewood red one. "Isn't it pretty?"

"You'll be beautiful in it," I assured her, finally smiling for real. I just hoped it wouldn't be too traumatic for Sal to be out as long as the wedding lasted.

"Emily seemed happier," Sal said as she laid the dress on the bed and she sat on the edge of the mattress. "She was so sad for a while."

"She was having a hard time."

My phone vibrated, and I pulled it out of my pocket to find a text from Alex asking where I was.

"I've got to go Sal," I said as I walked into her bathroom. The world outside the window turning black, I flipped the light on. Looking through her medicine cabinet, I found her sleeping pills. Filling a glass, I brought them out to her. Thankfully she'd been more cooperative about taking them lately and I didn't have to slip them into her food anymore. She swallowed the pill and took the glass back to the bathroom.

"Good-night," I said to her as she started brushing her teeth.

"Night!" she called through a foamy mouth.

I walked back to the house in the fading light. The sun hung on the tops of the trees, casting golden shadows on the world. The lake was perfectly smooth, all the tourists having gone inside from the day's wet and exciting activities. I breathed in a deep breath of fading summer air, welcoming in October.

"I know something is wrong with you," a voice said from the trees.

My heart jumped into my throat and adrenaline surged through my veins as I searched for the source of the voice.

I knew it would be Jeremiah before I found his beautiful yet terrifying face amongst the trees.

"What are you talking about?" I played dumb. "Why have you been following me?"

"You were taken to the afterlife and yet you are back. I know what you were, what you are no longer."

I stood there in the middle of the road, fighting both the urge to run away from him as fast as I could and attack him all at the same time.

"You killed a woman, did you know that?" I said as I stared at him with cold eyes. I was getting a clear look at him for the first time. His shoulders were broad and strong, his frame sturdy. His dark eyes were shadowed beneath his thick sandy eyebrows. The scruff of facial hair matched his shoulder-length hair. Everything about his features seemed strong.

"Such a tragedy," his voice was cold and uncaring.

"What do you want from me?" I demanded as I crossed my arms over my chest.

"To take you back to where you belong."

"She belongs here," a voice behind me suddenly said. I turned to see Alex walking out to the road. His eyes were cold and burning with rage. I noticed how the veins bulged out on the side of his neck. "That was the trade."

The black-eyed angel stared at Alex for a long moment. I could see the wheels turning in his head. His fingers clenched into fists.

"She doesn't belong here, she's not even fully alive anymore," he said coldly.

"But that was the trade," Alex repeated as he stopped at my side.

"You've given up so much for this woman, and yet there is so much she hasn't told you. Consider your sacrifice carefully."

And with a shift of the air, he was gone.

We both stood there for a long minute in silence. Everything within me felt ready to spring, waiting for something to happen.

Sliding his hand into mine, Alex led me back to the house.

As we walked inside, I kept waiting for him to say something. What Jeremiah had said was true, I was keeping things from Alex. There were things I could never tell him, at least not yet. It would be natural for him to question me as to what Jeremiah was talking about.

But he didn't say anything. He simply pulled me into his arms in the living room, pressing a kiss to my forehead, and held me for a very long time.

Eventually he released me, kissing me just once on the lips. "You look tired."

I could only nod.

"I'll let you go to sleep then. I'm going to start working on the cake tonight."

"Okay," I said quietly as he took a step away from me and started for the kitchen. I crossed to my room, pausing in the doorway.

"Alex?" I said quietly.

"Yes," he paused, his eyes looking slightly sad.

"I love you."

"I know," he said with an almost forced half-smile. "I love you too."

Trying to smile back, I stepped into the room and closed the door behind me. I leaned against it, letting my eyes slide closed.

I hated keeping secrets from Alex. I hated that I couldn't tell him that I was communicating with Cole, that I was begging for his help. I couldn't tell him that as of right now, I couldn't die, that I could never join him. I couldn't tell Alex that I was considering doing *anything* to save him.

But it was better to keep him safe. Even if it meant keeping the truth from him.

Taking a deep breath, I pushed away from the door and went into the bathroom to get ready for bed.

As I brushed my teeth, I studied myself in the mirror. I'd gotten used to the otherworldly perfection I'd acquired. It was still unnerving for me and everyone around me but I was used to it by now. But there was something different about my countenance.

It was that I wasn't running scared anymore. I wasn't just kneeling down and taking the beating the afterlife had dealt me my entire life. I wasn't shedding tears anymore, my hands didn't shake, my emotions weren't getting the best of me at every moment.

I was finally fighting.

I spit into the sink and rinsed my mouth out. I changed into my tank top and cotton shorts, glancing in the mirror at the raised scars of intricate wings that spanned my back. I had been only minutes away from acquiring my own real set of wings just before Alex died.

Strangely, I felt calm as I climbed under the cool sheets. I wasn't panicked, I wasn't scared. Only weeks before, Cole had terrorized me, was my worst nightmare. But now I sought out his presence.

I could face my worst fear if it meant saving the man I loved.

And then I closed my eyes, slowed my breathing, and let sleep take me over.

CHAPTER FOURTEEN

I sensed another presence in the dark as soon as I entered the world of the unreal. They shifted uneasily, their breath rapid and scared.

"Hello?" a voice cautiously called out. "Is someone there?"

I didn't know what to answer. I knew I wasn't supposed to be here. It seemed better that I didn't say anything.

"I know you're there," they said in a shaky voice. "Do you know what's going on? Where... where am I?"

A part of me wanted to reassure whoever it was in the dark, to tell them that everything was going to be alright. But that would be unfair. I knew nothing of the deeds of this man's life, what his scrolls contained. He had a fifty-fifty chance of being pulled into the fiery depths in just moments.

"I..." they stuttered. "I think something happened to me. I... I remember a car swerving in front of us. And then..."

As the person struggled to remember their final moments of life, I felt the air shift around me, turning icily cold. With a muffled scream, that other person was plunged into the afterlife.

I waited. If a trial was just getting over, it might take a little bit before Cole could escape unnoticed.

He arrived quicker than I had expected. The air suddenly chilled again, and I felt his presence behind me, standing very close.

"That was a very brave and very stupid thing you did," his voice saturated my ears.

"I couldn't let them take him," I breathed as I hugged my sides.

Even though I couldn't see through the dark, I sensed the smile that spread on Cole's perfect face. "You've grown, Jessica. You're not afraid anymore."

"I'm terrified," I said as I furrowed my brow, turning in the dark to face him. "Every moment I'm scared that I'll find that he's gone, that I can never join him."

"But you're fighting now. You have learned to stand up for yourself finally."

"Did they mean it?" I asked. "That they will give him a while longer?"

"Yes," Cole said as he started pacing. "But a while is not a long while. You've got to figure this out faster."

"Can't you just tell me how to save him?" my voice came out desperate.

"You think I have all the answers," Cole said coolly. "I know you have the ability to do it yourself. Jessica," he paused. "I don't know how you are going to save him. I do know that if they take him, it will be too late. He's dead. Once the council claims the dead, the dead don't get to go back. At least not permanently.

"And even if I did know what to tell you, I couldn't," Cole said, his voice lowering. "I would risk losing my position. As it is, it is already in danger. They watch me. My being here now is dangerous."

I reached out through the dark, searching for Cole. My fingers only met the cool air. "You've grown too, Cole." I couldn't help but smile.

"Don't mention it," he said sarcastically. "There is something else you should know," he moved on. "Alex's mother."

"Caroline?" I questioned. "What about her?"

"I can sense her. Her transition into my world becomes stronger by the hour. I felt her a few hours ago. She'll be under my leadership soon if you do not intervene."

"Where is she?" I asked, my voice coming out desperate sounding.

"She's in a place that's familiar to her. I can feel Alex's presence all around her. I don't recognize the place."

"The rental house," I breathed. My heart started hammering in my chest. "Thank you, Cole," I said, again reaching out for him. "I have to get back. We have to help her."

"Jessica," he called as I started willing myself to wake up. I paused, turning in his general direction. "You can't come back to this place. It's too dangerous. For both of us."

I nodded, figuring Cole would know I did. "Good-bye, Cole."

"Good-bye, Jessica," he breathed.

The air started to warm, my insides started shaking. And I opened my eyes to the pre-dawn lit ceiling.

"Alex!" I shouted, jumping out of bed, rushing for my closet.

Alex burst through the door, his front side covered in flour, panic in his eyes. "What's wrong?"

I pulled off my sleeping shorts, not even thinking about Alex seeing me in only my underwear. Pulling on a pair of jeans, I then threw on a long sleeved t-shirt. "We need to get to the rental house. Now."

"Why?" he asked, his brow furrowing.

"I just... have a feeling we should go over," I lied. Again.

"What..." he shook his head. "What's going on with you?"

"Please," I said as I stepped out of the closet and held his eyes. "Just go get changed. Quickly."

He looked at me a moment longer, the wheels in his head turning. "Okay," he said as he shook his head and walked out the bedroom door.

I whirl winded around the bathroom, trying to tame my hair, brushing my teeth. By the time I walked back into the living room, Alex was dressed and waiting with the truck keys.

"Let's go," I said, having a hard time meeting his eyes. Not saying a word, he followed me out to the garage.

We drove in silence for a long while, tension hanging in the air. My fingers were knotted together tightly in my lap, my palms sweating.

"Is there something you want to tell me?" Alex finally asked. He kept his eyes fixed on the road ahead of him, his left hand gripping the top of the steering wheel just a little too tightly. The veins in his forearm bulged out.

I just shook my head and stared out the passenger window. Through the reflection in the glass I saw his jaw tighten.

As soon as we pulled into the driveway of the house, I jumped out of the truck, before Alex had even put it into park. Not seeing Caroline at the front steps, I practically ran around the back of the house. I pulled my cell phone out of my pocket and started dialing 911.

And there she was, passed out on the back step of the house. We had only brought her here once to see all the improvements Alex had made but apparently she had a good memory. I wondered how long she had been lying there, unable to get through the locked door.

"Caroline?!" Alex shouted as he followed me. Moving faster than me, he was suddenly by her side, rolling her onto her back, and pressing two fingers to the side of her neck.

"She's still alive," he said, followed by a curse under his breath. "She reeks of alcohol and I don't even want to know what else. Call an ambulance."

I simply pressed send.

In less than five minutes we heard the sirens wailing and the saw the lights flashing in the early morning air. A man and a woman loaded her up and less than seven minutes since I made the call, Alex and I were headed to the hospital.

"How did you know?" Alex asked very quietly. His entire frame was rigid.

"I just had a feeling," I lied, hating myself.

"How did you know, Jessica?!" he half shouted.

I glanced at him, seeing his cold, hard eyes turn on me. "I had a dream about it, okay?" I said defensively.

Alex glanced at me from the road for a moment, gauging what I had said. Finally his expression softened, he let out the breath he had been holding.

"I'm sorry I yelled," he said, his voice still tight. Given my past experience with dreams, it was understandable that he believed me. "It's just everything about Caroline gets me so freaked out. Sometimes I think it was a mistake bringing her back here."

"No, it wasn't," I said firmly. "She needs you. And you should be able to need your own mother."

He reached across the seat and took my hand in his. He glanced down at the ring on my finger for a moment, a small smile cracking on his lips.

"Moving on," he said quietly as he looked back at the road, his smile quickly fading. I didn't have the will-power to ask what he was referring to in this instance.

By the time we arrived in the emergency room at St. Joseph's hospital, Caroline had already been taken to a room and was receiving treatment. There was nothing Alex and I could do but sit in the waiting room and fill out paperwork.

"I don't even know half this information," Alex sighed as he worked his way down the page.

"Just do what you can," I said quietly as I tried not to meet the eyes of every staring person in the room. People always stared. I didn't know why I had expected that to stop. Their eyes would linger on my skin, on my too bright eyes. They didn't seem to be able to help it.

Alex stood back up, walking to the reception counter. "I'm sorry," he said as he handed the paperwork back to her on the clipboard. "That was all I knew. Any of the billing can come to me."

After getting more paperwork handed to him, Alex sat back down next to me.

"At least we found her," I said quietly. I leaned forward, resting my elbows on my knees, letting my hair fall around my face. I hated feeling like I had to hide. But I didn't want all their eyes on me. "She'll be at the wedding now, as long as she's okay."

"Well, I don't want to get any of my expectations up," Alex said as he continued to work on the forms. "Like I said, she's going straight to rehab this time."

My phone vibrated in my pocket. Pulling it out, I found a text from my dad.

Is there anything you need us to help with? Our flight leaves tomorrow morning.

And then it hit me. I'd been so distracted the last week that the days had been slipping by without my even noticing them.

The wedding was only three days away now.

While my heart suddenly started beating faster in excitement and anticipation, my stomach sank, fear for losing Alex taking over. I didn't have much guaranteed time after the wedding.

Nope, I texted back. *We've got pretty much everything done. Just show up.*

I can't believe my little Jessica is getting married. Love you.

Love you too, Dad.

Alex walked up to the counter and handed the woman the rest of the paperwork. Sinking back into his chair, he rubbed his hands over his eyes with a sigh. "I can't wait to get to the beach and unwind."

I rubbed circles into his back as he leaned forward. "Just the two of us," I said with a smile.

"Just the two of us," he said as he reached a hand over and rested it on my knee. His hand was stiff though. Alex was still mad.

We sat there for nearly an hour before a nurse came to get us. My stomach twisted as I remembered Sal lying in one of these beds, of finding a feather tangled in her blankets, of waking in a hospital bed myself, and knowing that I had to get out of there as soon as possible. It seemed I was visiting this hospital all too often the last seven months.

We were led into a room with a doctor in a while lab coat fussing over Caroline's still form.

"You must be her family," the doctor said as he stepped away from her and shook each of our hands. "I'm Dr. Scoresby."

"Alex Wright, and soon to be Mrs. Wright, Jessica," Alex introduced. I couldn't help but smile. Maybe he wasn't too mad at me after all.

Dr. Scoresby nodded. "We're flushing Caroline's system out right now. She had a dangerous mix of methamphetamines in her system, as well as extreme amounts of alcohol. She would have been dead within a few hours, maybe less, if you hadn't found her when you did."

Alex just stared at his mother's body. "Is she going to be okay?" I asked when Alex didn't say anything.

"It's going to take a while to flush everything out of her system," the doctor said, turning his eyes on me. He stared for a second, as if he was actually looking at me for the first time. "Uh," he stuttered. "I'm going to recommend that she stay in hospital care for a few days. And if I may be frank, I suggest we immediately release her to rehab."

"That's the plan," Alex suddenly said, his eyes hardening as he continued to look at his mother.

"Is there any chance," I piped up "that she could be released by Saturday. Just for a few hours. That's the day of the wedding."

A small smile crossed his face for a moment. "Congratulations," he said. His smile then faded just as quickly. "We will see how treatment goes. She will need to be watched very closely. Drug addicts will do anything to get to their next fix. It might not be very enjoyable for the two of you to have to make sure she doesn't abscond during your wedding."

"We'll make it work," I said as I slid my hand into Alex's, giving it a tight squeeze. His fingers just hung loose.

"Well, we'll see how things go," the doctor said. "Right now we can just wait while her system flushes out. I don't think she'll wake up for a while. A nurse will be in soon to look after your mother. If you'll excuse me."

He offered one more smile before he let himself out of the door.

Pulling away from my hand, Alex walked to the side of the bed. Looking down at her, I saw his eyes harden, his jaw tighten.

"I'm so sick of her always screwing things up," he said through clenched teeth. "I don't know why I keep expecting her to change. To be a decent person."

I swallowed hard, stuffing my hands into my pockets, not knowing what to say. He was right though. She wasn't a decent person. She was trying to kill herself with the life she was leading.

"Do you still want her to come?" I asked.

"To the wedding?" he asked, looking at me. I hated how sad his eyes looked. I nodded. His eyes dropped back down to her still form. "I don't know. Maybe not. She might not even be able to come."

I came to his side, sliding my hand into his again. He loosely curled his fingers around mine. "Give her one more chance," I said quietly as I looked down at her. She was so scary looking. "If she can, let her come to the wedding. If she cares enough to behave for a few hours and goes to rehab without issues, maybe she can change. If that doesn't happen, if she continues her drama, be done. No one can blame you. She abandoned you all your life. She can't expect you to keep swooping in and saving her at the last minute."

"That's the thing," he said, his voice hinting at cracking. "She doesn't want to be saved. She doesn't want me saving her. She's already told me that herself."

"One more chance," I said, leaning my head against his shoulder.

I felt him nod, giving my hand a tight squeeze. Finally. "One more chance. But I'm not waiting around the next few days, holding my breath."

Just then the door opened again, a young looking nurse with slanted eyes and straight black hair walking in.

"I'm Caroline's nurse until she's transferred to her long term room," she said quietly. "I'm just going to take her vitals and draw another blood test."

Alex nodded, stepping out of the way as she started to work. "We're not staying actually," Alex said as he cleared his throat. I could tell how hard this was for him. "She's going to need to be watched closely. I'd say she's a flight risk. Have them give me a call when they know more."

"I will let them know," she said, giving Alex a sad smile.

Alex nodded, and grasping my hand tighter, turned and we walked out of the room. Just as we were about to walk out of the sliding glass doors, Alex's phone rang. He answered it with a curt sounding "Hello?"

I felt like there was a rock in the pit of my stomach. It was supposed to be filled with happy butterflies just days before my wedding. Instead I was terrified of my fiancé being pulled into the world of the dead, my soon to be mother-in-law was strung out and nearly dead, and everything just felt wrong. This wasn't how things were supposed to be.

"That was the tux shop. My suit is ready," Alex said as he slid his phone into his pocket. "Want to come with me to pick it up right now?"

"Sure," I said, my mood instantly brightened. This was more like it.

CHAPTER FIFTEEN

It only took us a few minutes to get to the tux shop. My heart started beating faster with the right kind of anticipation as I thought of seeing Alex in a suit in just a few days, about to bind himself to me for as long as we had.

Which I intended to make much longer.

"You know," I said as the woman helping us started to unzip the white garment bag that held Alex suit. "I think I'm going to wait outside while you try it on. I want to be surprised and see you in it for the first time at the wedding."

"How traditional of you," Alex winked at me and I stepped back into the bright sunlight outside.

My phone started ringing as soon as I sat on the bench just outside the doors. Pulling it out, I found it was Rita.

"Hi," I answered.

"Hey, sweetie," she said in her ever-kind voice. "I got Katlin to come in for your shift this afternoon. You're only days out from your wedding and I feel bad for scheduling you today."

"Don't worry about it," I said as I picked at a thread on the hem of my jeans. "It's not a big deal."

"Well," she said. "I've already asked her to come in and I think you might have other plans this afternoon."

"I don't, really, its fine," I tried to clarify.

"I've got it covered sweetie. Have fun today. See you after you get back from your honeymoon!" and then she hung up the phone.

I glanced at the screen, seeing "call ended" flashing at me. Shaking my head, I slid my phone back into my pocket. Just as I did it vibrated.

Where are you? a text from Emily read.

We have plans right now, another from Amber came through at the same time.

I shook my head, laughing to myself. So that was what Rita had meant that I had plans for this afternoon.

Be home soon, I texted back. *With Alex picking up his suit.*

I didn't have to wait long for Alex to come back out. His real Alex-smile spread on his lips as he walked out of the doors, white bag slung over one shoulder.

"So apparently I have plans right now," I said as we slid into the truck. "I'm a little afraid what Emily and Amber have in store for me."

"I guess I have plans too," Alex chuckled as he started the engine. "Rod called while I was in there. We're having a little 'party' tonight."

My face suddenly fell. "There aren't going to be any strippers involved, are there?"

Alex laughed as he looked over his shoulder and backed out of his parking space. "Don't worry, if the strippers come out I'll put an end to it. Maybe," he added.

"Alex!" I yelled as I hit his arm. My playful hit would have bruised a normal man.

"Kidding! Kidding!" he laughed. "Don't worry, Rod knows you'd kill him if he planned for strippers."

I just shook my head and laughed. "Man, a bachelor party," I said as we started back home. "This is getting pretty real."

"Not getting cold feet on me, are you?" he raised an eyebrow at me, a crooked smile on his lips.

"No way! You're not going to change your mind on me, are you?"

Alex's eyes got serious then as he glanced over at me. He took my hand in his again, pressing a kiss to the back of it. "Never."

By the time we pulled back into the driveway, everyone was there waiting for us, Emily, Amber, and Rod.

"Prepare to be ambushed," Alex said, hesitating to open the door.

"Yikes," I breathed.

And as soon as I stepped out of the truck, I was attacked with a pink boa, a plastic tiara, and forced into a pair of black lacy panties, over my jeans.

"These are your last days of freedom," Emily declared as she spun me around, taking pictures as I twirled. "We must live it up before you're tied down for eternity!"

"Why didn't you make him wear a speedo or something?" I asked Rod, giving him a mock glare. I could feel my face burning in embarrassment.

Rod raised one eyebrow at us, shaking his head. "Unlike you ladies, I actually like my best friend, and am unwilling to submit him to this kind of humiliation."

"You're just not as creative as us," Amber said, bounding over to press a quick kiss to his cheek. He couldn't help but smile.

"Rod," I said as the Emily started dragging me into the house. "No strippers, okay?"

He laughed out loud. "Yeah, right. Alex would have a heart attack as soon as the first bit of clothing was removed."

Amber suddenly froze behind us, turning back toward the guys. "Rod," she said seriously. "No strippers."

His face suddenly turned serious. "No strippers, baby."

She blew him a kiss before helping to shove me into the house. I barely managed a wave good-bye to Alex before he slipped into Rod's car.

As soon as I walked in the door, I froze in horror.

"Oh my…" I trailed off.

Posters were taped to the walls everywhere, each of them dominated by a man wearing only a tight pair of underwear, each of them sculpted to muscular perfection.

"You guys," I said as I shook my head, feeling my face flush with heat. "This is humiliating."

"Come on!" Emily said as she grinned mischievously and pulled me over to the couch. "Enjoy looking at a few half naked men before you aren't allowed to anymore."

"Why would I want to look at any other half-naked men when I've got Alex?" I said as I raised an eyebrow at her.

"You've got a point there," she said with a mock wistful sigh. "But, the real point is that these men *aren't* Alex."

"They're also two dimensional men," I teased her.

"That's enough!" Emily said in an authoritive voice, holding back her laughter. "Amber, get me the box!"

A giddy laugh bubbled from Amber's lips as she bounded to the bar and picked up a box.

"You aren't going to do anything to embarrass me further, are you?" I cringed as Amber bounded back across the room with a black box that had a pink lacy pattern printed on it.

"We intend to educate you," Emily said as she raised one eyebrow at me, a sly grin on her face. Taking the box from Amber, she opened the lid and handed it to me.

As I looked inside, I flushed a scarlet that made my face burn.

Well, they were right. This was one area I certainly had no experience in.

"What's the occasion ladies?" the waitress asked as she brought us our waters. "This wouldn't be a bachelorette outing, would it?"

"What gave me away?" I said as I looked down at the pink boa and touched the crown on my head. At least they had let me take the panties off. Emily and Amber snickered in their seats next to me. The waitress smiled.

"When's the wedding?"

"Three days," we all said at the same time.

"Congratulations," she smiled kindly. Getting back to her job, she took each of our orders and walked away.

"Guys, this place is way too expensive for what I know you make," I said as I looked around the darkly lit restaurant. I'd been there with Alex once upon a time and remembered the stack of cash he had to leave behind when we were done.

"Don't worry about it," Amber smiled slyly. "Rod's paying."

"To Rod," Emily said, raising her glass of water for a toast.

"To Rod," Amber and I echoed, raising our glasses.

Taking a long draw, we set our glasses down with a heavy clank.

"I really do think you should wear your hair like that," Emily said, fussing with the curls. "Minus the crown, maybe."

I touched the curls that were half gathered on the back of my head, half cascading down my back. I'd never had my hair look so tamed. The three of us had spent half the day fussing over my hair and makeup. "I do like it."

The waitress soon returned with our dinner. My stomach turned as I looked at my salad and bread sticks. I was liking to eat less and less these days.

"So are you ready for your parents to get into town tomorrow?" Emily asked as she swallowed a bite.

"Don't remind me," I mumbled as I picked up a piece of the hot bread. "I just hope I survive 'til after the wedding."

"You'd just skip over the wedding and all the memories and go right to the…"

"Emily!" I cut her off, blushing again. "You are terrible today!"

"Hey, ever since I stopped going out all the time and," she took a hard swallow "Cormack left, I'm a little…"

"Horney?" Amber said as she broke a piece of her own bread and popped it into her mouth.

"Amber!" I shrieked, looking around to make sure no one could hear her. I shook my head, chuckling at her.

"She's such a prude," Amber said to Emily, leaning into her side.

"So innocent," Emily batted her eyes. "Until Saturday that is."

"Oh my gosh!" I gasped, covering my flushed face with my hands.

"Excuse me miss. The man at the bar just sent these over," the waitress suddenly said. As I uncovered my eyes, I saw her set three glasses of what I assumed was red wine on our table. "He said to tell you good luck."

I whipped my head around toward the counter. It was empty.

"Who sent it?" I asked the young girl before she left.

She searched the room, a confused look forming on her face. "Oh, he was there just a moment ago. He must have just left. Enjoy though."

"Oh," Amber said. "A secret, mysterious admirer." She reached for her glass.

"Don't touch that!" I snatched it away before she could grab it, just a little too fast. My heart was pounding in my chest, every nerve inside of me saying something didn't feel right.

"You're only eighteen," I covered for my reaction.

"I'll be nineteen in three weeks," she wined.

"Still not old enough to be drinking," I raised my eyebrows at her. "And you," I said as I pulled Emily's glass away from her. "You should know better than to drink things strangers give you. Remember that night I picked up at like three in the morning?"

"True," she said as she tipped her head to the left, giving a little nod. "And you don't drink. What a waste of that guy's money."

Trying to be discrete as we started eating, I leaned forward and took a sniff at the wine. I wasn't familiar with how it was supposed to smell, but something didn't seem right. Then I noticed the tiny white granules at the bottom of the glasses, something not quite dissolved yet.

As I glanced up, I saw him, watching me through the darkening window outside. A sly smile tugged at Jeremiah's lips, and then he was gone.

He'd just tried to poison us. Knowing the waitress wouldn't have known which glass to give me, he had put something in every one of our glasses. He would have killed all three of us.

"I'm not very hungry anymore," I said as I pushed my plate away, along with the three glasses.

"Are you okay?" Amber asked. "You look kind of... greenish."

"It's all of you and Emily's sex talk," I said, just a little too sharply.

My phone suddenly vibrated. It showed a text from Alex.

"No phones during the party!" Emily said, quickly snatching it from my hands.

"Wait!" I shouted, just a little too loudly. "I need that!"

Emily glanced at my phone. "Alex can wait until we return you tonight."

"His mom's in the hospital," I suddenly blurted, glaring at her.

"Oh," was all she managed, looking at me with taken-aback eyes. "Why didn't you tell us?"

"I didn't exactly get a chance with everything you two have been putting me through," I said, grabbing my phone back.

Caroline woke up, the text said. *They're watching her. If she cooperates they said she could come Saturday.*

I just shook my head as I read the message. I could only really hope that she didn't screw this up.

"Is everything okay?" Amber asked in a quiet voice.

I slid my phone back into my pocket and took a long drink of my water before I spoke. "We found her this morning, all drugged up. Alex is pretty fed up."

"I don't blame him," Emily said, raising her eyebrows. "I mean it's nice that he found his mom after all this time but she is one screwed up woman."

"Are you ladies ready for your bill?" the waitress asked as she walked up to the table.

Amber pulled a card out of her purse and handed it to the woman before she could even set the ticket down. With a polite smile, the girl walked away.

"Is she still coming to the wedding?" Amber asked.

"We'll see how things go," I answered as I rubbed my eyes. I was suddenly dead tired. I'd been spending all my sleeping time in the afterlife and with Cole lately. "Alex is ready to send her to rehab and be done with her."

"We're a sad bunch," Emily said as she pulled a small mirror from her purse and checked her lip gloss. "We've all got some really screwed up parents."

"Hey, Rod's parents are normal," Amber chimed in. "At least they seem like it from the phone."

We just chuckled at her and finished paying. Walking out into the cooling early fall air, I couldn't help but glancing around, looking for my new stalker. He was nowhere to be seen.

I sat in silence with my forehead against the window as Amber and Emily drove me back home. Things were so crazy lately, I felt like I couldn't keep life straight. There were too many important things going on right now. A wedding, life, death. It was all just too much right then.

"Jessica?" a voice from the front seat finally said. I sat up, realizing that I had been dozing off. "You're home."

"Oh," I rubbed the sleep from my eyes. "Thanks for everything. I really did have a good time."

Amber and Emily said goodbye and headed back for their apartments. I walked slowly back up to the house, breathing in the cool air. Glancing over at Sal's house, I saw all the lights off, deciding it was too late to go and check on her. My eyes wandered down to Cole's house, looking empty and so forlorn.

I found that Alex was still gone when I went inside. Things looked normal, all of Amber and Emily's embarrassing posters taken down. Half stumbling into the bathroom, I changed and brushed my teeth. My hair came cascading down as I let out the bobby pins. A little sign escaped my lips as I slid between the cool sheets and pulled the blanket up to my chin.

"Jessica?" Alex's voice suddenly cut through the dark house, the door closing behind him.

"In here," I called sleepily. The fingers of sleep were already tracing their way down my back, pulling me down into them.

He walked quietly into the room, leaning against the doorframe, his arms crossed over his chest.

"Did you have fun tonight?" I asked with a yawn.

"Yeah, we went to a basketball game and then went out to the shooting range," he said quietly through the dark.

"So, no strippers?"

"No strippers," somehow I could hear his smile.

"Come here," I said, letting my eyelids slide closed.

I heard Alex slip his shoes off before he slid into the bed. Finding my familiar spot, I nestled myself into his side.

"I've missed you at nights," I said quietly.

"I've missed you too," he whispered as he placed a kiss on the top of my head.

"Will you stay here until I fall asleep?"

I barely heard him whisper "of course," before I was out.

CHAPTER SIXTEEN

The sun shone in brightly through the bedroom window, amplified by the reflection off the lake. I rolled over, pushing my hair out of my eyes, squinting against the light. The sound of the TV drifted into the bedroom.

Straightening my clothes, I shuffled across the floor, glancing at the clock. It was already ten-thirty.

Rubbing my eyes, I stepped into the living room.

"Whatcha' watching?" I said with a yawn.

And then I opened my eyes. My parents were sitting on the couch, chatting with Alex.

It hadn't been the TV I'd heard.

"Hey sleepy head," Dad said cheerfully as he stood and crossed the room to give me a hug. I suddenly stiffened, realizing I was wearing only a spaghetti strapped top. I could be thankful for my mane of hair to cover most everything. I also felt self-conscious for wearing extremely short shorts.

"Hi," I breathed as he wrapped his arms around me. "I didn't expect you guys so early."

"Well, the day is almost half over," he teased as he stepped away from me. My eyes shifted over to my mom, who sat stiff and tense on the couch.

"Hi sweetie," she said with a slightly forced looking smile.

"Hi mom," I said, attempting to smile back.

It was then that I noticed Alex trying to hold back a chuckle.

"What?" I demanded, glaring at him.

"Nice hair," he finally laughed, covering his smile with his fist.

"Oh my gosh," I said in horror, retreating back into my room. I could feel my face flood red. Dashing into the bathroom, I found it smashed completely flat on one side, and sticking up to a comical height on the other.

"I'm jumping in the shower," I yelled from the bathroom, and heard laughter answer me back.

Just breathe, I reminded myself as I stepped into the warm water. *You're a grown up. You have your own life, you're getting married. Stop letting her affect you so much.*

After pulling on a pair of jeans and a light sweater, I made extra sure my hair stayed in a general downward direction. My heart couldn't seem to decide if it wanted to be calm or try and hammer out of my chest.

By the time I made my way back out into the living area, my parents were seated at the bar and Alex was working on a brunch that would feed a small army.

154

"Better?" I teased Alex as I grabbed a glass from the cupboard and filled it with orange juice.

"Beautiful," he smiled, kissing me on the cheek.

"You two are so cute together," my mom said with a sigh, a real, happy smile on her face.

I genuinely managed to return it as I sat on the barstool next to my dad.

"So what can we help with this morning?" she asked as Alex set a plate of pancakes on the counter. "There's got to be a lot to do still, you guys threw this together so fast."

"Not really," I said, eyeing the pancakes, my stomach suddenly churning slightly. "We've got the venue all picked out and ready to go. Its outdoors so there's not really any decorating that needs to be done. The dresses are set to go."

"You picked one?" my mom beamed.

I nodded. "And then we just have to pick up the flowers tomorrow afternoon. Alex has the cake just about done. Um..." I tried to think. My mind had been in so many other places I felt like there was something I was forgetting. Somehow I felt cheated out of what was supposed to be the biggest day of my life. There were so many other things going on that the wedding felt almost unimportant. "Anything else, Alex?"

He shook his head as he forked pieces of bacon onto a plate. "I don't think so. Everything's pretty much ready."

"Well what about a reception after the ceremony?" Mom asked, her brow furrowing.

155

"There's not really any need," I said with a hard swallow. My stomach didn't feel right. "We literally only have eight guests coming. We're keeping it really small."

"Really?" Dad said in surprise. "What about all of your friends from down in California, Alex?"

I saw Alex's eyes flash to my face for just a moment. He shook his head, throwing on a small smile. "None of them could make it up on such short notice. I don't mind it being small though."

I hated Alex having to lie. He wasn't inviting his friends because he had cut off almost all ties now that he had changed so dramatically. It was easier this way. But still not right.

"It sounds romantic, sweetie," Mom smiled at me.

I smiled back, glancing down at the glass I held between my hands. My stomach felt like it was quivering. Small tremors worked their way from my core, out into my limbs and down into my fingers and toes.

Maybe I should have expected that going back to the afterlife, being mostly dead myself, would have repercussions.

My throat felt like it was caving in on itself as all of my insides tightened on me. Suddenly my body felt as if it was crushing itself from the outside in.

I glanced up at Alex and found him watching me with narrowed eyes. I felt my own widen as the breath caught in my throat, feeling like my lungs were slowly dissolving in my chest.

Suddenly the glass between my hands shattered.

Every one of us jumped, my dad leaping from his seat to avoid the shards that sprayed across the bar.

"Whoa!" Dad cried as he half tripped over himself. And then his eyes narrowed.

There was a shard of glass sticking out of the fleshy part of my palm. I yanked it out before he could even process the movement.

"Oh, I'm so sorry!" I jumped to my feet, trying to divert attention before my dad realized that he really had seen what he thought he had. Going to the pantry, I grabbed the broom and the vacuum.

"Are you alright?" Mom called, jumping to her feet to help. "What happened?"

"I…" I stuttered, trying to make my brain function again. It couldn't seem to come up with a believable lie in that moment.

"She must have grabbed the glass with the crack in it," Alex covered for me as he started sweeping the glass up on the bar with a rag. "I knew I should have just thrown it out when I saw the crack. Sorry, Jessica."

"I'm okay," I repeated, setting to cleaning up. *I'm okay*, I said again to myself internally. The earthquake inside of me started to calm.

Things settled back down quickly, my parents eating the meal Alex had prepared for them, Alex and I pretending to eat. But I saw how Alex kept looking at me, saw his eyes narrow.

He knew something was wrong. He knew my behavior, he knew me too well to not know something was wrong.

I didn't know if I could keep hiding everything from him.

In an attempt to avoid the conversation I knew would be coming with Alex, I insisted on spending every moment of the rest of the day with my parents. I may have wanted to avoid my mother, but I wanted to avoid having to explain everything to Alex even more.

That evening, my parents being entertained by Alex, Amber, and Rod, I excused myself to go and check on Sal.

The house was quiet when I first walked in, though every single light was left on. Checking the first floor, I found no signs of Sal.

Keeping my feet quiet on the stairs to not wake her should she be asleep, I descended. And froze on the bottom step.

I could hear Sal talking, her voice low and hurried. She made no pauses, didn't wait for a response, just continued her rushed speech.

For a few moments my heart leapt into my throat. There shouldn't have been anyone in the house. Who was she talking to? Silently, I followed the sound of her voice, into her bedroom, and peeked around her bathroom door, which was just barely cracked.

Sal stood in front of the mirror, hurriedly speaking to her reflection, her eyes wide and blood-shot looking. Her hands twisted around each other, occasionally flitting to her mouth, covering her lips, though she never ceased her mumbled conversation.

"You... you..." she stuttered, looking at herself in the mirror. "Never should have talked to you at the beach that day. Never should have said hello. Hitting, hitting. So much hitting. I said stop, I said stop, but you, you couldn't listen."

I swallowed hard, remaining silent just outside the door. She was talking about her husband.

Or maybe talking *to* him.

"I..." she took a gasping, rattling breath, squeezing her eyes closed for a moment. "I can't remember what it felt like. I felt it moving. I know I did. But I can't remember..."

I thought back through what I knew about Sal's past, trying to recall what she might be talking about.

"You..." tears started streaking down her cheeks. "You took him away! The blood... Mine... his. You killed him! You killed our baby boy!"

Goosebumps flashed across my skin and my blood chilled as I finally understood what Sal was ranting about.

Sal had been pregnant when Roger had nearly beaten her to death. She'd lost the baby because of him. That explained why he'd been sentenced to jail for the rest of his life.

He'd nearly ended two lives that day.

I never knew about that part.

"Sal?" I called, my throat tight. The word cracked as it came out.

She jumped violently, her hands finally falling still at her sides. She whipped around to face me, her eyes wide, and almost guilty looking.

"Are you okay?" I asked as I pushed the door open.

She pressed her lips tightly together and gave a small nod.

"Are you sure?" I saw her hands start to tremble.

"Uh huh," she said with a shaky breath, wiping away one of the tears that rolled down her face.

"Why don't you come lay down?" I asked, stepping into the bathroom and placing a hand on her back. Gently, I started guiding her back toward her bed. "It's getting really late."

"Yes," she said, a small, very fake looking smile spreading on her face. "It's very late. Very late."

Sal crawled into her bed and I pulled the covers up to her chin. Sitting on the edge of her bed, I brushed the hair away from her face without thinking about it. She twitched away, her eyes squinting closed, her face cringing.

"I'm sorry, Sal!" I said, horrified, regret instantly filling me. I should have known better. She didn't like to be touched in general and considering the state I had just found her in, this was the worst time I could have touched her.

"It's okay," she said, squeezing her eyes closed again for a moment, taking a deep breath. "You won't hurt me."

"No," I shook my head. "I would never hurt you."

"Never," Sal said, shaking her head with her eyes closed.

"You know if something is going on that you can talk to me, right?" I asked.

She pressed her lips tight together again and nodded her head. A moment later she opened her eyes. As she looked up at me I saw fear hidden somewhere in them.

"Will you be okay tonight?" I asked, feeling my heart sink. It was so unfair, everything she had to go through. "I could stay tonight if you wanted."

She shook her head once. "I'll be okay, Jessica," she said, a small smile spreading on her face. "You're a good girl."

"So are you," I smiled back and stood. "Good-night, Sal."

"Night."

I glanced back at her just once more as I walked out her door. She was staring wide-eyed at the ceiling above her, the faintest movement forming on her lips.

She was getting worse.

As I got to the top of the stairs, I pulled out my cell phone and dialed Alex. He picked up on the second ring.

"Hey," he answered. I could hear everyone laughing in the background.

"Hi," I said quietly. I didn't want Sal to hear me. "Um, I think I'd better stay over here for the night. Sal's not doing too good."

"What's wrong?" he asked, his voice concerned.

I sighed, pacing the floor. "Sal's been acting strange lately. She keeps seeing her husband who's in jail. She hasn't been sleeping well. Just now I found her in her bathroom having a full-fledged conversation with herself in the mirror. She was really upset."

"Do you want me to come over there with you?" he asked, I could hear him shutting a door behind him, like he had walked into the bedroom for privacy.

"No," I breathed. "I'll be okay. I'm just going to try and get some sleep on her couch. You keeping the troops entertained?"

"Yeah, everyone's just playing a game right now," Alex answered on the other line.

"Will you tell them that I'm sorry to cut the night short?"

"Sure."

"Alex," I said, pausing for just a moment. "I love you."

My heart sank into my stomach for just a second when Alex paused for an instant too long. "I love you too."

CHAPTER SEVENTEEN

Sal had muttered for an hour straight before she finally quieted. My eyes looked up at the ceiling, wide with the horror of hearing the frightening, nonsensical things Sal repeated over and over again. I breathed a sigh of relief when she finally fell asleep.

I didn't sleep more than two or three hours myself. As the sun made its way to the tops of the trees I slipped out Sal's front door. I didn't want to upset her further by being caught on her couch unexpectedly.

The house was quiet as I walked in the door. I chuckled as I found Amber and Rod asleep on the couch in the living room, the two of them tangled in each other in an uncomfortable looking way. Amber snored softly. I assumed my parents had made their way to their hotel room late last night.

I found Alex out on the back deck, standing at the railing, leaning with his forearms rested on it. His scars were in plain view on his bare back, his legs crossed at the ankle, covered in a breezy pair of sweats.

As I walked toward the door, he turned to look at me. The light danced in his grey eyes, the sun making his flawless skin glow. His face lightened in a quick smile as he saw me. I couldn't help but return it as I crossed the room and walked out onto the deck.

He wrapped his arms around me as I stepped into him, his breath tickling the skin on my neck.

"How's Sal?" he asked quietly.

"Alright, I guess," I replied. "She had a rough night."

"Did you get any sleep?"

"Maybe three hours," I answered honestly.

Alex shook his head. "You'd better watch out, I may just slip some sleeping pills into your dinner tonight so you get rested up before the big day."

My heart jumped into my throat. "Tomorrow."

"Tomorrow," Alex said with a smile as he looked into my eyes.

"I…" I struggled with words. "I didn't really ever think this day would come. It still doesn't really feel real."

"This is real," he said as he smiled, and then pressed his lips to mine. "This is real," he moved them to my neck. "You're real. My beautiful, strong Jessica."

His lips met mine again, moving with well-practiced movements. But the kiss deepened for only moments.

"Can't you guys wait until you're alone tomorrow night?" Amber said groggily, squinting through the bright light.

"Hey, this is our house," Alex teased as we stepped away from each other. I just chuckled and glared at her.

She grunted something incomprehensible and shuffled toward the bathroom. Rod gave a loud snorting snore on the couch, rolling over, and falling to the floor. He continued to snooze away. Alex and I broke out into muffled laughter.

"It's going to be a busy day today," Alex said quietly as he stepped back into the house, me following him.

I nodded, sitting at the bar. Alex opened the fridge and poured a glass of orange juice. He looked at it for a moment, longing in his eyes.

"It couldn't be too bad if I just took one sip, right?" he said, his eyes never leaving the orange surface.

"Yeah, 'cause it's so fun trying to hack it back up," I said as I shook my head and held my hand out for the glass.

"Fine," he said with a sigh, handing it over, a hint of a smile threatening to take over his face.

"So," I said after a long draw. "I'm going with my mom to pick up the flowers this afternoon. You've got the cake about done?"

Alex nodded. "You going to be okay with her on your own this afternoon?"

I shrugged, keeping my eyes glued to the countertop. "I'll have to be I guess. We'll see how things go."

"I'm really proud of you, you know that?" he said as he took one of my hands in his. "You've taken 'moving on' to a whole new level, way more than I expected you too."

"Tomorrow proves you have too," I said cautiously. Bringing up the last few months was a delicate subject.

Alex didn't have time to respond to that before his cell phone started ringing.

"Hello?" he answered. "This is him. Uh huh. By tomorrow? Is the facility ready for her?" Alex paused, listening. "Alright, thank you for keeping me updated." He sighed and set the phone on the counter.

"Caroline?" I guessed.

Alex nodded and pressed his hands over his face, rubbing his eyes. "Yeah. They said her system is pretty flushed out by now. They said she will be cleared to come tomorrow if someone can come get her and then the rehab facility will come and pick her up directly after."

"That's great," I said encouragingly. "So she'll be there."

"We'll see," he sighed as he straightened.

Rod suddenly grunted from the floor, and pulled himself onto the couch.

"Morning sunshine," Alex teased.

"Shut up," Rod half growled, half groaned, narrowing his eyes at Alex. "Dude, put some clothes on."

Alex chuckled and headed down the stairs to his bedroom. His for the next twenty-four hours anyway.

"Where's Amber?" Rod asked, rubbing his eyes and yawning.

"In the bathroom," I replied, turning on the stool to face him.

"Is Sal okay?" Amber said a second later as she came walking out of the bathroom.

"I think so," I said. Just then the front door opened and in walked Mom, Dad, Emily, and surprisingly, Austin.

"Well hello," I said, my eyebrows rising in surprise at the crowd that suddenly filled the house. "Morning everyone."

"Morning," Dad said cheerily for everyone. His face was practically beaming. "I thought I'd take everyone out for brunch."

"Um," I struggled to answer. I hated trying to pretend to eat at meals with everyone and knew Alex was just undergoing torture during these times. "I guess?"

"Sure," Alex said as he emerged, properly dressed, a bright smile on his face. "Let's go."

Less than fifteen minutes later, everyone filed back outside and each couple pulled away in their own car and started heading north into town.

"So, Austin and Emily..." Alex trailed off, his eyes on the road.

"I have no idea," I said as I shook my head. "She was talking to him at the bookstore the other day and then they hung out after. Do you think they're dating?"

"I hope so," Alex said in a half joking, half serious tone. "Maybe then Austin will stop checking you out every time you walk by him."

I chuckled, shaking my head again. "And Emily can focus on someone other than Cormack. Geeze, I feel like a crappy friend. I don't even know if my best friend is dating the guy I work with."

"You've kind of had a lot on your mind lately," Alex said as he took my hand in his. Somehow the statement felt heavier than it should have.

Brunch passed in a blur. I hardly got more than five words in the entire time as everyone talked over each other, excitement bubbling up about everything and nothing. I watched Emily and Austin closely throughout the meal, watched for glances of affection, brief touches. I didn't see anything, but I saw the way that both of their eyes seemed to glow just a little bit. It had been a long time since I had seen either of them look so happy.

The rest of the day passed in much the same way, one big blur. Austin had to head back to the hospital but Amber and Emily had thankfully ended up going with my mom and I to pick up the flowers, saving me from any awkward moments of having to talk about angels, wings, or nightmares.

Everyone ended up back at the house that night. Sal had been fast asleep when I went to check on her so I had made my way back. It felt kind of nice to have the house and living room so crowded. It was almost like I was a normal human being with a family and friends. It was almost as if everything was just perfect.

But there was this sinking feeling in the pit of my stomach.

Even though I loved the people in this room, I was keeping a secret from each and every one of them. Each of those secrets felt like a crushing lie.

I didn't know how long I could keep it up before it all smothered me.

Pushing my thoughts aside, I pulled myself back into the atmosphere and told myself to simply enjoy it. Who knew how long it was going to last.

When Emily excused herself to use the downstairs bathroom as the upstairs was occupied, I recognized my opportunity and dismissed myself downstairs as well. I sat on the floor of the basement family room, leaning against the wall, and waited for her to walk back out and ambush her.

Emily jumped violently when she walked out. "Holy crap! Are you trying to give me a heart attack?" she accused.

"Sorry," I apologized and patted the ground next to me. She gave me a sly grin as if she knew exactly what I was up to, but sat next to me. "Spill," I said simply.

She chuckled, shaking her head. "I don't know what to say. We've hung out a bunch recently. I met most of his family over the last little while. We're friends."

"Friends?" I asked, giving her the suspecting eye.

"Who…" she dragged out as she thought. "I might not mind letting evolve beyond that?" she said in an unsure tone.

I bit my lower lip, trying to not let the smile on my face become too huge. "I'm really happy for you," I said, reaching and taking her hand in mine.

"Hey now, I'm not exactly getting married to the guy," she laughed. "I've just made a new friend."

"Either way," I said, giving her hand a squeeze. "I'm really happy for you. I was worried about you for a while."

"Me too," she said with a small, sad smile. "I don't want to go back to those dark places though."

"Hey!" Dad shouted from above. "What's going on down there?"

Emily and I both broke out into laughter. "Coming," we said in unison, which made us laugh all the harder. Jumping to her feet, Emily pulled me up to mine. Still hand in hand, we walked up the stairs.

"Look out Alex," Rod joked as we emerged. "Looks like you've got some competition."

The room erupted into laughter. Emily dropped my hand, folded her arms across her chest, and stuck her tongue out at me. I mimicked her. Everyone laughed all the harder.

And for the rest of that night everything felt perfect. Like maybe, just maybe, everything was going to work out alright.

That night, after everyone had said their good-nights and Emily and Amber teased the heck out of me about this being my last night as a virgin, Alex and I cleaned up and slowly started getting ready for bed.

We were both quiet, each seemingly lost in our own thoughts. But for some reason the air felt heavy, there were words that needed to be spoken hanging around us like hand-written notes attached to strings from the ceiling. But they were words neither of us seemed able or willing to say.

As the hour neared midnight, I wrapped my arms around Alex, resting my head against his chest. Just breathing him in brought on peace and comfort.

"We're alright, right?" he asked me quietly.

"Of course," I said, my stomach clenching up. "We're getting married tomorrow."

"Okay," he breathed. Tilting my head up, my lips sought his. It was brief, but in it I remembered everything we had gone though, everything we had given up to be with each other.

"I love you," I said softly against his lips.

"I love you too," he said, squeezing me for a moment. "Good-night, Miss Bailey."

"Good-night Mr. Wright." And then I took a step away, giving a small smile, and walked into my bedroom alone for the last time, and closed the door.

As soon as the door was shut I leaned against it, letting my head hang and my shoulders slump. It wasn't more than a full minute before the first tear started streaking down my face. Within another minute I couldn't stop the torrent of them as they fell down my cheeks.

My shoulders shook, my chest heaved. Everything inside of me quivered.

Everything was wrong. This wasn't how you were supposed to feel twelve hours from marrying the man of every woman's dreams. I wasn't supposed to feel this sense of sick, to feel like I was dirty from all the secrets and the lies that I had buried myself in. I wasn't supposed to be dreading my wedding day because I had no guarantee that the man who would be my husband in just hours was going to stay with me.

It was all just so wrong.

I dragged myself to my bed and collapsed onto its soft surface. And I cried myself to sleep.

CHAPTER EIGHTEEN

"Get up!" a loud voice shouted. With my enhanced hearing it felt like it was screamed right into my brain. My eyes flew open to see Amber, Emily, and my mom bustling around my room and bathroom.

"Get up!" Emily yelled again, this time jumping onto my bed. She took my shoulders in her hands and gave me a rough shake. "Wake up Jessica!"

"I'm up, gosh!" I half yelled at her, giving her a glare. "What time is it anyway?"

"It's nine-thirty!" she said in an exasperated tone, climbing out of the bed.

"What?" I gasped, leaping out of the bed, tripping over the sheets that were tangled around my feet, and falling flat on my face on the floor. "Why didn't anyone wake me up earlier?!"

"We assumed you would have been up before we got here," Amber said as she plugged the curling iron in and fussed around the bathroom. "It's not like you're normally one to oversleep."

"Why didn't Alex wake me up then?" I said, my voice sounding irritated as I headed toward the shower.

Amber and my mom shrugged but I noticed the way Emily stiffened, her eyes shot to my face.

My stomach dropped into my feet.

Without even trying to be tactful to not alarm Amber or my mom, I grabbed Emily by the arm and hauled her out into the living room.

"What?" I demanded, looking frantically around. Alex was nowhere to be seen.

"He's not here," Emily said in a low voice. "He wasn't at Sal's this morning, I checked when I went to get her ready."

"He's..." my voice cut out for a moment. "Gone?"

Emily's eyes widened in fear. They turned red and filled with tears that threatened to spill onto her perfectly made-up face. "I don't know," she whispered.

Everything inside of me froze and black spots formed on the edges of my vision.

"Sweetie," Mom said as she cautiously stepped out of my room. "Is everything okay?"

And right at that moment the front door opened and in walked Alex, wearing a pair of basketball shorts and a t-shirt, looking worn out and tired.

I rushed across the room, a bit faster than I should have, and squeezed him so tight I would have broken his ribs if he'd been normal. "Yeah," I answered. "Everything's perfect."

"What's wrong?" he asked. "Did I miss something while I was out on my run?"

Emily and I both chuckled with relieved sighs. I didn't even care about how he wouldn't have looked worn out from a run. But he would have looked worn out from fighting the call of the dead.

"No, you didn't miss anything," I said quietly, squeezing him again.

"Just Jessica panicking when she realized she's overslept by about an hour and a half," Emily chimed in. "Speaking of which," she grabbed my arm and started dragging me back to my room, "we need to be getting her ready or she'll be late for her own wedding."

I blew Alex a kiss before I was shoved into the room.

"Shower, now," Emily said as she pushed me toward the bedroom. "Quickly."

"Yes ma'am," I saluted as I closed the bathroom door behind me.

I barely even got all the shampoo out of my hair and my legs shaved before Emily was yelling outside the door to hurry up. As soon as I stepped out I was ambushed into lacy white panties and a strapless push-up bra I certainly hadn't picked out.

"Trust me," Emily said as she rolled her eyes at my embarrassment, partially at how I looked and partially at having all three of them seeing me in so little, "Alex is going to like it."

Throwing on an old button-up shirt of Alex's I wore to bed sometimes, I was sat in a chair and was subjected to having my hair pulled, twisted, curled, and pinned. The three of them argued over the exact amount of make-up that needed to be applied to my apparently already perfect face. And then the rest of my entire body was lotioned down and buffed and shined.

I looked absolutely unearthly by the time they were done.

"You look…" Amber breathed as they stepped back and observed their work. I squirmed under their scrutiny.

"Like an angel," Mom said as she gave me a cautious, tight-lipped smile and hugged me.

Nice word-choice, Mom, I thought to myself, rolling my eyes as I hugged her back.

"Alright people," Emily said a bit too loudly. "Let's move. We need to be there in less than a half hour!"

In a whirl-wind, I was forced into clothes that I would change out of when we got there, my dress was grabbed, the girls loaded their dresses into my mom's rental car. Emily dashed over to collect Sal, and with Rod and my Dad behind us, we headed to the facility. Alex had already left to go pick up Caroline from the hospital.

I sat with my forehead leaned against the glass, looking out at the partially cloudy October day. I felt oddly still inside. Perhaps a little too still. I wasn't feeling excited, I wasn't feeling nervous. I wasn't feeling much of anything.

I just felt there.

We pulled into the parking lot and I stepped out into the warm air. Alex parked next to us, flashing me a brilliant smile before walking around the truck and opening the door for Caroline. Dad and Rod pulled in next to him.

I simply went through the motions of grabbing my dress, of following Mom, Amber, Emily, and Caroline up the gardened path toward the front door. The smallest of movements caught my attention from the corner of my eye.

There was Jeremiah, standing at the edge of a garden, hands tucked into the pockets of his tuxedo.

A small smile spread on his lips as he stared at me with his black eyes.

I finally felt something.

Panic.

Turning my gaze away from him, I hurried inside with all the girls and we were directed to the dressing rooms.

I think everyone was trying to talk to me as they undressed me, pulling me into my dress. But I wasn't hearing anything. I had a million thoughts rushing through me, a million feelings. Everything that had happened in the last nine months was coursing through my head, all the choices I'd made, all the lies I'd told, all the secrets I'd kept.

And the things that Jeremiah had said to Alex.

Before I knew it, I registered my mom say that it was finally time. We were shuffled to another small building situated at one end of the garden we had chosen to be married in. Music started playing softly, bouquets were handed around, one was pressed into my clammy hands, and the girls started filling out the ornate doors that swung closed behind each of them.

Something within me told me I needed to open those doors and walk down the aisle of flowers that would lead me to Alex and the rest of my life. This was what I wanted, what I had been fighting to have for so long.

But I couldn't move.

You've given up so much for this woman, and yet there is so much she hasn't told you. Consider your sacrifice carefully.

I didn't deserve to have Alex. He had given *everything* for me. And I'd lied to him, about so much.

I didn't deserve him. I couldn't marry a man that I didn't deserve.

My legs sank me onto a white wicker chair, my elbows resting on my knees, my beautiful flowers resting loosely in my hands.

Everything inside of me felt dead again.

Just like the most of me was.

I barely registered the music stopping, heard the voices murmuring outside.

The door opened quietly and glancing up, my eyes already filling with tears, I saw Alex step inside.

He looked perfect. There was no other way to describe him. Everything about him was seamless from his face, to his hair, to the black tuxedo he wore. He was glorious.

He crossed the small space and without saying a word, he crouched down in front of me. Taking the bouquet from my hands and setting it on the floor next to him, he took my hands in his. A single tear escaped onto my cheek as his eyes met mine.

"I can't keep lying to you," I half whispered. "I can't marry you like this."

Alex's face didn't even falter, his eyes never wavered as he kept looking into mine.

"I can't die, Alex," I said, sniffing and wiping the tear from my face. "And I mean literally can't die. That was what Cole and I talked about when we were in England. I haven't changed at all since you died. I'm not even aging. I'm stuck. I can't progress, I can't move forward. Cole told me that while you're dead and while I have what was your life, I can't die. Too much of me had already died. So I'm stuck.

"I should have died, so many times since you did. But I didn't," my voice cracked slightly. "The car accident, in a fire, Cole throwing a knife into my chest to test this theory, so many times. You're going to be pulled back soon, and I can never go with you. Ever."

Alex continued to look into my eyes, his face unchanging. But I could see the wheels turning in his head.

"The angel who's been following me has been trying to figure out what is wrong with me. He thinks that if he can find a way to drag me back he can become the next Cole. And..." I hesitated, my eyes dropping away from

179

Alex's for a moment as I gathered the courage to tell Alex the worst part. "I've talked to Cole recently. A few times."

"Since Cole went back?" Alex asked, his voice shaky.

I met his eyes again, and nodded slowly.

"You've been back to the afterlife?" Now the fear showed in his eyes.

"Kind of," I scrambled as I gathered my thoughts, sorted everything out in my head. "One of those times I should have died that other angel was there, I grabbed him and somehow he pulled me back."

Alex's grip on my hands tightened slightly.

"He wanted to keep me there. Cole got me out. But I begged for his help. He told me to come see him when I slept."

"You went back again," he half stated, half asked.

"Three times," I breathed. "Alex, I watched them argue over when to take you back. That day you collapsed to the floor, when you found me next to you when you came to. I went back to the afterlife and Cole convinced them to let you have a few more weeks, enough time to make it just past the wedding.

"The other time he told me what it was the man who's been following me wanted. And then the last time he told me that he didn't know how to save you, just that I had to figure it out faster. That's how I knew about Caroline, where she was and that she was nearly dead. Cole told me."

I took a gasping breath, pulling one of my hands out of Alex's to cover my mouth as ragged breath's came in and out.

"Is there anything else?" Alex asked quietly.

I let my breath out with a whoosh, meeting his eyes again. I felt something inside of me harden. "Even if you don't want to marry me anymore for lying to you, I will still do anything, *anything* I have to to keep them from taking you."

He didn't say anything for a minute, just held my hand and looked at me. I could see thoughts flashing across his eyes. I wasn't sure if I wanted him to ever say anything or not.

"I wish you had told me sooner," he started. "I could have helped you bare all of this, helped you figure this out.

"But I am so proud of you I can't even put it into words. You're the bravest person I know. And that you're willing to take on the entire afterlife for me," his own voice cracked.

"I want to marry you," he said after taking a moment to gather himself. "I *need* to marry you, Jessica Bailey. You are *air* to me, you are *life*. And I promise that I will do everything, *everything* to stay here with you. I can't," he faltered again, his eyes dropping to the ground as he tried to compose himself. Another tear rolled down my cheek. "I can't leave you."

Just as if a thousand pound weight had been lifted from my shoulders, I felt a release wash over me. I felt like I could breathe again. A few more tears rolled down my cheek, this time out of relief.

And suddenly everything was okay. In that moment I knew that everything had to be okay.

"Then let's go get married, Alex Wright," I said quietly, placing my hand on his flawless cheek.

His eyes rose to meet mine again, hope, fear, relief, and one hundred other emotions flooding them. "Let's go get married," he whispered.

We both rose to our feet. I grabbed my bouquet, checked my face in the mirror, wiped away the stray tears. Slipping my arm into his, we opened the doors together and stepped out into the warm fall air.

The music softly picked back up, floating through the flowers and trees from an unseen source. Confused and slightly panicked looking faces turned towards us in unison. Alex and I both gave smiles as arm and arm, we walked up the aisle toward the pastor who stood uncomfortably before everyone.

We both managed to ignore the lone figure, standing off in the distance, watching us all.

Finally we came to a stop before my parents, Caroline, Emily, Amber, Rod, Sal, Rita, and Austin. I wore the beautiful lacy dress I had seen in Idaho, with my wings in full view for every single one of them to see. I was done hiding.

Everyone settled as Alex took my hands in his, the smiles returned to their faces and the music faded away.

The pastor spoke poetic words of love being strong and enduring, of it lasting beyond death. That with love we could do anything.

"Jessica, do you take Alex Wright to be your husband?" he finally asked.

I thought my heart would beat out of my chest and that my chest might burst from how it swelled with nothing but pure joy as I said "I do."

"And Alex, do you take Jessica to be your wife?"

"I do," he said, his brilliant smile cracking on his face.

Emily handed us the rings and in a gesture as old as civilization, we slid them onto each other's fingers.

"Well, I guess I pronounce you two husband and wife," the preacher said with a light-hearted chuckle, a smile breaking across his own face. "I suppose you could kiss her now," he said with a wink.

I thought my own smile would crack my face as we both leaned forward. My hand wrapped around the back of his head, Alex's arms circling around my waist and for the first time, I kissed my husband.

There were no angels, there were never any nightmares, there was no death and fear.

There was simply the joy I felt as Alex's lips were pressed against mine, as my family and friends watched us share the moment we both feared would never come.

Despite all the obstacles that had been placed in our way, we were here.

CHAPTER NINETEEN

Butterflies filled my stomach as we went through the motions of our tiny "reception" after the ceremony. The wedding cake Alex made was divine, as little of it as I actually ate. Caroline was picked up by a worker at the rehab facility and Emily ran Sal home when it all started to be too much for her. We changed afterward and went to some fancy restaurant. Apparently my dad had a goal of running his account dry as he encouraged everyone to order more and more.

The entire day I kept stealing glances at Alex. And I kept catching his eyes on me. The heat behind them was enough to make my knees feel like melting butter. His hand would brush against mine, I would feel his breath against my bare shoulder. His fingers slipped beneath the lacy fabric of my dress at my back, his body positioned so that no one else could see.

The anticipation was going to kill me.

Eventually the good-byes were said, Alex and I loaded our bags into the GTO and made the two hour drive down to SeaTac airport, arriving just in time to catch our flight.

184

With all of the excitement of the day, all of the nerves I had felt, I slumped into Alex's side and let sleep wash over me.

And finally, nineteen hours later, we parked at the house on the beach.

I opened the door of the rental car and stepped out into the brilliant morning light. The bluest water I had ever seen lapped softly at the sand, light dancing off of the tiny granules. Palm trees nearly swarmed the small house, two hammocks swinging lazily in the light breeze.

A pair of strong arms wrapped around my waist, Alex's chin resting on my shoulder. Just his simple touch was enough to send my heart racing.

"What do you think of it?" he asked quietly.

"It's perfect," I couldn't help but smiling, reaching up and placing my palm against his cheek. "A week, just the two of us."

"Just us," Alex said suggestively, squeezing my midsection.

I bit my lower lips as the smile crept back onto my face. Yet butterflies filled my stomach.

"Come on," Alex said as he stepped away back toward the car. "Let's get our stuff inside."

The house was small but it felt perfectly comfortable with its oversized chairs and couches, terra cotta tiling everywhere, indoor and outdoor showers, and massive all white bed in the master suite.

Another round of butterflies filled my stomach as we stashed our suitcases in the closet attached to the enormous bathroom. We stood there for a moment, neither of us saying anything, just staring at our bags on the floor.

"Are you scared?" I asked finally.

"Terrified," he said seriously. And then he laughed.

I couldn't help but chuckle with him. "Why is this so scary now?" I shook my head. "With as many close calls as we've had before it shouldn't sound so terrifying."

"Because we always knew before that we couldn't ever actually do it," Alex said as he slipped his hand into mine. "Now we can."

"Wow," I breathed, looking up into Alex's face finally.

"Wow," he repeated, a smile cracking at the corner of his lips.

And then the awkward moment was broken by the sound of my stomach growling.

"Hungry are we?" Alex asked as he raised his eyebrow at me with a smirk.

"I'm never hungry," I said. I could feel my face blushing already.

Alex chuckled and led me out into the kitchen area. "It's the nerves," he said as he opened the fridge we had just unloaded a few things into. "If I still ate I would be hungry right now."

"You were *always* hungry," I chuckled as I sat at the small table and propped my sandaled feet up on the other chair. I felt myself finally start to relax.

"What sounds good?" Alex asked, his head in the recently loaded fridge.

186

"You," I teased, feeling my face blush all the more. I was trying to think how Emily might talk in an awkward situation like this.

"I'm what's for dessert," Alex said as he pulled out the makings for a sandwich.

I chuckled, shaking my head at him. "I could make that for myself you know."

"I know," he smiled as he spread the mayo. "I just... miss cooking, so even with how little you eat anymore, it's still some cooking."

"I like when you cook for me too," I said, smiling as I watched him. "It's sweet."

He glanced up at me, his eyes lingering on my not quite human looking face for a moment. I sensed a shift in his line of thought. "So it's true then," he suddenly said, turning his focus back to the sandwich. "You're more... angel than human?"

I nodded, even though he wasn't looking at me. "That's what Cole said. I'm basically more dead than alive. He said I was as close to death as I could come and not be dead. I've felt, just... really disconnected from everyone normal lately."

"Neither of us has been normal for a while now," Alex said as he put the sandwich on a small plate and handed it to me.

I nodded and took a bite. "I've never really been normal though I guess."

Alex gave me a sad smile. "Sometimes being unique is better than being normal. It's what brought us together."

"What do you mean?" I asked him, furrowing my brow at him.

"Well, if you hadn't have had your nightmares, you never would have run away from home. If it wasn't for them you never would have met Jason, he never would have broken up with you because he thought you were crazy, and you never would have fled to Washington, gotten the job from my grandparents. And I never would have found you in the stairwell with a baseball bat."

A small smile spread on my lips. "I've never thought of it like that I guess. That if it wasn't for them I wouldn't have met you. Makes it all worth it. All the hell I experienced."

A few bites was all it took to fill my stomach. I washed the plate, and together we headed out to one of the gigantic hammocks next to the water. Folding myself into Alex's side, I closed my eyes for a moment, just breathing in the warm air.

"Feel better now?" he said quietly into my ear.

"Yeah," I said, hugging his chest.

"Are you tired?"

"Are you kidding?" I asked with a chuckle. "I probably slept for five hours on the plane."

Alex laughed. "You were out. I've never seen you sleep like the dead like that before."

"I think I was just so relieved to get all that stuff of my chest that I finally just... relaxed. So no," I said. "I'm not tired."

"Good," Alex whispered, tilting my face up to his. His eyes smoldered as he looked into mine, and very slowly his lips met mine.

It felt like my blood surged with electricity as our lips connected. They touched briefly at first, the anticipation of action enough to drive me into a furnace of heat. Gradually, our lips moved in unison, my tongue sliding over his bottom lip, his hand coming to the back of my neck. I smiled as I felt the cool surface of his wedding ring on the back of my brand.

Shifting his hands on me, Alex maneuvered me until I was straddling his waist. Our lips never leaving each other, Alex's hands slipped under the thin fabric of my tank top and slowly slid it up and over my head. His eyes lingered briefly on the blue lacy bra I wore underneath, a million thoughts rushing through his body all at once. I could see it in his eyes.

"I've wanted you so bad for so long, Jessica," he whispered as his lips connected with my skin again, traveling to my throat. At the same time, his hands slid down to my denim shorts.

"I'm all yours now," I breathed as I closed my eyes. "There's nothing stopping us now."

A light breeze picked up, rocking the hammock softly. My hands slid under the fabric of Alex's shirt and I let my hands run over the surface of his stomach and chest as I drew it up. As it dropped to the sand below us, I couldn't help but stare at the perfection that was Alex.

"I love you, Jessica Wright," he said as my shorts were maneuvered off.

Everything inside of me surged at finally hearing the name and knowing it was actually mine. "And I love you. Forever"

CHAPTER TWENTY

My hair blew into my face, tickling my nose, pulling me from my dreams that were recapping the previous twelve hours. I opened one eye, squinting in the brilliant morning light. The sun reflected on the ocean water, the scent of sand heavy in my nose. Lying on my stomach, tangled in an oversized white towel, I propped myself up on my elbows.

After a swim in the water long after the sun had gone down, Alex and I had lain out on oversized beach towels to dry off and apparently I had fallen asleep. As I shifted to sit up, a piece of paper floated off of my bare back. Grabbing it off the sand, I recognized Alex's handwriting.

Went for a run, be back in a bit.

Smiling in nothing but happiness, I climbed to my feet and went back in the house to shower. Dressing in a breezy white sun dress, I pulled a brush through my tangled curls, and lotioned my dried out skin. With the dryer weather, the ocean water and sand, I felt like a lizard.

When I walked back out into the living area, I found Alex sitting on the couch, flipping through a familiar book.

191

"What are you doing with that?" I asked, my voice coming out tighter sounding than I meant it to.

"Are these what I think they are?" he asked, not even looking up.

I sank onto the couch next to him, my eyes scanning down the lists. "The names of the dead," I replied.

"The ones you stood trial for?"

"Most of them," I answered, my previous happiness sinking slightly. "I didn't realize they were real people for a long time, I started recording the names afterward. And toward the end there I was too out of it to even recall the names."

"There's *hundreds* of names here, Jessica," he breathed, his face looking horrified.

I didn't say anything, just read down the list.

Isabel Isaacs.

Tamara Bishop.

Matthew Barnes.

George Vasquez.

"Do you mind if I ask why you brought it?" he asked.

I shifted uncomfortably. "I don't know. I guess I just feel like maybe there will be some answers in here." Opening up to the back of the book, I pulled out a few sheets of folded paper. Opening them up, I showed Alex my drawings. "We're running out of time. Maybe there's something here."

He took the pages from my hands. I had only brought four of them. One of the chairs the council sat in, the ones mounted directly into the wall. One of the endless angels who sat on the spiral staircase that wound around the cylinder. There was one of Cole, leaning forward, his greedy eyes boring into me even through the page. The last was of myself, being pulled by one exalted angel and one condemned.

"These people," Alex said, looking back toward the list of names. "They owe you everything for standing their trial. I mean, just from when I was there, it was terrifying. And they didn't have to go through it because you did it for them."

All the trials, all the scrolls with the deeds of the dead upon them, all the brandings, everything flashed through my head. I squeezed my eyes closed as I thought of Alex possibly having to go through that soon.

"You okay?" Alex asked, his fingers intertwining with mine.

"You can't leave me," I breathed, slowly opening my eyes to meet his grey ones. "You can't leave me." Before I let any coherent thoughts form, I leaned forward, my lips meeting his, my hand coming to the back of his neck.

The book of names and the drawings fell to the floor.

The sound of music started to fade away as Alex and I walked hand in hand back from the small coastal town. Managing to drag ourselves out of the massive white bed for just a few hours, we wandered down the dirt road that eventually led to small shops and restaurants.

I had gotten a small lunch and then we wandered through the street market. I laughed as I pulled on an enormous hat with an even bigger pink flower on the brim while Alex snapped pictures. Browsing through the tables and rickety racks, we found matching necklaces for Amber, Emily, Sal, and Caroline.

Everywhere we went people stared.

I sighed in relief when the sun started to set and Alex and I slowly walked back to the house.

"Did you hear those kids that were staring and pointing at you?" I asked as I leaned my head on Alex shoulder as we walked hand in hand.

"Angel! Angel!" he did a perfect mimic. I felt him shake his head. "Just look at you. You'd think more people would guess it."

"Even though I'm not," I tried to sound joking. It seemed like we couldn't ever just have a normal day. It always came back to angels.

"Not quite," he said as Alex kissed the top of my head.

He was quiet again as we continued down the dirt road. The long breezy dress I wore wrapped around my legs as a breeze picked up off the water. I felt the wheels in Alex's head turning.

"What?" I asked, knowing there was something.

"Explain how the trial works to me," Alex said after a moment of hesitation.

I lifted my head from his shoulder, looking him briefly in the eye. Everything in me didn't want to talk about the trials at that moment. But I knew we didn't have much time left.

"Well, in my nightmares I always started out in this cell. Cormack would walk down this long tunnel and get me. Then he would take me down the tunnel and out onto the catwalk and leave me there. The council would show up and state that the deeds of the person's life would be made known. And then the other angels would swarm the cylinder. Then the council would produce the scrolls of the person's life."

"Scrolls?" Alex questioned, his brow furrowing.

I nodded. "They would have two scrolls. One had all of the good deeds of a person's life, the other one had all the bad. They'd read aloud those things. Some people have done really horrible things in their lives," I shook my head, recalling all the things I had heard. My stomach turned. "They read it for everyone to hear. No one ever forgets what you've done.

"Then they sentence. All ten of the council members determine where they think you should be placed, up or down. If you're sentenced below, Cole brands the back of your neck to mark where you belong." As I spoke, the hairs surrounding my own scar stood on end.

"And then you get your wings," Alex filled in when my voice faltered.

I nodded again. "Once your judgment has been placed you get your own set of wings. It doesn't feel too good."

"I remember," Alex made an attempt at joking. I just half glared at him. He gave me an apologetic smile. "Then what?"

I thought back to all the trials, thinking what the answer to that question was. "And then... whatever side you're placed on claims you."

Alex didn't say anything for a moment, mulling that over. "So it's not even the council who claims someone?" Alex questioned. "It's their minions."

"I guess you could say that," I thought. "I mean, the council decides where you go, there's no question about that. You can fight and scream all you like but they determine that. But yeah, the condemned either drag you down to hell or the exalted escort you into the above."

Alex's eyes stared out over the ocean. I could almost see the wheels turning in his head. "There has to be something there," he said. "With them claiming someone after they are judged."

We neared the end of the dirt road and walked past the hammock that now had a lot of good memories associated with it. My mind kept turning over and over as we walked back into the house. Stepping into the bedroom, Alex flopped down on the bed and I sat on the edge of the mattress.

I reached over to the nightstand and grabbed the drawings that had been left there. Shuffling through them, I stopped at the one of me being used in the tug of war between good and evil. "What...?" I started, my brain forming a line of thought in jagged patterns. "What if the dead wouldn't claim someone? What if they refused to take someone judged to join them?"

Alex didn't say anything for a minute, just stared up at the ceiling above him. "If a judged person has nowhere to go, where do they go?"

And it flashed into my mind like a white hot light. "Maybe back," I breathed, hardly brave enough to say it for fear of letting myself dare to hope it.

"It makes sense in a way," Alex said, his voice rising just slightly in excitement. "If there was nowhere for me to go they may as well send me back. If the afterlife stops trying to pull me back to judge me, maybe things can... go back to normal. Has anything like that ever happened before? That the dead didn't claim someone?"

"Not that I ever witnessed. I have a hard time imagining that it ever has."

"But how do we get them to do that?" Alex said, his voice already sounding disheartened. "From what I remember of the afterlife, half its residents don't seem the type to want to do anyone a favor."

I thought about that for a long while, simply staring at a blank spot on the wall. Glancing back over at the nightstand, I grabbed my book of names.

"We simply ask them," I breathed as I started scanning through the pages. My hope and nerves grew at a rate I feared would consume me.

"Ask them?"

"You said so yourself yesterday," I said, my heart starting to pound in my chest. "Those that I stood trial for owe me everything."

"So you would ask them what?" Alex asked, his voice sounding nervous and excited all at the same time.

"To not accept you," I breathed, reading through the pages in a nearly frantic way. "I have to go back and find them."

"Go back," he said. "Back to the afterlife that wants you back so badly?"

"They want you back more, Alex," I said, meeting his fearful looking eyes. "I could go unnoticed."

"That seems unlikely."

"I have an ally there," I said, feeling my stomach knot up.

Alex paused, his expression blank and unreadable for a moment. "Did he really change that much?" he asked, something sad and painful in his voice.

"Cole is still a bad, selfish man," I explained, recalling those final few hours we had together before he went back to the afterlife for good. "But he... he's moved on too, in his own way.

Alex gave the faintest of sighs before he rolled onto his back, folding his arms above his head as he stared up at the ceiling again. "I don't know that I can ask you to do this for me, Jessica. A million things could go wrong."

"But if I do nothing, you won't be here for much longer," I whispered as I set the book and the pages aside and curled into Alex's side. "How much harder is it getting?"

Alex just stared up at the ceiling for a moment. "Sometimes it feels like every single moment is a struggle," he answered, taking in a quivering breath. "Every day gets harder and harder. It's all I can do to keep the wings contained."

"Cole told me that he couldn't keep his hidden, those last few days. His entire body started looking like this," I said as I traced my fingers along the veins that were starting to bulge on his forearms. The skin was already looking tighter. "The skin around his eyes started turning black, almost like he was diseased. His veins rose up. And he was losing a lot of feathers."

"I lost a few this morning while you were in the shower. I had to let them out, just for a bit. Three of them fell to the ground."

"See," I said against the skin of his chest. "We can't afford to wait any longer. It could just get to be too much at any time and I could lose you."

Alex didn't say anything for a minute and I could almost feel the war he was fighting in his head. He knew how dangerous this was going to be. *I* knew how dangerous this was going to be. Things could go so horribly, terribly wrong. Who knew what they might do to me if I got caught.

"You gave up everything to keep me alive" I said quietly. "Now it's my turn."

"Okay," he finally breathed. He gave me a tight squeeze, kissing the top of my head.

I lifted my lips to his, running my hands under his shirt and over his chest, feeling every bump and valley of his body. I let my fingers trace down his stomach. Shifting my weight on top of him, I let my lips move with his. Alex's hands fisted in my mane of hair.

"I refuse to let them take this away from me," I growled as I moved my lips down his jawline, to his throat. "I intend to enjoy you, my husband, for a very, very long time." My lips continued to move down to Alex's chest.

Alex gave a little moan, tilting his head back. "I refuse to go!" he half shouted, half growled toward the ceiling.

Later that evening, I sat alone in the hammock, the soft breeze pulling my hair away from my face. Alex was inside, enjoying a long shower. The warm air felt good on my almost completely bare skin, the only thing I wore a breezy, lacy nightgown.

I lay back in the hammock, my eyes staring up at the palm leaves that partially blocked out the perfectly pink evening sky. I felt strange inside. A very big part of me was on the verge of a panic attack. Going back to the afterlife to do what I was going to do was petrifying. I had lived in terror of the afterlife all my life. My world had been ripped apart because of it all. Yet I felt an odd sense of anticipation. I was finally going to be able to fight back. I was not going to let them take him. I was going to take back what was mine. I had earned Alex after all they had done to me. And I was taking a huge step toward saving Alex.

If they decided to keep and punish me, it would be no worse than having Alex ripped away from me anyway.

I thought back to all those trials I had stood, all the names that I had been called. All the times Cole had branded me for someone else.

I had experienced the death of others, over and over again in trade for evading my own.

Something in my stomach hardened. Alex was right. Those people owed me everything for bearing what I had for them. They owed it to me to do what I would ask them.

The sun started to drop below the horizon, the sky turning from pink to a deep purple. I rose from the hammock, my stomach filled with nervous butterflies. Just as I stood, I saw Alex leaning in the doorway, watching me. His face looked almost sad, and yet his eyes were filled with nothing but love, the kind of love that came around only once every hundred lifetimes.

I closed the gap between us, stopping just in front of him, and wrapping my fingers around his lightly.

"I'm scared, Jessica," he whispered.

"Don't be," I breathed. "I'm ready for this."

His eyes searched mine for a long while, the fear so obvious in them. I finally looked away from him. If I thought about Alex's fear for too long I would scare myself out of this.

And I couldn't back out now. I wasn't lying when I had said that I was ready for this.

Stepping away from Alex, I walked back into the house. Finding the book of names on the coffee table, I grabbed it and slowly walked back into the bedroom. I faintly heard the sound of Alex following behind me.

I stood at the foot of the bed for a long while, simply staring at it. I ran over everything in my mind again, pictured the hell that I was about to put myself into.

And I recalled the way Alex looked when he said the binding words of "I do" in front of everyone who mattered to me.

Taking a hard swallow, I climbed into the bed and under the thin sheet. Alex slipped into the bed next to me. Clutching the book to my chest, I curled into Alex's side. He wrapped his arms around me protectively, his chin resting on the top of my head.

"Don't let go of me until I wake up," I said, my voice shaking more than I would have liked it to.

"I won't," he breathed, squeezing me all the tighter.

Letting the names flow through my head, I closed my eyes, and started willing myself back into the world of the dead.

CHAPTER TWENTY-ONE

Letting myself slip under was a bit like willing myself into death. I suppose for me it really was. It was as close to death as I could ever come. I willed my heart to slow, to almost stopping. I focused on my blood slowing, on my organs slowing down. I focused my brain on not being active anymore.

And then I was in the world of the dead.

I appeared on the staircase, in a shadowed area, facing the wall opposite of the stone council chairs. As soon as I arrived, everything inside of me felt like it was being shredded to pieces. Everything within me shifted, faded away, wanted to transform, needed to be dead, to be changed. But it couldn't settle on whether it was human or angel.

Because I wasn't quite either.

There was no one around me when I arrived, but as I looked down at the catwalk below me, I understood why. A man led a figure out onto the catwalk. As far as I could tell it was a woman. Her head was covered in the white bag mine had always been, her body sheathed in the same white robes, her hands bound in front of her body. I could see her hands shaking even from my lofty position. The man whom I could only assume was Cormack's replacement turned and walked back into the stone tunnel.

And I then heard the rustle of wings. Voices talked quietly, and one by one, the council members landed in their appointed chairs.

I watched them from the shadows as they started the trial. They were all so beautiful. There were three exalted women, each with a face that would make a normal man sell his soul just for a few hours with her. The exalted men were equally beautiful, their faces and bodies flawless.

The unfair thing was that the condemned were just as beautiful. They were just as perfect looking, just as breathtakingly flawless. The two women looked like goddesses, and the three men, including Cole and Jeremiah, were just as incredible.

"You're actions must be made know," the leader of the exalted said, his voice ever sad as he looked at the faceless woman before him.

My barely beating heart hammered in my chest as I heard the mass rush of wings. Numberless angels ascended from the fiery depths and swooped down from the blue skies above. And suddenly I was surrounded by blue and black-eyed alike. I pressed my back against the cylinder, trying to hide the fact that I myself did not have a pair of wings.

A few eyes turned to me, but they did not linger before they moved onto their fellow comrades in exaltation or damnation. I may as well have been one of them. That, or they simply didn't care that I was there. But I seriously doubted that.

The air came in and out of my lungs in gasping breaths as my eyes turned back to the woman on trial. Black spots formed on the edge of my vision. Everything inside of me hurt. It felt like my organs kept being burned away and then re-growing in my ribcage.

The deeds of this woman's life started to be read and I felt real panic.

I didn't have endless time to do this. I couldn't waste my time being terrified and hiding in the corner so to speak.

"Excuse me," I said hoarsely to the woman next to me. She didn't even turn her head in my direction. "Excuse me," I said again, raising my voice just slightly. She turned her brilliant blue eyes on me. I sighed a little breath of relief. "I am looking for someone. I wondered if you could help me?"

She gave me a confused look for a moment, and I worried for a second that she might not answer me at all. "Are you alright, child?" she asked, her face concerned looking. "You don't look well."

"I'm... I'm fine," I stuttered. "I'm looking for Rose Roberts. Do you know where I could find her?"

As soon as I said her name, my eyes were drawn to a place on the staircase about fifteen yards away. As I saw the red haired woman, her eyes instantly locked with mine.

"Looks like you don't need my help anymore," the first woman said, her eyes still concerned looking. I shook my head once. Slowly, I started making my way toward the red-haired woman, being careful to keep along the wall and my back pressed against the stone.

No other angels seemed to notice our odd behavior as I approached her. Their eyes were firmly locked on the woman on trial. As I came to her side neither of us said anything for a long time, we simply stared at each other.

"You're her," she finally said quietly. "The proxy."

I could only nod.

"I am so thankful," she said, her head shaking just slightly. "I've see the trials, how terrifying they are. I didn't have to endure that, because of you. And I am so sorry. It wasn't fair."

I stared back into her beautiful blue eyes, trying hard to swallow the hard lump in my throat. "No, it isn't."

She continued to look at me for a long moment, and it was a bit before I realized I needed to say something. "I need your help."

Knowing my time was running out, I rushed through an explanation. Everything that was happening to Alex, everything we had been through. All the struggles we were going through to be together.

When I finished, she stared at me with sympathy in her eyes, but there was something else there that I couldn't place.

"I know what he did, honey," she said, placing a hand on my shoulder. "We all know what he did. Never before has one made a plea like that and be allowed to return. What he did for you was incredible. But..." she trailed off.

"But what?" I said, slightly too demanding sounding. I felt the panic surge in my blood again, everything inside of me feeling so completely wrong.

"But things are changing around here. The council. Things must change to remain fair. Some of us have talked. We know your Alex doesn't have long left up there. He is a good man. Good men like that don't come along very often."

She paused for a long moment, staring back into my eyes. I tried yet again to swallow that hard lump.

"What are you saying?" my voice came out as barely more than a whisper. "That... that you want him... as a council member?"

"That's exactly what I am saying," she said, looking around to check that no eyes were watching us.

"But..." I stumbled over my words. "But he has to stay with me. He can't leave me."

"But when it's time for someone to go, it is their time."

"No!" I practically shouted, taking a quick step away from the woman. "No, that's the point. It wasn't his time.

The leader of the condemned, he killed Alex! It wasn't Alex's time to go. It wasn't fair."

"Nothing in life is really fair," Rose said, her eyes sympathetic again. "I had just given birth to my third child, a little girl, when I found out I had breast cancer. I only had eight months to be her mother. Only eight months to fit in a lifetime of mothering to my children."

I stared back at this woman, my mouth hanging open, knowing there was more I needed to say but unable to make my brain work to recognize what it needed to do.

"If you ask me to not accept him, I will do it, for what you did for me," Rose said quietly, again glancing around to make certain no one was listening. "But it is a wonderful thing, what we want for him. He would be an incredible leader."

"Thank you," I managed to whisper, my entire body starting to vibrate with the pain that was growing in my body.

Just then those with the black eyes sprang from their seats and leapt at the newly branded woman. I glanced back at Rose, trying to manage an appreciative smile.

And in the midst of the chaos, I leapt into the depths below.

A gasp ripped from my throat as I sat straight up in the pillowey white bed. Alex jumped in surprise, his form barely visible through the nearly non-existent light.

Air continued to come in and out in gasps. My lungs felt like they weren't there. It felt like my stomach wasn't there. It felt like my heart had filled my entire chest cavity, pulsing, throbbing, pounding painful blood through my shifting system.

"Jessica?" Alex said through the dark. A moment later the light flipped on. Spots formed on the edges of my vision as I met Alex's terrified, wide eyes. "Jessica!"

I barely felt it as Alex placed his hands on the sides of my face. Forcing my eyes to focus on his, I tried to even my breathing. But it felt like I couldn't find my lungs.

"Jessica? What happened? What's wrong?" The fear and panic were so obvious in his eyes.

I continued to gasp, clutching my chest. No longer able to keep myself sitting up, I collapsed back onto the bed.

"Jessica!" Alex screamed, panicked. "What do I do?!"

I reached a hand out, frantically searching for his. Finding his forearm, I clung to it like my life depended on it. Alex leaned over me, gripping my other forearm, and looked into my eyes.

"Focus on me," he said, trying with everything he had to calm his voice. "Focus on me, Jessica. You will stay with me. You will not be pulled back into that place. You don't belong there. You will stay with me. You are my *wife* and I will *not* let them take you from me."

"You're..." I gasped again, feeling something inside of me starting to solidify again. But every part of me wanted to go back. "You're wife."

"Yes," he said, his eyes burning as he looked into mine. With every passing moment, my breaths came easier and smoother. "You are my wife, and you promised to stay with me. Just like I promised you."

I nodded, letting go of one of his arms, and rubbed at my chest, never breaking eye contact with him.

It was then that I noticed the small black vein that bulged around Alex's left eye. Lifting my free hand, I touched it lightly.

Alex placed his hand over mine, holding my palm against his cheek. I saw his lower lip quiver, saw the pain in his eyes. Had he been capable, there would have been tears.

"Is this going to happen every time you go back?" he asked in a quivering whisper.

I bit my lower lip for a moment, to stop my own trembling. Slowly I nodded. "I think so."

Alex squeezed his eyes closed, the pain and fear rolling off of him. His entire frame trembled slightly.

"I won't let them take you," I breathed, my whole body shaking as well.

Alex took a sniffling breath, and then let it out in an unsteady whoosh. "I'm so scared, Jessica."

Wrapping my arms around Alex shoulders, I pulled him into me. I wanted to tell him not to be scared. But I knew he had every reason to be. So I just held him instead until the sun came up in the east.

X

The next four days came and went in waves of panic, urgency, pain, and despair.

I continued to return to the world of the dead. I went in every chance I could force my body to sleep, sometimes multiple times a day, with a list of names. I no longer hid in the corner, fearing being caught. I ran. I sprinted through the concourses of angels, searching frantically for the faces I somehow always knew. And I explained in desperation what I needed from them. What I wanted and tried to demand from them.

But I continued to get the same answers. The exalted wanted Alex as one of their new leaders. The condemned simply wanted to punish him out of jealousy for being allowed more time to return. Our plan was backfiring. In a major way.

I sat up from the bed with a gasp, clutching my chest in pain. My lungs were like soggy sponges. My vision blurred as I tried to focus on Alex's face before me, tried to find the details in his features. And slowly they did. Each new black vein around his eyes.

"Jessica," I faintly heard Alex say through the painful haze that was my entire existence. "Jessica."

Slowly my lungs became detectable and my body stopped pulsing and shifting. My eyes met a bed with a handful of feathers atop it.

"Alex," I breathed, picking up one of the perfectly white feathers. My eyes started filling with moisture as I met his. That was when I noticed his hands shaking.

"It's coming, Jessica," he said in an unsteady voice. "I..." he faltered. "I don't think I can fight this much longer."

I shifted on the bed, kneeling in front of him. I took his forearms in my hands, placing my face just an inch from his. "You can do it, just for a little bit longer. We just need a little more time."

Alex met my eyes, something all too close to despair radiating in his own. "Just a little more time," he repeated.

But I think we both knew that was a lie.

It was going to take more than time to save Alex.

CHAPTER TWENTY-TWO

I watched the water drip from the faucet in the bathroom. It circled around, gathered heavy and weak against the pull of gravity at the mouth of it. Slowly, it stretched, trying to cling desperately to the stainless steel, before it couldn't fight anymore. It fell into the abyss of the drain at the bottom of the sink.

My eyes rose to meet my reflection. Odd perfection stared back at me. Perfect skin, perfect eyes, perfect lines and surfaces, given to me, unwanted and now hated.

Again I felt that rocket, that bomb ticking inside of my head. We had slipped past double digits into single. No matter how hard I was trying to find more numbers to put back on the clock, they just kept falling and slipping away.

Turning the water on full blast, I pooled it in my hands and pressed my face into its cool surface. Everything about my being now felt strange. I didn't even feel like a human anymore, but didn't quite know how to feel like an angel either.

I'd managed to track down seven of the people I had stood trial for last night. And couldn't breathe for several minutes after I woke up.

Pain. That was all life felt like these days.

A ringing in the bedroom caught my attention. The high pitched ring-tone told me it was my phone and not Alex's.

Wiping my face dry with a hand towel, I made my way into the bedroom, spotting two feathers resting so innocent looking on the floor at the foot of the bed. Trying my best to ignore them, I reached for my phone on the dresser.

Emily.

A rock formed in my stomach.

"Hello?" I answered.

I heard a sniffle on the other end and it was a second before Emily's voice came through on the other end. "Jessica?"

"Hey," I said. "What's wrong?"

"Oh, Jessica," Emily sobbed again. A round of tears cut her voice off.

"Emily," I practically shrieked. "What's the matter?"

"It's Sal," she half whispered, her voice cracking. "She's gone."

The rock in my stomach grew heavier. "Did she wander out of the house? How long has she been missing?"

There was silence for a moment as Emily gathered herself. "No Jessica," she said, her voice becoming a little more solid. "I mean she's gone. Sal died two hours ago."

And then those organs inside of me that felt so dead just disappeared.

"Jessica?" Emily said, her voice sounding very far away.

"Yeah?" I barely managed to whisper.

"You and Alex need to come home."

"Yeah." My hand snapped the phone closed.

Neither Alex or I said much as we headed back to the airport, sat on the plane for hours that felt like seconds. We loaded our bags into the GTO when we got into Seattle and then the wheels were meeting the pavement of I-5. In what felt like only minutes since we left Costa Rica, we arrived home at two in the morning.

I had texted Emily when we arrived at SeaTac Airport, and she pulled into the driveway just five minutes after we walked into the door. She looked like hell.

Neither of us said anything as Emily wrapped her arms around me. It felt like I had gallons of tears threatening to break from my eyes, but I could only hold Emily with stiff arms and hold my breath.

"What happened?" I finally managed.

Emily stepped away from me, wiping her cheeks with the back of her denim jacket sleeve. Alex stepped to my side and slid his hand into mine.

"The doctors said it was a brain aneurysm. I just found out a few hours ago, got the report. They said she had probably had it for a while and it was just getting worse the last few months."

"That's why she was hallucinating and seeing her husband," Alex said. I felt the rock in my stomach grow all the heavier.

Emily nodded, her eyes shining with tears yet to fall. "The doctor said it seemed unlikely that she wouldn't be hallucinating. They said it was just a time bomb ticking in her head. But they wouldn't have been able to operate on it, 'cause of where it was in her brain."

That didn't ease the guilt I felt in the pit of my stomach. I had known she was hallucinating. What if I could have done something? Maybe there would have been some other kind of treatment if we would have found it sooner.

"I'm so sorry, Jessica," Emily said in a trembling voice. Two more tears traced paths down her cheek.

I just nodded, my eyes slipping to the floor.

And then I felt Alex's hand start to shake in my own. As I looked at it, I saw the veins rise from his skin, bulging out against his tightening skin.

Alex's breath caught in his chest and as I looked up at him, he closed his eyes, his jaw clenching tightly.

"He doesn't have much longer left, does he?" Emily asked.

I met her eyes, saw her new fear. Something inside of me felt like it was trying to claw its way out. I pushed it back down, afraid what it might present itself as if it managed to get out. "No. We're working on it."

Alex worked his way over to the couch with my help and tucked his knees up into his chest. He just sat there with his eyes squeezed closed, trying with everything he had in him to stay. In unneeded hushed tones, I hurriedly explained to Emily what we were trying to do, that I was putting myself back into the afterlife. And then I had to explain how I had been going back before, how Jeremiah had been following me.

"They just won't stop," she said, holding my hand tightly in hers. "Will they?"

"Not until they get me back," I said, staring at nothing, shaking my head. "And Alex."

"Don't stop fighting," Emily said, squeezing my hand. "You've earned a life. After everything they've put you through. You deserve a real life."

I gave Emily a tight lipped smile, squeezing her hand. Every one kept feeling sorry for me and giving me their sympathy. So many had said that everything "wasn't fair" or that I deserved better, but now it was just starting to feel like meaningless words. All the talk in the world wasn't going to fix anything.

"I'd better get going," Emily said with a sigh, pressing her hands into her reddened cheeks. "I have to teach in the morning and I'm meeting up with Austin later."

"So the two of you are dating then?" I asked, grateful for the change in conversation.

"I don't know," she said, shrugging. "We hang out a lot and I've spent quite a bit of time with his family. We held hands once but that was about it. I like spending time with him."

"I'm glad," I said, giving her a small smile as she stood.

"Hang in there, Alex," she said, giving him a sorrowful look. He just managed a nod before she stepped out the front door.

As soon as the door closed, I collapsed back into the couch, my breath coming out in a big whoosh.

It felt like I had the world sitting on my chest and eventually I was just going to be crushed through the couch, into the ground below the house, and be swallowed up into nothing.

Alex's hand slid into mine and I looked over to see his frame relax slightly. There were a few new black veins protruding around his eyes though. Everything about him seemed tight and unnatural.

"Better?" I asked wearily.

"Not particularly," he said, and I could tell he was forcing his body to relax.

I studied his changing face for a few long moments. His eyes weren't to the point that Cole's were yet, but they weren't far from it. Already, Alex was becoming less beautiful to look at, and more frightening. His skin stretched over his bones, like he was being sucked into himself.

"I'm tired," I said, my eyes never leaving his gray ones.

"Are you really?" he breathed, his eyes never wavering either.

I finally broke away, staring at the black glass of the back door. "I don't know," I said as I shook my head. "I'm not even sure what real tired feels like anymore. But I have to go back."

And without saying anything, because there was nothing new left to say, we both stood, and walked into the bedroom. We went through the motions of getting ready for bed, brushing teeth, changing clothes. Without a word spoken, we climbed between the sheets and I curled into Alex's side. He slid his arms around me and rested his chin on the top of my wilder than normal hair.

As I let my eyes slide closed, I did feel tired. Not tired as in wanting to sleep though. Tired of angels, of death, of always trying to fight so hard.

I just wanted a few normal hours. That was all.

But I knew that wasn't going to happen. Alex and I had reached the peak of our climb together. We were staring down at the avalanche that was going to take us to the bottom, not quite able to see where all of this was going to end. But there was no stopping this.

So I jumped off that peak, and let sleep take me.

CHAPTER TWENTY-TWO

The shift inside of me hit me like a punch in the gut as I felt stone beneath my feet. In the all too familiar gasp, my lungs searched for air. After a few moments of nothing, hot, suffocating oxygen finally filled my quivering lungs.

Looking up, I saw the chairs of the council members, saw the bottoms of perfect bare feet. A figure stood on the catwalk, their sobs audible, even clear down here, so close to the fiery depths.

"There she is," I heard the hissed whispers from across the cylinder. My eyes flashed to the speaker and found a woman whispering to a small group of other's. All at once, their eyes found mine and I stood frozen as they started shifting through the mass toward me.

The group seemed to grow as they made their way around the large space, descending down the staircase toward me. I could only stand frozen as they approached, standing with my back pressed against the hot stones behind me.

"You are the proxy," a man with black eyes spoke as the group stopped, just a few feet away from me. Nearly a dozen pairs of black eyes settled onto my face.

I simply nodded my head.

"We have heard what you are trying to do," he spoke again. The light of flames danced on the surface of his perfectly white teeth. "Hushed word is being spread around the afterlife about a female proxy, asking favors of those she stood for. You aren't supposed to be here."

"I know that," I said, my voice sounding more confident than I felt. "And I ask that you not inform certain angels about my presence."

The man and a few of those behind him chuckled. "Mischief and rule-breaking is part of what granted us the brands on the back of our necks and the color of our eyes. Trust us, none of us are going to tell on you for doing something you're not supposed to be doing."

"Do you know why I am here?" I asked, hiding my shaking hands behind my back.

"Someone who kept you from joining us is in danger of not being around anymore," he said casually.

I nodded. "And when he comes back, I need you all to not accept him. I need him sent back."

Several members of the group laughed, glancing back and forth between each other. "You've got spunk. You're a brave one. But naive. He's dead. His life is gone. He can't be sent back and be dead."

221

"Just say that you'll do it," I said harshly, anger starting to brew in my system. "You all know what I've done for you. The hell I experienced for you. When the time comes, just say you won't accept him. You owe it to me."

The man who had been speaking for the others gave me a hard look, the wheels in his head turning. "I make no promise. But I will not forget what you have done for me," he said, his eyes narrowing.

I heard a scream from above as a newly branded angel was dragged down into the fiery depths. Suddenly the cylinder was chaos. And I felt him before I saw him.

Cole and Jeremiah were on the staircase just above us, descending. Toward the group that surrounded me, and myself, hiding against the wall.

The man I had been talking to looked at me with wide eyes, glancing between me and the two council members. In a split second, he threw me over the edge of the staircase just as Cole glanced in my direction.

Violent tremors shook my hands as I cupped water in my hands at the kitchen sink and splashed water over my face. Something shook my insides. Or maybe it was more violent than that. It felt like a jack-hammer had been set loose inside of me.

Things had gotten worse overnight. For both Alex and I. The pain was so much worse after I woke up. My insides wouldn't settle. I felt half in the afterlife, half in this world I wasn't supposed to be a part of. And I'd woken up to Alex with his wings visible, glinting in the sun, the light breaking through them in too many places. The blackness around his eyes was more pronounced, his skin frightening and shrinking on his bones. His entire frame trembled.

The real life situation didn't feel any less dreary than my supernatural one. I'd contacted a funeral home and they had agreed to take care of the funeral arrangements. I'd also called Sal's attorney and she was taking care of everything else. My voice sounded dead even to me on the phone as I made the calls.

"Jessica?" a voice called from the master bedroom.

Closing my eyes tight for a second, I attempted to still the hurricane that was inside of me. Letting the oxygen flow in and out of my lungs should have made them feel real, but they didn't.

"Coming," I said as I stepped away from the counter. Every step I took across the hardwood floor seemed to echo maddeningly, my angelic senses in overdrive.

I stepped into the bedroom, the weight of everything a physical thing in the air. Amber sat in the rocking chair by the window, her eyes fixed on Alex's form on the bed. He sat with his knees drawn up to his chest, his arms curling up and around his head. His entire frame was so tight looking it seemed he might shatter at any moment. Every feather of his wings shook.

"I have to go into work soon," Amber said, the fear of this impossible situation obvious in her voice. "I'm sorry."

"It's okay," I half whispered, my voice sounding awful. "I'm fine."

She stood and wrapped her arms around me for a brief minute. "I'm so sorry," she breathed. She let go and a moment later I heard the front door close.

I watched Alex for a while. After I'd woken at five that morning and seen how bad Alex was, I was too afraid to let him out of my sight for even a moment, afraid that if I did, he would be gone. But as panic started to eat at me, my nerves were strung out, I had called Amber to come sit with him while I gave myself a break for two hours.

"Hey," I finally said as I sat next to him on the bed, placing a hand on his bare shoulder.

He didn't say anything in return, just took a sharp intake of breath.

"I'm..." my voice wavered, afraid to voice the thoughts I wasn't sure I could turn into actions. "I'm thinking about taking one of Sal's sleeping pills, so I can start going back more often." But everything in me screamed *no!* against that statement.

"Jessica," Alex said, his voice sounding pained in every way. "You know you can't handle much more of this. You are already sleeping almost as much as you are awake. I can practically smell the pain you're in."

A single tear rolled down my cheek as I bit my lower lip for a moment to try and control myself. "At least it can't kill me," I breathed.

"But what kind of existence are you going to have after all of this?" he asked, his eyes terrifying as they met mine. I had to force myself to keep looking at him. "You're shredding yourself to pieces. I can tell something in you doesn't come back each time you sleep."

"I am *not* giving up!" I suddenly hissed through clenched teeth. My hands shook all the harder. "Don't you dare give up on me Alex Wright, and don't you *dare* try and stop me from saving you!"

My breath came in and out in ragged draws as Alex looked at me with wide, surprised eyes. I let mine drop from his, feeling the fire that suddenly filled me die out.

"I'm sorry," I said in a rush. "I'm sorry. I just..." I squeezed my eyes closed and pressed my fists into them, feeling my shoulders slump in on me. "I'm just..."

"Shh," Alex said and I felt his shaking arms wrap around me. "I know."

"I just don't know if what I've done is going to be enough," I said, my voice finally starting to calm. "They want you back so bad. I just don't know if I've talked to enough of them. If I can just talk to more, they can help spread the word, maybe then it will be enough."

"It will have to be," Alex said as he stroked my hair. "Or I'll start my own war in the afterlife."

225

Amber came back later that afternoon. Having next to no food in the house, I had to go get something. It made me sick to think that I no longer had to run over in my head what Sal might be in need of. My entire body felt heavy as I loaded the two grocery bags into the back seat of the GTO.

The clouds had been building all day and as I parked in front of the bookstore they finally couldn't hold anymore. The rain felt oddly comforting. Rain felt normal.

The bell on the front door sounded as I stepped inside. Katlin was working the front counter. I didn't know her well since we worked alternating days.

"Hey," she said with a bright smile. "I thought you were still on your honeymoon?"

I tried to force a smile onto my face. "We needed to come back a bit early."

"Is everything okay?" she asked, her face growing concerned. "You don't look your best."

That fake smile on my face faltered. "I don't exactly feel my best. Is Rita here?" I changed the subject.

"She's in her office," Katlin said, pointing toward the back of the store.

Barely remembering to say a thank you over my shoulder, I made a bee-line toward the back. As promised, I found Rita in the cramped, over-crowded closet of an office. I gave two knocks on her open door, drawing her attention away from her daily log book.

"Jessica!" she said in surprise. "Back already?"

I nodded, feeling everything inside of me squeeze. It felt like my entire body wanted to cry.

"Is everything alright?" she asked, pulling her reading glasses off, her brows knitting together.

I shook my head, fighting back the sting behind my eyes. "No."

Rita cleared a stack of books off the chair in the corner of the office and eased me into it before closing the door. "What's the matter?" she asked, her voice ever caring and kind.

I took a deep breath and let it come out in one quivering note. "You know the lady I help take care of?" I started. "Sal?"

Rita nodded.

"She passed away yesterday morning," my voice shook. Rita's face fell all the more. "She had an aneurysm that burst. The doctors said it had been there for a long time. Emily called yesterday to let us know, so we flew home."

"Oh sweetie," Rita said as she pulled me into her thin arms. "I'm so sorry."

I nodded, hugging my sides tight underneath Rita's embrace. "There's something else," I breathed into her wildly curly red hair. She sat back, her eyes focused on my face.

"Alex is sick," I said. It wasn't exactly the truth, but it didn't fully feel like a lie. "I mean really, really sick."

"Is he going to be okay?" she said with a small gasp.

I shook my head. "He probably doesn't have more than a few days left," my voice cracked. My eyes fell to my lap, my arms squeezing my sides all the tighter. "I think…" I struggled to make my voice continue to work. "I think I won't be coming in anymore for a while. I need to be with him."

"Of course," Rita said, her voice sounding light and airy, as if she was still trying to process everything I had just said.

"Will you be okay with the shop?" I asked, wiping my nose with the back of my sleeve.

"I'll be alright, sweetie. Austin is taking some time off with the surgery today but he'll be back in a few days."

"Surgery today?" I questioned, grateful that the conversation was moving in a different direction.

"His little sister and Emily?" Rita said, her eyes looking a bit confused.

"What does Emily have to do with any of it?" I asked, my own expression growing more confused by the second.

"She never told you?"

I shook my head.

"You know Austin's little sister needed a new kidney. Well, Emily talked to Austin about it, and just out of the blue volunteered to be tested to see if she was a match. And she was," Rita's eyes shone with tears and mixes of joy and sadness.

"Emily is giving his sister her kidney?" I said, my voice rising in pitch slightly.

228

Rita nodded. "The surgery is supposed to start in less than an hour."

For the first time in what felt like a long time, something inside of me felt a little brighter.

Emily was going after redemption. In a big way

I squeezed my eyes closed, and relished in the small smile that spread over my lips. "She told me last night that she had plans with Austin today," I chuckled.

Rita chuckled as well.

I opened my eyes again with a sigh. "Well," I said as I stood. "I'd better be getting back home. Amber is sitting with Alex. I don't want to leave them for too long."

"Okay," Rita said as she stood as well. She pulled me into one more quick hug and walked me to the front door. "Tell Alex that he is in my prayers," Rita said as she watched me walk to my car. "You are too, Jessica. If you need anything, and I mean anything, don't hesitate to give me a call."

"Thanks," I said with a sad smile, and slid into my car.

My cell phone rang as soon as I shut the door. It was the funeral home and they gave me all the details, let me know that everything would be set in three days. Sal's attorney had let me know that according to Sal's will she wanted to be cremated. We could pick up Sal's remains and have our own service Saturday.

The rain continued to come down as I made my way to the freeway. I tried not to think about how I had lost a woman who felt equal parts best friend and foster child. I tried not to think about how I might also be losing my husband just days later.

And I tried not to think about ways to lose myself should he be lost.

Instead I realized I hadn't seen any traces of Jeremiah since the wedding. This was almost alarming to realize that I had paid so little attention to that face. Something felt off there. Jeremiah didn't seem the type to just let something like this go.

Amber seemed relieved when I entered the house. She'd never been good at handling stressful situations and the whole angel thing had always freaked her out. She practically ran out the door when I said she could go.

Alex shuffled around the kitchen, attempting to cook something with his unsteady hands in desperation to distract himself.

"Being babysat kinda' sucks," he said as he slid a sheet of chocolate chip cookies into the oven.

"Going to the afterlife kinda' sucks," I said as I joined him in the kitchen and wrapped my arms around his chest. I was somewhat relieved that his wings were gone. He felt slightly more solid.

"You have a good point," he said as he pressed his lips to mine.

I leaned my head against his chest and breathed Alex in. That distinctive smell of his was growing stronger. I closed my eyes and tried to pretend that none of this had happened, that he wasn't an angel, that I wasn't almost one as well.

"This isn't how I pictured life just after our honeymoon," Alex said quietly against the top of my head.

"Me either," I confessed.

"Don't get mad when I say this, okay?" Alex breathed, squeezing me gently.

"Okay?" I answered cautiously.

"We need to make sure everything gets transferred to you properly, should I... go," he said, his voice tightening slightly. "I made up a will before, just after I got pulled back last time, but now that you're my wife, things will need to be adjusted a bit."

Everything in my chest tightened and I squeezed my eyes closed. I wanted him to not have spoken the words, to not have them be a threat. "Okay," I managed to say.

"I'll call Ted and have him make the adjustments tomorrow morning."

Ted was Alex's hefty priced, powerful attorney. With as much as Alex had to meet with him, I had yet to see him in person. Though with Alex's current physical appearance he would be doing his dealings over the phone. I wouldn't be meeting the man any time soon.

"On the brighter side," Alex pushed on. "I got the other house rented out."

"That's great," I tried to sound enthusiastic. I was pretty sure I failed. "I just found out some interesting news."

"Oh yeah?"

I nodded my head against his chest. "Emily's is donating one of her kidney's."

"That right?" Alex said, his voice sounding relieved as well at the change of subject.

I nodded against his chest again. "To Austin's little sister. She's probably in surgery right now."

Alex was quiet for a moment. I could feel the thoughts that were rolling through his head. "I'm happy for her. She doesn't deserve to be branded, despite what she's done."

"No, she doesn't deserve that."

I stepped away from Alex, wiping at my nose again with the back of my sleeve. I suddenly felt disgusting.

"I need a shower," I said, hugging my sides, letting my eyes drop to the ground. I realized my dilemma then. That would require taking my eyes off of Alex.

As if reading my thoughts, Alex took my hand in his, and led me into the bedroom. Closing the bathroom door behind us, Alex's lips met my neck, his hands coming under my top, slowly pulling it over my head. I tipped my head back as his lips made their way to my collar bone. His lips never leaving my skin, he reached over and started the water in the shower.

"This is how I imagined we'd spend our days following our honeymoon," he said in a rough voice against my skin.

I couldn't help the smile that finally crossed my face.

CHAPTER TWENTY-THREE

That evening, after a call to Rita for an update on the surgery, Alex and I headed out of the house. We had to carefully consider how best to cover up the being Alex was becoming. Pushing a baseball cap down as far as he could on his head, he also wore a long sleeved t-shirt and I had my first experience in putting make-up on a man. Even with the cover-up, the blackness around his eyes was frightening.

The light was quickly fading as Alex parked the truck at the hospital we seemed to be making far too many visits to. My stomach knotted as I remembered all of us who had been housed in these walls for a time. I'd spent far too many hours there.

Silent visitors walked the halls. But as we got toward the end of the one we had been directed to, laughter and happy chatting could be heard from one of the rooms. We slowed as a crowd of people spilled out into the hallway, and I couldn't help but glance in their direction.

"Jessica!" a voice from inside the crowded room called. I did a double-take, and caught a glimpse of Austin's face through the crowd of people.

"Hey," I tried to sound cheerful as he pushed his way through them towards Alex and I. I swallowed hard as Austin caught a glimpse of Alex's face, and he stopped just a little too short, his eyes growing wide.

"Hey," he said, his voice slightly too quiet as he looked at Alex's face again. Finally pulling his eyes away, he met mine, a genuine smile spreading on his face. "How was Costa Rica?"

"Pretty," I said simply, stuffing my hands into the pockets of my jacket. "I assume that's your sister's room?"

Austin glanced back toward the doorway and all the people. "Yeah. I'm surprised the nurses haven't come back down here to yell at us for not letting Callie rest. Everyone's just so excited about the surgery. We've waited a long time for this."

"I'm really happy for you and your family," I said, trying to give a small smile. It felt like I'd forgotten how to.

"Emily's amazing," Austin said, his face cracking into a brilliant smile. It wasn't hard to tell he was already head over heels. That did make me smile just a bit.

"Yeah, she really is," I agreed with him. "We're going to see her now."

Austin nodded, his smile still spread. "I'll be down there in a few."

"Okay," I said hollowly and started back down the hall. I didn't miss Austin's wary glance at Alex's face again. Or the way Alex was unnaturally silent the entire time.

"Did he see it as bad as it is?" I asked quietly as we approached Emily's room number.

Alex just shook his head.

Another small stone was added to the pile in my stomach. Alex hated messing with people's heads.

I gave three quiet taps on the door before being told to come in. We stepped inside, this room looking exactly like the one Sal had resided in before being transferred to the mental institution.

"Hey, guys!" Emily said cheerily, smiling at us from where she sat slightly propped up with a few overly starched white pillows. "Guess you found out my secret."

"Rita accidently narked on you," I said, trying to smile for her as I crossed the room and hugged her. I then sat on the bed next to her. Emily reached for one of my hands and held it tightly.

"Blast," she said, though a wide smile covered her face.

I just shook my head, a real feeling smile tugging at the corner of my mouth.

"Well, you look like hell," Emily said as her eyes turned to Alex who stood just behind me.

"Thanks," Alex said with a chuckle and a shake of his head. "I kind of feel like hell."

"It's getting worse?" she asked, her voice suddenly serious.

"Much," I said. My rock-filled stomach gave a little twist and shudder, my insides still not solid. "So when are you going to be able to go home?" I changed the subject. I was getting good at that.

"I talked to the doctor," she said with a slight sigh. "They agreed to let me out for a few hours so I could go to Sal's service. One of you will have to come pick me up. They'll talk your ear off about being careful, not letting me do too much, blah, blah, blah. Then I have to come back for a few more days. Hopefully I can go home in a few days."

"Uh, you're not going home by yourself," I said, my eyes turning a glare at her. "You're not going back to sit in that empty apartment by yourself. We've got that whole house to ourselves and an entire apartment sitting empty downstairs. You'll be coming to stay with us."

A small smile spread on her face again, her eyes practically glowing. "Okay," she said, her voice showing hints of emotion. "Thanks you guys."

"You're always welcome," Alex chimed in.

There was a knock at the door and a moment later Austin stepped inside, a familiar grin spread on his face.

"Hey," he breathed.

"Hey," Emily said airily back.

I just shook my head. They so liked each other and were so oblivious to how bad it was.

"So what is the University doing while you're out of commission?" I said, turning back to Emily. Austin had taken a seat next to her bed, sitting with his socked feet on the edge of the mattress.

"My students are being tortured with book work. Did you know there were entire books written on yoga?"

"I do work in a bookstore," I chuckled.

"Oh, right," she said, her face flushing red just a little bit. "Well, I didn't really think about that. I just did yoga. Anyway, the University requires that I have some sort of text curriculum which I've been putting off so that's what they're doing while I'm gone. Book work. Independently."

I nodded, grateful for such normal conversation.

I felt Alex lay a hand on my shoulder from behind. The trembling in them was getting violent again. I got the message.

"Well," I said as I stood, letting Alex's hand slip into mine. "We'd better be going. I'm glad that you're doing okay."

I gave Emily a hug, hesitating awkwardly before giving Austin one too. Alex just hung by the door, struggling to keep it together before we could get back to the truck.

"Take care," I said to Emily as I joined him at the door.

"You too," she said with a sad smile. "Hang in there Alex. You're not allowed to go."

"Thanks, Emily," Alex replied in a shaky voice.

As soon as we closed the door behind us, Alex practically ran back to the truck. The sun had fully set by that point, the hospital looking unnaturally bright from the outside. Throwing the passenger door of the truck open, Alex flung himself inside.

And the next moment his jacket and shirt were shredded as his wings burst out.

I hesitated outside, just one more rock dropping on the pile forming inside of me. Alex kneeled on the seat, clutching his arms around his head, shaking in a way that I could see even from here.

Gathering my courage, I swallowed hard, and opened the driver's door. I felt like I should have asked Alex if he was okay, but it was obvious he wasn't. So instead I put the key in the ignition, started the truck, and backed out of our parking spot.

Alex didn't move the entire drive back. We didn't say a word as we moved through the night. As we got back to the lake, I stopped in front of Sal's house and got out before Alex could say anything.

I fished for Sal's keys and let myself in.

All the nights Sal and I had spent together, all the episodes of *Touched by an Angel* I had tried to ignore, all the meltdowns and leisurely afternoons came back to me. I'd never hear Sal's nonsensical voice again.

Pushing the memories aside, I made my way downstairs into Sal's bathroom. Opening her mirror, I found her prescription sleeping pills. My hands threatening to shake, I twisted the lid off, found twenty-something-odd pills still inside. Slipping the bottle into my pocket, I walked back upstairs, and locked the front door behind me again.

By the time I got back into the truck, Alex looked more composed, his wings gone. His face looked tired, but not quite so dead. I hadn't expected him to remain silent after I got back in and parked the truck in our garage, but he didn't question me.

We walked into the silent house, still neither of us saying a word. I sighed as I set my purse on the table, bracing my hands against its wooden surface. I let my eyes slide closed, feeling so heavy and so exhausted.

I heard Alex walk out of the bedroom, assuming he had gone to get a new shirt. He hesitated behind me in the living room. I could feel the turmoil inside of him. It reached out to me, meshed with my own.

"We're going to go to Italy next spring," he suddenly said, his voice louder than I expected it to be, like he was trying to convince himself of their sureness. "Next April. We're going to go spend two weeks in Italy. We're going to ride a gondola, or whatever they're called. We're going to go stay in some really expensive villa with goats or something that grazes the land."

"Goats?" I said, my eyes still not leaving the surface of the table.

239

"Or something," he said. I heard him take two steps toward me. "And then next November we're going to go to Greece. I've never been."

"I'd love to see Greece," I said, feeing a few of those rocks in my stomach disappear.

"Next month we are going to go to your sister's wedding. We're going to watch her and Rod say their vows. And someday, you and I will be aunt and uncle to their kids."

And then one more rock dropped back in.

"And when we feel ready, we're going to adopt some kids of our own," Alex was standing just a foot behind me now.

"Three," I said softly. "I always wanted three, when the time came."

"Three it is then," Alex said as he touched my shoulders lightly. Almost as if he didn't quite dare wrap his arms around me. "And then we're going to remodel this house. We're going to decorate a nursery, put a swing on the branch that hangs over the backyard.

"We're going to have our own family, Jessica Wright. We will make our own *life*."

I turned around to face Alex. His eyes burned with intensity as they looked into mine. I wrapped my arms behind his neck, bringing his face close to mine. I touched my forehead to his and closed my eyes. "We are going to move on to the rest of our lives."

"Yes we are," he said, letting his lips brush mine as he spoke.

"Thank you," I said with a sigh, letting myself relax into his embrace. It felt nice to be supported, to just finally let go of everything inside of me.

Alex didn't say anything, just brushed his lips against my temple and squeezed me tighter.

CHAPTER TWENTY-FOUR

I collapsed to my knees as the afterlife materialized around me. It felt as if my body were trying to turn itself inside out. My organs tried to expand and explode their way out of my skin. My entire body quaked.

Lifting my head took every ounce of strength I had. Trying to place myself, I found I was on the staircase, directly across from the council's seats. The new Cormack had just walked back into the stone tunnel leaving a recently deceased person standing alone on the catwalk.

As I heard the rustling of wings, I threw myself back against the wall, trying to make myself as small as possible.

I couldn't even dare a glance toward the council as the trial got underway. I didn't want to know if they could see me or now. I wasn't sure if I should feel panicked or relieved when the condemned and exalted started flooding into the cylinder. They hid me from the eyes of the council, but my odd behavior was like sending out a flare. Yet no one acknowledged my presence; they simply sat in rapture of the trial underway.

I looked around as I got to my feet, the names of the dead running through my head.

But I didn't have to search for long. A pair of blue eyes locked with mine, and as usual, I just knew that was Philip Clearwater. As he started walking toward me, two others joined his side, and a moment later, three more. As he approached me, he gave a nod of his head, indicating that I was to start up the staircase. I understood. We were in too obvious of a spot.

As we made our way up, the crowd behind me seeming to grow, I dared one glance sideways toward the ten council member's.

A dull throb pulsed through my chest as my eyes settled on Cole. Our final hours together before he was pulled back filled my thoughts. The honesty he had finally allowed to come through put a lot of strange feelings into my chest.

Suddenly, as if I had spoken those thoughts directly into his ear, Cole's eyes lifted from the man before him. He scanned the staircase for just a moment, and then his eyes met mine.

I could tell he was trying hard not to react to me. But I could see the fear in his eyes, the panic he must have been feeling. And then his eyes flashed to the other side of the cylinder, to the stairway that wound up and down. I followed his line of sight, feeling a strange sensation crawling along in my blood.

I saw myself from across the cylinder. I stared down at the man on trial, my face serene and calm looking.

Jane.

The woman Cole had loved for centuries. The woman who had cheated on her husband with Cole. The woman he had fathered an illegitimate child with. And the woman who had forsaken him.

The woman who was the reason Cole had come after me.

My own eyes slid back to Cole. I didn't even think to be more tactful to compose my shock-saturated face. Cole's eyes met mine again, his expression both saddened and shameful looking.

I was prodded from behind, and I stumbled forward, my body feeling numb.

"Keep moving," a voice mumbled from behind.

I just kept glancing back and forth from Jane's oblivious face to Cole's deepening disturbed one.

He caught my eyes once more, and shook his head in a very clear way.

I swallowed hard and turned my eyes back in the direction I was supposed to be going. Gathering my wits, I committed myself to not look at Jane and her blue eyes again.

Finally out of view of the council, I turned back to the people behind me, realizing that the group had grown to over a dozen angels.

"We know why you're here," a woman with black eyes said. Surprisingly her voice was calm, not the normal hate-filled hissing they usually spoke with. "And while not all of us agree, I will do what you ask. I haven't forgotten the branding you endured for me."

"But the council needs him," a blue-eyed man said, his eyes turning hard on the woman. "You've seen the chaos. Only one council member has been committed for the next term but the contention continues to get worse. He will be a needed addition."

I glanced back to the council. A blue-eyed man I had never seen before sat with the rest of them, one of the women now gone.

"He didn't deserve to be taken when he was," the woman said, her voice hardening as she met the man's glare. "It wasn't his time."

"It must have been if he's dead!" another of the black-eyed angels said.

"Please," I said, my voice just a little too quiet to be heard. I swallowed hard, squeezing my eyes closed. "Please," I said more loudly, letting my eyes slowly open again. "Don't accept him when they judge him."

They were quiet for a while, their eyes not quite meeting mine.

"Not like it matters," one of the ones with black eyes said. "We all know where he will be placed. It doesn't matter if my kind agree."

"He's right," a blue-eyed woman said. "We all know where he's going. You really only have to get those of us he would join to agree with you."

"Than do it," I said, my voice sounding desperate. "I can't let him be taken back. And I need you to help me. I can't reach everyone in time. He only has a week, at the most. I need you all to help find those I stood trial for and get them to agree."

They were silent again for a moment that felt too ominously long.

"We can't make that promise," a young looking blond woman said quietly.

I met each of their eyes, reading the same answer in each of them.

"Fine," I said, my voice shaking, threatening to crack. "But can you just tell me one thing before I go?" I took their silence as a maybe. "Have any of you seen a Sally Thomas?"

They glanced between each other, something spreading through them that felt like an inside secret.

"That's enough," I said, closing my eyes again. "You don't have to tell me. I just wanted to know if anyone had seen her."

Without waiting for any more heart-sinking words, I stepped off the ledge.

The following two days passed in a slow roll of anticipation and dread. I continued to go back to the afterlife as much as I could, aided by Sal's pills. But I was getting the same answers. A few would do what I asked, but most wanted him on the council. We were losing this battle.

Alex couldn't even keep his wings in anymore. They were patchy and frail looking. Feathers were strewn throughout the house.

Alex finally looked like the terrifying being Cole had become, just with gray eyes instead of black.

As per Sal's wishes according to her will, Sal was cremated and her remains were given to me in a beautiful black urn. I dressed solemnly that morning, black feeling so fitting for the day. At six in the morning, there was a soft knock on the door and as I stepped into the living room, Emily and Amber walked in, just the two of them. Emily moved with care, obviously still tender from the surgery. I hadn't dared leave Alex to go pick her up. Amber had agreed without a fight.

We didn't say anything as I gathered what was left of Sal's physical body. Emily and Amber's eyes both grew wider as Alex stepped out of our room, his wings exposed, the truth of what he was undeniable.

"Oh Alex," Emily breathed, crossing the room to wrap her arms around him. He simply squeezed his eyes closed and hugged her back. Amber just stood there, eyes wide and frozen. I couldn't blame her. I felt like that too sometimes.

"Let's go," I said, my voice raw. "Before the neighbors wake up."

Without waiting for a response, I opened the front door and stepped outside into the misty October morning.

We all silently made our way up the hillside. The ground was slightly slick with the morning dew and all the mist. The dense evergreens around us felt warm and cold at the same time. Something about that mist that hung low to the ground made the moment not feel real, like this was a scene from a movie and this was the solemn part where a single choir voice would sing out a high-pitched, sad sounding note.

Light shone on the peak we hiked to, the sun casting shadows on the ground that added to the surreal feel of that morning. We gathered on the rocky top, each taking in the view that dropped away back to the lake on one side, the other side spanning out to the ocean and the islands in it.

I clutched the urn tightly to my chest, feeling like if I loosened my grip I might just finally break down. I was already filled with too many cracks, if I let the sand start to leak through one of them, the entire spider-web would shatter.

"Sal was one of the most innocent people I knew," Emily said, always the clear-headed one in situations where I couldn't be. "She was always so sweet and always honest. I have been lucky to have been able to call her my friend."

It was quiet for a moment then. I couldn't seem to make my eyes move from one of the islands out in the water, not really seeing anything.

"Um," Amber cleared her throat, her voice sounding slightly uncomfortable. "I didn't know Sal well, but she was a good person. You can just tell that about people sometimes. Sal was a beautiful being."

Alex's arm came around my shoulders, his wings brushing against my back. "Sal was genuine," he said, his voice coming out strong and clear. "There are a lot of fake people in this world and a lot of people pretend to be something they are not. But Sal wasn't one of those people. I always appreciated that about her, not that she could have been different, but it's always nice to know that someone isn't saying one thing to you and thinking another. Sal was real."

I closed my eyes, feeling as if everything inside of me was sinking into my feet. A single tear broke from my eyelashes and rolled down my cheek. I felt the cracks spreading inside of me.

Alex squeezed his arm tighter around me, pressing his lips to my temple. "You don't have to say anything," he said quietly. "We all know you loved her. Sal knows you love her."

Emily came to stand in front of me, placing her hands on the urn. "It's time sweetie," she said softly. A light breeze picked up off the ocean, pulling her curls around her face. I stood there, looking into Emily's eyes for a moment, squeezing the urn with all the pain inside of me. But finally I nodded my head, and let her take Sal from me.

Emily took the lid off and carefully, turned it on its side.

Slowly, the pieces of Sal's left behind body were carried away down the hillside on the wind.

When the urn was empty, Emily replaced the lid, and then hugged the porcelain herself.

"Sal saw things for what they were."

Everything inside of me stilled at that voice. Everything about that accent, the timbre of it, the tone of his voice brought back a flood of memories and emotions.

Everyone turned at once. And there he was, standing on the hill top, back in the world of the living.

"Cole," I breathed.

His black eyes seemed alight, reflecting so many emotions I felt fanning out inside of me.

"She saw me for what I was," he said, his voice low.

"How?" I said, my voice not fully wanting to work.

"I don't have long," he said, his again flawless looking face almost pained looking. "A few minutes. If they realize I'm gone I will for certain lose my position on the council."

It wasn't until then that I thought to look at Alex. But I was surprised when I looked at him that he seemed controlled. His face looked wary, but he wasn't seething as I had expected.

"What are you doing here?" Alex asked, his voice careful.

Cole met his eyes, his face a mix of the old jealousy and sadness. "You feel like hell, don't you?" he asked.

Alex simply nodded.

"I came to tell the two of you the time is coming. Quickly. I would be surprised if you have two days left. Probably shorter."

"Is there anything else we can do?" I asked. Cole's words from a few months previous echoed in my head. *If they can't claim you, what are you willing to do to save him?*

"Pray for a miracle," he said, his voice sounding as defeated as my thoughts felt.

We both stared at each other for a long moment. Everything inside of me felt knotted up, such a tangled web of panic, determination, despair, fading hope. I would never be able to distinguish all the pieces of me again.

"You've grown so much, Jessica," Cole said, something in his eyes softening. "When I told you to fight back I didn't expect this. I understand now, just how much you really do love him. To go back to my world and fight for him like that."

I slipped my hand into Alex's.

And before our eyes, Cole's skin started tightening, a few black veins rose around his eyes. He wasn't lying when he said he only had a few minutes.

251

"There's really nothing you can do for him?" I said, suddenly taking a step toward him.

"At this point I don't think anyone but you can save him," Cole said, the black veins rising on his face more quickly. He was decaying before our eyes.

I swallowed hard, feeling my hands start to tremble. It felt like they never stopped doing that these days. Everything inside of me started to quake, seeing Cole being pulled back into his world seemed to remind my body that was where it belonged now.

"Cole," I said in a hoarse whisper. "What about Sal? Is she..." my voice cut out. It hurt too much to think of sweet, innocent Sal having to stand a trial.

"She's in a happier place," he said, giving me a sad half smile. I saw something flash in his eyes, similar to how the angels in the afterlife had reacted.

A tear slipped down my face then and I could only give a little nod.

"Use your time wisely," Cole said. Glancing over at Emily, Cole's eyes grew sad. "It was good to see you again, Emily."

And then he was gone.

I could only hear the sounds of my breathing for a long while. The air flowed in and out of my lungs slowly, expanding and then contracting. The breeze had stilled, the world feeling silent and dead.

Not even realizing what I was doing, I had looked to the side and finally felt like I slipped back into my body when I took in Emily and Amber's expressions.

Amber's face was filled with nothing but pure horror. Her eyes were wide and distant looking, her jaw just slightly slack. But Emily's eyes were filled with tears, her lower lip trembling. She looked absolutely exhausted. And her face was pale white.

"Let's get you back, Emily," I said, turning back toward the house. "You can't be getting all worked up."

"It's happening again," she said in a weak voice. "I'm having them again."

"Having what again?" I asked, turning back toward Emily.

"The nightmares," she half whispered.

I didn't say anything for a moment, trying to make my brain process what Emily had just said. "That's what Cole meant?"

Emily nodded. She then turned and pulled her curly blond hair from her neck. Her brand was freshly red and painful looking. "My first time back and I was branded."

"Oh Emily," I said, crossing the space and pulling her into my arms. "You know what this means, don't you?" I squeezed her tighter.

Emily sniffed, nodding her head. "I'm neutral now."

"It's more than that," I said, my voice sounding excited and finally hopeful. "You're not condemned anymore, Emily. You have a wonderful future before you."

She sniffed again, a breathy sounding laugh escaping her lips. She stepped away from me, wiping at her tears, a small smile spreading on her face. "You're right," she said. "And while this is terrifying, to know I'm going to go through this again every time I sleep, it feels good. It's worth it. Just like Cormack said."

"I'm so happy for you," Alex said, stepping forward to join us, his smile both brilliant and pained.

"I'm not really sure what is going on," Amber said. "But it sounds like having nightmares is a good thing. I guess I'm happy for you too."

We all chuckled a little at Amber, everyone coming close together, and embracing in a very real and very needed four-person hug.

"We really should get you back," I said to Emily as we released each other. With a nod from her, we all started silently back down the hillside.

Amber and Emily didn't even come inside when we got back to the house. They both climbed in Amber's car and pulled onto the road. I was relieved that they did, I heard Alex's labored breathing the whole way down, saw how his feet seemed so unsteady on our unmarked path.

Alex was practically gasping as we walked through the doors. Before I could even say anything, he was suddenly in the kitchen, moving faster than a human ever could, and was pulling half of the contents of the fridge out, and a mountain of pots and mixing bowls.

"Alex," I said, unsure of what to say. Because, really, what was there left to say?

He shook his head, his breathing still hard and sharp. "I need…" he struggled to speak. "I need to… make something. I need… to stay here." He paused in cracking half a dozen eggs and braced his hands on the countertop, squeezing his eyes closed. His whole chest expanded and contracted as he took in mouthfuls of air. His wings trembled, the morning sun coming in through the window and reflecting off of them.

Alex no longer looked like something you'd read about in a romance novel. He was no longer perfect and glorious looking. He looked like something out of a horror movie. Like something from your worst nightmare.

In that moment I felt so selfish. It was obvious how much pain Alex was in. I had caused every moment of this pain. If he hadn't have met me he never would have died at the age of only twenty-three, his neck snapped by a demented angel. He never would have become an angel himself, until it was his time at a very old age. He wouldn't be holding onto reality with every painful fiber of his being.

Maybe it would be better for him to move on. All the other angels I had pleaded with said what a wonderful thing it was that awaited him. To be an exalted council member had to have its benefits. And it sounded like it was pretty much a guaranteed thing. I was keeping him from that. I was being selfish again.

But I couldn't stop being selfish.

I couldn't stop loving Alex.

I couldn't let him go where I could never go permanently.

The phone suddenly rang, causing me to jump violently. Alex took one more deep breath, and moved back to whatever it was he was making. I numbly walked to the handset and picked up the phone.

"Hello?" I answered. Alex paused, watching my face as I listened to the voice on the other end. "Uh huh," I said. Swallowing hard, I forced myself to answer the woman on the other end's question.

"I don't know if that will be possible," I said. "I'm afraid my husband will probably be leaving soon and I'm not sure when he will be returning." Alex's eyes continued to watch mine. "Okay. Thank you."

I hung up the phone and sank onto a barstool.

"That was the rehab facility," I explained, Alex's hands continuing their work.

"And?" he said, measuring out some flour.

"Caroline's doing really well. They said she's really progressing. She wanted to set up a meeting with you."

"Oh," was all Alex said, his hands pausing for just a moment as he placed my responses with the words the woman on the phone had spoken.

And I sat at the counter the rest of the day as Alex cooked a meal that would have fed fifteen people.

CHAPTER TWENTY-FIVE

I couldn't do it that night. Everything in my head was telling me that I had no choice, that I had to go back, that I had to keep fighting, to keep pleading.

But I couldn't do it. Everything inside of me was screaming against my brain. My entire being shuddered at the thought of having to go back one more time.

I just couldn't do it that night.

The air was cold and damp that night as I sat on the wooden swing on the deck. I could hear Alex inside, putting the remains of his cooking frenzy away. The wood planks below me were cold on my toes as I pushed myself slowly back and forth. Drops of dew were already forming on the seat around me, creating a ghost around my body where it warmed the wood too much for the water to collect.

I closed my eyes, tipping my head back against the swing. Breathing the night air in felt good. Yet I still felt like I was suffocating. So much of me felt dead.

The back door opened but I didn't open my eyes until something light but large in size was placed on my lap. I opened my eyes to see Alex keeping my guitar upright and balanced on my lap. In his other hand he held his own guitar.

"It's been a long time since you've played it," he said, letting go of mine. He settled on the ground in front of me, crossing his legs, and letting his own settle in his lap. His eyes holding mine, he let his fingers start to pick their way through chords.

Something in me wanted to smile at this gesture of normality. Alex was right. I couldn't even remember the last time I had played my guitar. I played so infrequently the last year or so that there wasn't even a hint of the callouses that once covered the fingertips on my left hand.

Looking down at the strings, I placed my fingers on them. And then my other hand started picking at them, bringing notes out that reflected how I felt inside. Broken and lost.

Alex picked up with a fitting harmony, his notes complimenting mine but in a hopeful uplifting tone. I met his eyes as I continued to play, searching for answers there. But all I could think about was how the gray was soon going to be blue again, and I was never going to be able to see them.

It took a moment for me to realize my picking had faded away. Alex started to hum to his notes. After a minute I recognized the tune. Alex started to sing softly.

"You're the closest to heaven that I'll ever be

And I don't want to go home right now.

And all I can taste is this moment
And all I can breathe is your life.
'Cause sooner or later it's over,
I just don't want to miss you tonight.

And I don't want the world to see me,
'Cause I don't think that they'd understand.
When everything's made to be broken,
I just want you to know who I am."

"The Goo Goo Dolls," I said when Alex stopped singing, his fingers still moving though. "I've always loved that song."

"I always kind of thought *Iris* described us," he said, his eyes looking a little sad still. "It's always been our song to me, I guess."

"It's perfect," I said.

We were quiet for a moment, simply looking at each other. There were a million words that needed to be said between us, and all I wanted was a lifetime to say them.

"In case this doesn't work," Alex said, his voice sounding rough. "In case they take me, I just want you to know that I don't regret one second of the past year. I would do it all over, every moment of it. It's been worth it all."

Feeling so still inside, I set my guitar on the deck and kneeled down in front of him. He set his own guitar aside, keeping my eyes. I reached my hand toward him, letting my fingers trace the blackness around his eyes. I let my hands drift to his lips, feeling their smooth surface.

"This can't be the end," I breathed, letting my eyes linger everywhere but his eyes. "Everything has just started for us. This can't be the end."

He didn't say anything and I could feel his eyes tracing over every surface of my face, letting them trail down to my body. I felt my pulse quicken, electricity running under my skin. Alex's right hand came up, trailing lightly along my bare arm. I traced my fingers along the edges of his lips, recalling how they tasted and felt against my own.

Alex's hands went from my arm to the hem of my shirt, lifting it over my head. The cool air caused goosebumps to flash across my skin. He just looked at me for a moment, his eyes taking in every detail. And finally his eyes came back up to mine, his alight with love and anticipation. His hand came to my cheek.

"You're perfect," he said, his voice barely above a whisper. "You've *always* been perfect."

A small smile crossed my lips then, and for the first time in what felt like a long time, I actually felt happy.

For that moment, being there with him would be enough to last me forever.

CHAPTER TWENTY-SIX

I knew this was the day.

There wasn't any reason for thinking it. Any more reason than there would have been for it to have happened yesterday.

I simply knew that today would be the day.

My eyes slid open to meet the ceiling above me, the realization that I had missed my last chance to go back and make a plea making me sick. I wasn't going to get to go back before Alex would be sucked away. This was the black date, all the numbers on the bomb had fallen. Today was the day everything was going to implode.

I rolled over to see Alex sitting on the side of the bed, a pile of feathers beneath his wings. He sat with his forearms braced against his knees, his head hanging low. He held his wedding ring in his fingers, turning it over and over, the sun reflecting off of its surface.

And watching his face, I knew that he knew this was the day too.

"Would you make me some French toast?" I asked. I was proud for making my voice sound so normal.

He looked over at me, his face haggard looking. He looked so worn out. And decayed. He reached a hand out toward me and tucked a stray lock of hair behind my ears. "Sure," he said.

Alex stood and headed for the door, two more feathers falling before he even made it out into the living room. His skin was so tight on his bones it looked painful. His veins rose out in a terrifying way.

It felt like I had a thousand tiny knives inside my chest.

I stepped into the shower, trusting my instincts that Alex wouldn't disappear before I could get out. As I lathered my hair, I noticed something inside of me felt different. I felt in control. I felt grounded. Like I was going to make this work.

Like maybe, just maybe, Alex might make it through this day. Somehow.

Seeing the rain that was coming down as I toweled off, I pulled on my favorite green sweater and a pair of worn-out jeans. Feeling like today of all days I shouldn't have to hide what I was, I twisted my locks into a messy bun on the back of my head.

Alex looked up at me when I exited our room and paused for a moment, simply staring at me.

"What?" I asked, feeling suddenly self-conscious.

"I've never seen you wear your hair up before," he said, a hint of a smile cracking in the corner of his mouth.

"I can't remember the last time I did it," I said, taking a seat at the bar. Alex passed a plate of French toast across.

Next came the butter tray and a bottle of Alex's homemade syrup.

I realized then that I wasn't hungry in the least.

Dutifully, I poured the syrup and took a bite. As usual, it was perfection, even if I wasn't hungry.

As he cleaned up, I watched Alex. At times, it seemed as if the edges of him blurred, as if he wasn't quite there all the way. He had to reach for the egg carton twice, his hand seeming to pass right through it the first time he tried.

There was no question that today was the day.

"I want you to do something for me today," he said as he finished and I ate my last bite. He rested his forearms on the counter and looked at me.

"Anything," I promised, knowing that I would.

"I want you to draw me," he said, his eyes never wavering.

"Draw you?" I questioned, my brows knitting together.

He nodded. "Like those drawings you showed me before. How long has it been since you last drew anything?"

I shook my head. "I don't know. Probably since I was about thirteen?"

"Draw me," he said again.

I understood then why he was making his request. We both knew what was going to happen today, and just in in case he didn't come back he wanted to leave one more reminder of him for me. Even though we both knew that I didn't need it. "Alright," I said, my voice sounding scratchy.

Alex walked into our bedroom for a moment and emerged with some blank pieces of paper and a pencil. Taking my hand in his, he led us out onto the back deck. Rain dripped off the overhang, over the side of the deck railing. I pulled up one of the chairs, resting a notebook on my knees, balancing it and my pages before me. Alex sat in the other chair, ten feet away, his forearms resting on his knees, his wings folded behind him.

I just looked at him for a long time, not saying a word. I used my sharpened memory to recall the way Alex looked, before Cole killed him. His skin was a bit rougher looking, like he'd already spent too much time out in the sun. His hands were more calloused. And his eyes. His beautiful, blue eyes.

Looking down at the page before me, I hesitated. It had been so long since I had drawn anything. I knew I had had talent, but talent didn't tend to stick around when you didn't use it.

I let the pencil meet the paper, letting them use each other to create lines and planes. I glanced up every so often, letting my eyes trace over the shape of Alex's forearm, the way his shoulder rose to meet his neck.

The pages fluttered to the ground as I filled them and shuffled to blank sheets, the sun moving from the east above our heads. We sat there in silence, each studying the other.

I drew Alex's eyes, as they were now and as they used to be, on the same page. I drew his hands, the way they hung together, his arms draped over his knees. I drew his silhouette, framed by only his wings in their former glorious state.

I felt emotions trying to build up inside of me as I filled the pages. But I pushed them down, knowing that if I let them surface I wouldn't make it through this day. Every part of me felt exhausted from the effort. And when I couldn't draw anymore, couldn't make any other surface of him appear on the page, I slumped back in the chair and let my eyes slide closed.

I lay like that for a long time. I heard Alex stand, gather my filled pages, and slip inside, but I didn't have the energy to follow him. I couldn't even open my eyes. I knew what was coming later. I was going to need every ounce of fight I had in me in a few hours.

Through the panes of the windows and the sliding glass doors, I heard Alex making phone calls. I recognized the first as Emily, simply from the way he spoke. Emily had been released first thing that morning but instead of coming to stay with us, Austin had gone to stay with her. Alex thanked her for being such a good friend to me. I assumed Emily had started crying as he tried to assure her, not quite able to find comforting words in a situation that involves you basically dying all over again, this time for real.

He next called Rod. He'd tried to keep the conversation light, joking around in their usual banter. Then he had tried telling Rod that he hadn't been able to hang out lately because he was sick. I heard him assuring Rod that no, he didn't need him to come over. He made an attempt to say that he was going to be alright, but no one would have believed it.

After saying good-bye to Rod with a shaky voice, Alex dialed Ted, his lawyer. The phone call was brief. He simply asked if everything had been taken care of. He said good-bye to Ted as well.

Ten minutes later, Alex came out onto the back deck again, closed the door behind him, and leaned against it, watching me. He cleared his throat and then said "I need you to do something for me, if…" his voice cut out.

"What?" I asked, letting my eyes finally open, staring at the underside of the boards of the upper deck.

Alex took two steps toward me and I looked over to see him place a simple white envelope with Caroline's name written on it in my hand.

"I need you to give this to her," he said. "Everything I have to say to her is in there."

I let my head lean back against the chair, letting my eyes stare vacantly upward again. "Okay," I agreed.

He was quiet and I could tell there was something he wanted to say. He shifted from one foot to the other. "Please come inside," he breathed, pain obvious in his voice.

I finally looked at his face again. He looked terrified. He looked like he was in an immeasurable amount of pain. And he looked so inhuman.

Rising to my feet, I clutched the envelope tightly between two of my fingers, and took Alex's had in mine with the other hand. Together, we both went back inside and walked into our room. Closing the door behind us, we both lay on the bed. I reached over and set Caroline's letter on the nightstand. Alex lay his head on my chest and I wrapped my arms around his shoulders, resting my chin on the top of his head.

It felt almost as if I was holding a person made of sand. Nothing about Alex felt solid.

Today would be the day.

"I know you don't want to talk about this, Jessica," he said. "But we have to consider that this is probably going to be my last day. I need to know that you'll be okay when I go. What will you do after?"

I let my eyes close, feeling another half a dozen rocks drop into my stomach. "I don't know," I answered, my voice cracking.

"I think you should move back to Ucon," he said, his voice trying hard to sound like we were having any normal conversation. I could tell he had thought a lot about this. "You shouldn't have to deal with this on your own. Your parents love you. They will want to help you through this. And you'll have plenty of money to buy a house there if you don't want to move in with your parents."

I shook my head, my eyes still closed, even though Alex couldn't see it.

"You could open up your own bookstore too," Alex said, trying to force excitement into his voice. "You'd do good at that, if you put your focus on it."

Everything in me wanted to tell Alex to stop talking. But I couldn't do that. Not when these were Alex's final hours. Or minutes.

"You have to promise me that you will keep going on," Alex said, his grip tightening around my mid-section. "You have to promise me that you will be okay and that you will keep living."

A sharp breath caught painfully in my chest as I tried to breathe. My ears rang.

"Promise me, Jessica," Alex repeated, his frame shifting more. His hands started shaking. "Promise me."

I held my breath for one second, willing myself not to fall apart. I couldn't crack now, not with Alex like this. "I promise," I whispered.

He fell silent then. His frame continued to quake, his breath starting to grow more ragged.

I reached for my book on the nightstand. Propping it up in front of me where Alex could see it as well, I opened it to the beginning, to the very first page.

Eliza Booth's name was followed by John Killerman. Who was followed by Trace Laggen and hundreds of others. "These people will come through for us," I said, forcing myself to believe my words. "They will make it possible for us to stay together."

"They'll come through for us," Alex repeated, his voice barely understandable. His grip tightened on me.

I watched the hands of the clock on the opposite wall. The minutes seemed to slow down and speed up in alternating shifts. Time didn't feel consistent and I waited for it to run out.

That distinct smell Alex picked up ever since his change grew stronger and stronger. It was pure and fresh but it was tainted now with fear and pain. He continued to shake, his breath coming in sharp spurts.

Five o'clock rolled slowly around, and in desperation to distract myself, I observed every detail of our bedroom. The blankets around us were wrinkled and tangled around our legs. The book of names lay next to Alex, propped open to a place near the end. The dresser had one drawer pulled open, a few of my shirts hanging out of it haphazardly. The door to the closet and bathroom were both cracked open just a bit. The nightstand next to us held a book I'd started reading before the honeymoon, Caroline's letter, a lamp. A bottle of pills. Sal's sleeping pills.

Alex gripped me tighter suddenly, his breath going in in one hissing gasp. I could see his entire frame shift before me.

"Jessica," he half cried, half moaned. "Jessica."

"I'm here," I said, everything suddenly flowing to the surface. All the emotions and feelings I had been fighting all day long finally pushed its way up, bringing on a string of tears with it.

"It's time," he gasped. "I'm sorry. I can't... can't... fight it anymore."

"I know," I said, more tears slipping down my face. "I know."

It took everything he had in him, but Alex lifted himself up onto his forearms and looked me in the eyes. "I love you," he said, his voice straining to come out. "I love you with everything that I am."

"I know," I said as I placed a hand on the side of his face. Slowly, I leaned in, and pressed my lips to his. "I love you too," I whispered.

And then the air seemed to change. The edges of Alex shifted and faded. The blackness around his eyes started spreading down his face, blackness growing from his chest at the same time. His skin continued to shrink.

Alex squeezed his eyes closed in pain, his breath catching sharply.

A gut retching cry erupted from his lips.

A pulse pushed through the air, emanating from Alex's body. The blackness of his skin consumed Alex. He seemed to fade from the inside out.

And in the space of one second, he was gone.

I sat there stunned for a moment. Just a moment.

The reality of this situation had failed to fully hit me. In a way I think I had been in denial that Alex would ever actually go. Alex was the most real thing of my existence. So him not being around at some point would never have felt real.

The time was here. And already gone.

Closing my eyes, I ran over everything in my head. How many had agreed not to claim Alex? I wasn't sure the exact number but I knew that it would never be enough. The afterlife wanted him. The exalted wanted him.

But so did I.

Swiping Sal's pills from the night stand, I was in the kitchen half a second later. I filled a glass with water and unscrewed the lid of the container. Tipping it back, my mouth was filled with as many pills as I thought I could swallow. Tilting back the glass of water, cold liquid spilled over and ran down my neck as I swallowed the painful lump and forced them down into my stomach

Knowing it would never work fast enough, I dumped three pills onto the counter and started throwing drawers open. Settling on a wooden rolling pin, I started crushing the pills into a fine powder.

I'd never even been tempted by drugs my entire life, but I knew that snorting a drug got it into your system a whole lot faster than if you took them orally.

My eyes watered and everything in me wanted to force the powder out of my body. But I made myself keep sniffing the white stuff off of the kitchen counter.

About to run back into the bedroom, I paused for a second, my eyes catching on the cordless phone on the counter. Snatching it up, I carried it with me back into the bedroom. I swept the feathers off of the bed, gathering the blankets and sheets up around me.

"I'm coming Alex," I said to myself as I dialed.

"Jessica?" Emily's voice came through on the other end.

"You're at home and okay today, right?" I asked, my voice sounding a little too demanding.

"Yeah, Austin and I got back this morning. He's staying with me. What's up?" she asked, the concern in her voice rising.

"I need you to come over as soon as you can. And you're probably going to have to call 911 when you get here."

"Whoa," she said, her voice at full attention. "What's going on Jessica? What... what did you do?"

I simply hung up the phone.

My ears were starting to ring by that point and I could feel the gentle tug at the back of my eyes. As I lay back in the bed, I felt my limbs grow heavy and relaxed.

It was working.

"I'm coming, Alex," I said, staring up at the ceiling. Lines were starting to get blurry. "I'm coming."

CHAPTER TWENTY-SEVEN

It felt like I'd been shot back into the afterlife with a cannon. I hit the floor with such force it knocked me off of my feet. Trying to orient myself, I crawled to my knees and looked out at the cylinder.

The afterlife was in total and complete chaos. Angels flew everywhere, hissing escaped many throats. And there was so much yelling.

There was a gathering of angels on the narrow catwalk, creating a circle. In the middle I could see Alex. Other's flew at them, shouting horrible things, trying to get to Alex and do what I could only assume was drag Alex down below. Endless angels argued with each other along the staircase, some of the debates growing heated and violent. Only about two thirds of the council were at their seats, the rest of them scattered about the cylinder trying to bring peace to the masses.

My eyes went back to Alex, watching his face, feeling everything inside of me harden. His eyes were wide as if he was afraid, but I saw the firm set of his jaw, that determined way he held his shoulders.

He looked flawless and perfect again.

I stood and attempted to get myself out of the way of all the chaos. Two angels made their way up the staircase by way of shoving each other and shouting.

"He must go back," one said roughly.

"He doesn't belong there anymore!" the other shouted. "He belongs here! We need him! Look at what his going back has already done to our world."

As I tuned into what the masses were saying, it was all pretty much the same thing. A few wanted to send him back, but most were determined to keep him.

"Enough!" two voices roared, deafening in its volume and power.

Every body fell still and turned toward the council's seats. The leader of the exalted sat stiff in his seat, and Cole's black eyes cut through the cylinder as he turned them on those causing the chaos. Together their voice had been powerful enough to cause the stones of the afterlife to quake.

"That is *enough*," the leader of the exalted repeated, his blue eyes narrowed, his lips set hard. "You will all calm yourselves and let the proceedings go as usual. I will not have a war starting under my watch.

And then I remembered Alex's words. That he would cause a war if our plan didn't work.

What had he said when he arrived?

Movement to my left caught my eye and I looked up to see Jeremiah shove another black-eyed angel off of him.

Straightening himself, Jeremiah coiled his wings and flew back to his appointed seat. Cole's jaw tightened and the two of them looked stiff enough to snap.

There was other muttering but the masses calmed themselves, sitting and standing along the staircase, their attention turning back to the council. Those that surrounded Alex returned to their positions. The last to leave Alex was the new Cormack. He eyed the angels around him one more time, his jaw set hard, and when he determined that no one was trying to attack Alex anymore, walked back into the tunnel.

Alex stood there alone, his wings glorious, his frame held high.

He looked like a leader.

"You, my boy," the leader of the exalted started, turning his eyes on Alex. "Have caused a great deal of stir around here. The voices of most have been heard. Can you tell what is happening here lately?"

No wavering or hesitation in his voice Alex replied "The council is changing."

"And do you understand what is wanted from you?"

This time Alex did hesitate, his eyes falling for just a moment before returning to the man's face. "I am wanted to join you."

The leader looked at Alex for a moment, a million judgments behind his eyes, and slowly nodded. "Most admire what you've done. They've seen what is inside of you. And they want you to lead them."

Alex gave an almost imperceptible nod.

"I know the desire of your heart. You wish to return. We were generous in allowing you a bit more time back. Never have we granted a request like that before. But you possess no spark of life. It is elsewhere, and while you are dead you belong with us."

Alex's head dropped. I saw his shoulders slump just slightly.

It was hard to fight against the council's wishes. It was like trying to fight against the gravitational pull of the moon.

"You would be foolish to not want what most are offering. While yes, being a council member requires passing judgment, your existence is fitting of what you have earned. Bliss, happiness, peace. Power. And you would give that away to go back to a world filled with pain, war, greed?"

"Yes," Alex said, his voice a little too quiet. He lifted his head and fixed his hard eyes on them.

"See," one of the black-eyed council hissed. "He doesn't deserve this. He doesn't even want it. He would not be able to perform his duty. Why give it to him? Place his judgment and get this over with."

"You will not speak until it is requested of you," Cole chimed in, turning eyes that could burn on him. He fell silent.

Now with attention back, the leader of the exalted continued. "You must understand that you cannot return in your state. You would not survive. We did not expect you to last half as long as you did."

"I wasn't feeling so great," Alex said.

A small twinkle could be detected in the leader's eye as he looked at Alex. "No, I don't suppose you were."

A few more scuffles broke out along the staircase. Fists flew and feather's fluttered down toward the fiery depths. The council's eyes darted to them.

"I said that's enough!" Cole roared, power seeming to radiate from him. Again the cylinder fell still.

"Alex Wright," the blue-eyed leader said. Every eye settled on Alex. "The deeds of your life have been accounted for and judgment will be passed. Your actions must be made known."

"No!" I screamed with a scream that made my chest feel raw. My legs were sprinting as I pushed my way up the staircase. Angels looked at me alarmed, dodging to get out of my way as I barreled up. As soon as I knew I could reach it, I leapt off the staircase and landed on my hands and knees on the catwalk.

"No," I said again, looking up into the eyes of the council. It felt like a fire had been lit in my chest giving me bravery I never knew I had. "You cannot take him."

"Jessica!" both Cole and Alex said at the same time. A primal hiss escaped Jeremiah's chest.

I met Alex's eyes, rising slowly from the ground. Something inside of me twisted, like my stomach and my lungs were trying to mesh together.

"Jessica," he said again, his eyes looking desperate. "This wasn't the plan. You aren't supposed to be here."

"Neither are you," I said, crossing the space between us and intertwining my fingers with his.

"What is she doing here?" a black-eyed council woman hissed. "She should not be here. She is not even dead."

"No," the leader of the exalted said. "She shouldn't be here. What are you doing in the land of the dead child?"

I swallowed hard, my fury only rising at being called a child. "I won't let him be taken," I said, my voice firm. "It is my fault he is here. It wasn't meant to be his time."

"You understand that he cannot go back," he said, his eyes boring into mine. "His life is gone."

"I know," I said with a nod. Until then I hadn't fully accepted that cold hard fact. Alex couldn't go back and be dead. He wouldn't survive.

But something stirred within me. There had been something that I had been missing all this time.

The trade.

Alex had given his life to me.

A small, satisfied smile started to curl in the corner of my lips.

...the only advantage you have against them to save him...

"He can have it back," I said, too quiet for anyone but Alex to hear. He looked over at me, his brow knitted together.

"Jessica," he breathed, panic rising in his eyes. "No."

Keeping his eyes, I said, "I have to. There's no other way. They want you too much." I turned to the council before us. "Alex gave his life for me. That was the trade, his life for mine. I can't have it anymore. It isn't mine. I wish to return it and you have to send him back. If he has life in him you can't take him."

The cylinder was silent for one moment, everyone, including me, trying to process the possibility of my words.

Before anyone even breathed a word or twitched a finger, Cole leapt from his seat with a powerful beat of his wings. He landed on the catwalk in front of me, his eyes boring into mine. But before I could even process the hard but proud expression on his face, Cole thrust his hand into my chest.

The air caught in my throat as I nearly collapsed in on myself. Cole's hand was buried in my chest up to his wrist. And as quick as he had driven it there, he pulled it out.

Everything within me felt like it was being ripped in half as Cole pulled out. As if my very soul were being ripped apart, layer by layer.

As I collapsed to my knees, I saw the small white orb Cole held in his hand. He looked at it for half a moment, as if this was indeed something rare, something that even he had never seen before.

And before Alex could even cry in protest, Cole shoved his hand into Alex's chest in the same fashion. Alex collapsed in on himself in much the same way I had, crying out in pain. As he dropped to his knees, Cole's hand retracting, his wings started quivering, re-solidifying and disappearing.

Moments later there was nothing left of them.

"Alex," I breathed, everything inside of me feeling like it had been turned into a bloody, pulverized mess.

Just as Alex started to lift his head up to meet my eyes, Cole shoved Alex off of the catwalk. A scream ripped from my throat as I searched over the edge for him. I caught one short glimpse of the bottoms of his feet before he disappeared.

My head both spun and pounded as I let myself fall to my stomach on the cold stone. My limbs cried out in agony. It felt as if my brain had caught fire. Everything inside of me wrenched and seemed to stop.

This was what death had felt like before.

Death was where I was at again.

I rolled onto my side, back toward the council. I felt a pair of hands help me to sit up, and barely managed to lift my head to look into Cole's black eyes.

"Thank you," I muttered, my eyes losing their focus. The thudding in my chest came in sporadic, painful beats.

The next moment Cole was gone, landing silently back in his seat.

"That..." the leader of the exalted said through clenched teeth. "That may have been the final nail in your coffin my brother. This judgment may well be your last."

With those words, the afterlife finally erupted.

"How is that possible!"

"What just happened?"

"He's just back?!"

"Brand her!!"

The screams were maddening. My head pulsed and throbbed. Something in my chest felt like it was going to explode.

Through the haze of pain and blackness that tried to overtake me, I saw Cole pinning Jeremiah to his seat. Jeremiah's eyes were maddened as he looked at me. He fought with everything in him to get passed Cole and at me.

"Silence!" the leader of the exalted bellowed. All did as he commanded. Jeremiah's cold eyes turned to Cole for a moment, and finally he slumped back into his seat.

The blue-eyed leader turned his cold-as-ice eyes on me. He seemed contemplative for a moment but my foggy brain couldn't seem to care what he wanted to do with me now.

Pain was all I could comprehend.

The thudding in my chest stopped.

I wasn't sure if it started up again.

Was this how it felt to be dead?

"Jessica Wright," he said, his voice hard. "The deeds of your life have been accounted for and judgment will be passed. Your actions must be made known."

I felt the nervous excitement that picked up from both sides. Wild whoops and cries echoed off the stone walls.

"You're deeds will now be revealed."

I couldn't even focus on the two scrolls that were produced. My head hung from my shoulders, struggling to keep upright. That beating in my chest started again just once, and then stalled again, sending my entire body into panic.

I could have sworn all the blood in my body rushed up into my throat, threatening to suffocate me.

But there it was again, a dull thud beneath my rib cage.

It took me a moment to realize the words the man before me was speaking words that made up my entire being.

They say before you die, your life flashes before your eyes. Mine was being read aloud, for all to hear.

Calling my sister a bad word.

Helping my mother in her garden.

Thinking horrible thoughts about the girls who taunted me at school.

Sitting with my grandma and helping her around her house.

Abandoning my family.

Learning about Sal and taking care of her.

Having lustful thoughts about Alex.

Rescuing that woman from the burning SUV.

Defying the council.

My entire life was laid out for everyone to hear. Cormack's words echoed in my foggy head. *The deeds of your life may only be read once but no one ever forgets or lets ya forget what you've done.*

What felt like a lifetime later, which in a way it was, they read the last of the lists. Everyone was still and silent as I continued to lie there in death and agony.

I knew what came next. The part that had always echoed how unjust my previous presence there had been.

Sentencing.

The exalted leader sat there for a long time, thoughts and decisions rolling behind his eyes.

"I think now it is time to let our second new council member place her first judgment," he finally said. Something in my chest felt like it had been quickly yanked in a different direction. This was unexpected.

One of the blue-eyed men looked at the leader with hate and betrayal in his eyes. "You think *now* is an appropriate time to replace me?"

"I think now is a perfect time to implement the switch," the leader said patiently.

Not waiting to be told a second time, the man spread his wings and took his place along the staircase with the others.

"Will our new exalted council member please join us?"

From a place high above me, I caught the sight of a set of wings flapping. A figure slowly made their way down, and ever so gently, settled into the empty seat, alongside the other council members.

"Sal," I breathed.

"Hello Jessica," she said with a smile. Her face was flawless, the tiredness and fear she constantly held had washed away. She looked glorious and perfect. And her eyes were bluer than summer sky.

"Judgment will now be placed," the leader said, the faintest hint of a smile crossing his face. And taking one more contemplative moment, he breathed, "Up."

Something in my chest relaxed, just a tiny fraction. Meanwhile my head continued to spin. I wanted to throw up. My hands gripped the stone beneath me, clinging to anything I could to keep me from spinning right off the walkway.

The woman sitting next to the leader considered for a long while, watching my face. "Up," she finally said.

"Up," Sal said without hesitation.

The next man looked at me with malice in his eyes. I knew what his answer was going to be before he parted his lips. "Down."

It felt as if my entire frame sank again. Any hope still left in me started to smother itself.

The last blue eyed man looked at me, his face looking torn. We sat there for nearly a full minute before he spoke. "Up."

The first of the condemned sentenced. "Down."

The next woman passed her judgment. "Down."

Another "Down."

Finally it came to Jeremiah. He had been silent throughout this entire nightmare that was now reality. His black eyes bored into me and if possible, I would have burst into flames. "Down."

Everyone seemed to take an intake of breath all at once and the cylinder fell still as all eyes settled on Cole.

This was it. All that was needed was Cole's vote to bring me under his rule.

My offer still stands.

I was going to be receiving my own brand in just a moment.

But when Cole's eyes met mine, I felt nothing but calm inside. Something else grew in my chest. Something that felt like hope, or anticipation, or just plain stupidity.

"Up."

Everything within me felt like it disappeared.

No one moved or said anything.

Never before had there been a tie. No one's judgment had ever been split right down the middle.

I had not even considered that Cole would send me above, for this fact.

What was to be done in a tie?

"What…" one of the blue-eyed's stuttered. "What do we do now?"

They all looked to the blue-eyed leader for direction. And he just sat there, staring at me.

"We let them decide," Cole broke the silence. His hand indicated those along the staircase. "Let those who want her take her."

Something jumped into my throat as my insides came back to me. Something tingled in my toes and fingertips. Something flickered to life in the back of my mind.

The council looked between each other, each as unsure of what to do as the next. Slowly, they all nodded their heads.

"It comes to all of you," the exalted leader said, his voice so unsure. "You all have watched us make tens of thousands of judgments. Now it is your turn to decide this woman's fate."

Only silence reacted.

I gathered what little strength I had then and lifted myself up to my feet. I looked around the cylinder, meeting their faces. Some smiled back at me knowingly, others listened as whispers started frantically sweeping around the staircase. Others looked at me darkly, but they nodded their heads as my eyes met theirs.

"Claim her!" Jeremiah screamed.

And still no one moved. The cylinder was deathly quiet, the only sound coming from the rustle of feathers.

I closed my eyes as my head spun more, the ground beneath me seeming to tip and sway. Pulses of pain pushed their way through my brain.

"What do we do now?" a blue-eyed woman half whispered to the leader. He just shook his head, his eyes wider than normal, at a total loss as to what to do with me.

Again the beat in my chest stalled and painfully restarted.

Cole coiled his wings once more, launching himself across the space to me. He landed just a foot away, his nose so close to mine.

"I told you to use their mistake against them," he whispered so only I could hear.

"You knew this would happen?" I breathed, my brow furrowing.

"Not exactly," a smile cracked in the corner of his lips as he studied my eyes. "But I knew you would find the answer."

And making me jump a little, Cole placed his hot hand on my chest. His grin spread all the more on his face. His eyes danced as he looked at me. Turning back to the council, he didn't take his hand from my chest.

"Her heart still beats," he said loudly and clear. "This woman is not dead."

Again there was a cylinder-wide gasp, followed by loud chatter.

"Of course she's dead," one of the black-eyed council members shouted. "We've just judged her!"

Cole shook his head, the grin spreading on one side of his mouth. "I can feel it beating inside of her. It's not strong," he said as he looked back at me. "And it wants to stop. It's just like it was before he made the trade."

It should have been obvious, but I hadn't pieced it all together until then. With Alex's life given back to him I was back to the same state I'd been in before the trade. I was sick. Sick and on the edge of death. Again.

But I wasn't dead *yet*.

"Send her back," Cole said, turning back to the council, dropping his hand from my chest. "She cannot be here if she isn't dead. Let her live out the rest of her human life. In her condition it won't be long. We can figure out what to do with her when she can join us for real."

"No!" three of the council screamed. Jeremiah leapt from his seat, his hands already outstretched, ready to choke the remaining life out of me.

Cole's fist connected with Jeremiah's face with a crack that echoed off the walls. Jeremiah collapsed to the catwalk. Cole stood above him, and grabbing him by the very flesh of his chest, Cole picked him up and threw him across the cylinder back toward his seat. With a demonic cry, Jeremiah caught himself in the air with a powerful beat of his wings.

"You will not touch her!" Cole bellowed. An emotion beyond hate in his eyes, Jeremiah perched like a rabid bird on the edge of his seat.

"It's an abomination!" another black-eyed council member cried, ignoring Cole and Jeremiah's scuffle. "A judged human?! Walking about in the world of the living? *Still* living!"

"What else do you suggest we do with her?!" Cole bellowed, loud enough it seemed a tangible thing that filled the entire cylinder. "They will not claim her and we cannot try her again! She has no place here, at least not yet. Send her back!"

The council argued with themselves for several moments. Finally, Sal spread her arms before her, as if she were trying to keep two fighting children apart.

"Enough," she hissed. Her eyes settled on me. It was strange how different she seemed. She was so normal without being normal, and yet there was still the Sal I knew and loved in there. I could see it in her eyes. "This girl has been through enough. And we must see logic during this time. What our brother has said is true. She doesn't belong here yet. She can't exist here. Let her run her course."

"It won't be long," Cole said again, though I felt it was more for me than for anyone else.

The council was finally still again, thinking to themselves. My strength seemed to drain out of me and my knees suddenly wouldn't hold me anymore. I sank to the stones below me.

"Fine," the leader of the exalted said, his jaw set. "We can all see she doesn't have long. What is it going to matter anyway, if she's given another day?" He looked to his neighbors, and slowly they each nodded their heads. Jeremiah just continued to stare at me with blood and ice in his eyes.

"Thank you," I managed to mutter, relief somehow fluttering in my stomach through the storm that raged there.

Cole turned to me and knelt in front of me. His eyes burned with intensity as he looked at me. He took one of my hands in his.

"I mean it when I say you don't have long. Just like before, you are *at* death. Get help the moment you return. I want this to be good-bye for what I hope will be a good long time," he said in a low, rushed voice. "I'm afraid to

289

say that I don't think I'll be able to keep my offer on the table any longer though. After this, I am fairly sure I will lose my position."

"I don't think it's a bad thing to not be the leader of the damned anymore," I tried to say lightly. He only gave me a sad smile, placing his hand lightly against my cheek. "You've changed so much," I breathed. Oxygen wasn't coming in and out very easily.

"You deserve something better," he said. "Something better than a lifetime of being chased and tormented by beings like me."

"Thank you," I whispered.

"Good-bye, Jessica," Cole said.

He pushed me off the ledge.

CHAPTER TWENTY-EIGHT

One.

There was a hint of warm air against my face.

Two.

I felt the surface underneath me hit my back like being slapped with a wooden plank.

Three.

Pain.

Four.

A scream leapt from my throat.

Five.

I rolled over and vomited on whatever surface I lay on, my stomach heaving.

Six.

Someone screamed.

Seven.

My eyes finally opened.

CHAPTER TWENTY-NINE

"Wait a minute!" someone screamed. "There's one more!"

I couldn't quite place myself as I stared up at the ceiling. The fan above me seemed to be spinning, but after a moment I realized it was *me* who was spinning, not it. Or rather my brain was spinning. There was blood on the tan carpet and on the bed that I could just make out in peripheral vision. There were red lights flashing against the walls.

"Jessica!" a familiar sounding voice said and the surface I lay on suddenly jostled and shifted. A beautiful albeit white and terrified looking face leaned across my field of vision.

"Holy shi..." I heard someone else breathe near the doorway. I thought it sounded like Austin.

"Emily?" I said, my voice barely audible.

"Jessica!" she said, her voice terrified and relieved sounding. "We thought..." she started choking on her words. "We thought you were gone. Oh my... Jessica. Your eyes."

But I wasn't comprehending her words. Blackness was starting to close in on the edges of my vision. That strange thumping that seemed to start and stop in my chest was back. My entire body felt chilled, despite the fire that was back in my brain.

"Alex," I muttered. "Where's Alex? Is he alright?"

Emily stilled for just a moment, holding something back.

"What?" I tried to demand, my voice to week to sound demanding. "Just tell me."

"He's back," she said, her voice cracking. "He's in pretty bad shape though. He looks like he's been run over by a semi."

"He's..." I tried to understand. And then it clicked. "No, he's had the life nearly beaten out of him by Cole." Alex had come back in the same shape he'd left as well. Right before Cole snapped Alex's neck Cole had beaten him to death.

Suddenly two people dressed in uniform rushed in and started barking questions.

"What's wrong with her?"

"Who is she?"

"Where'd she come from?"

The blackness was closing in on me faster though as I felt my body being lifted and then set back down. I felt wheels rolling underneath me and the air grew cooler. Suddenly I could smell trees and rain. Turning my head to the side, I forced my eyes open.

Just before they closed the back door to one of the two ambulances, I saw the bottom of one of Alex's favorite shoes, completely covered in blood.

I let the darkness take me.

X

There was a certain smell. That was the first thing I was aware of. It was subtle but familiar. With that smell came a sense of dread in the pit of my stomach.

They say the sense of smell is the strongest in triggering memory.

Mine was filled with times of worrying about Sal, of times after being in an accident with Austin, of wondering if Caroline would survive.

A hospital.

That was where I was.

My entire body felt sluggish and achy. And my eyes felt so heavy. It took everything I had in me to force them open.

The ceiling tiles above me looked blurry and yet not, at the same time. I kept waiting for all the small little details to slide into focus, to start noticing all the tiny cobwebs, the cracks in the walls, anything. But they didn't.

Forcing the muscles in my body to work, I lifted my head and took my surroundings in.

I was in a hospital room, that was for sure. Another bed lay empty across the room. There were balloons and flowers spread across the two bedside tables, a handful of cards were to be found. As I looked down at myself, I realized I was in a hospital gown. Attached to me were tubes and wires, an oxygen cannula sticking in my nose. A monitor beeped that I was still alive.

I was alive.

And while I didn't feel great, I didn't feel like I was on the verge of dying either. My head wasn't spinning or pulsing, my body was sore but didn't feel like it had been hit with a bus.

My stomach actually growled.

I was alive.

As I heard footsteps, noticing how quiet everything sounded, I realized the door to my room had been left open.

Panic flooded me for just a moment. Where was Alex? What had happened to him? I remembered blood and there being paramedics but not much else.

And then a moment later, a wheelchair was pushed into the room by a towering man with black as night skin.

"Alex," I breathed, feeling tears prickle at the back of my eyes.

"I'm here," he breathed as they stopped just inside the door. His eyes instantly turned red and it took only a moment for a tear to break onto his cheek. Actual tears.

My breath caught in my throat as I looked at his eyes. Brilliant blue. Human, Alex blue.

Finally, I took the rest of him in. Those beautiful eyes were framed with rings of black, his nose had a bandage on it, obviously broken. His left arm was casted as well as his right leg. The rest of his visible skin looked pretty black and blue as well.

"I'll give the two of you a bit of time alone," the other man said as he wheeled Alex closer.

"Thanks Derek," Alex said with a smile, glancing in his direction before he left and closed the door behind him.

I drew in a quick breath, biting my lips together, a tear of my own slipping onto my cheek. Slowly I reached a hand out, letting it brush Alex's yellowed cheek. He may have been broken. But he was alive. And he was human.

"Hi," I breathed. The smile that spread on my face hurt a little, yet it felt so good.

"Hi," he said, his face breaking out into a smile too. He winced, an *ouch* slipping between his lips, followed by a chuckle from the two of us.

"We're alive," I said, my voice filling with wonder.

"We're alive," he repeated, taking my hand in his uncasted one. "I am so proud of you. You were…"

"Stupid?" I said with a chuckle.

He laughed. "Stupid, yes. But brave. Beyond brave. I can't even think of a word for it."

I just smiled at him, in wonder of the being that was Alex. "Are you going to be okay?" I finally braved to ask.

He shrugged, wincing as soon as he did. "No big deal."

"This kind of looks like a big deal," I said, narrowing my eyes at him. "Cole beat you to death."

296

Alex shrugged. "My left arm and right leg are broken. So is my nose. I had a pretty major concussion but the doctors don't expect any permanent damage. So yeah, I'm going to be okay. I'll need quite a bit of physical therapy. That's who Derek is, my therapist. But in a few months, I'm going to be right as rain."

I smiled again, feeling something inside of me that had felt tense for what seemed like a lifetime relax.

"What about me?" I finally asked, feeling a little scared again. "What happened with me? I feel... better."

A sly grin started spreading on Alex's face. "That's one I'm going to let the doctors explain."

"What do you mean?" I started to question, when suddenly a doctor in a white lab coat and a nurse stepped in.

"Mrs. Wright!" the man with the thickest gray hair I had ever seen said joyously. "You're awake!"

"How long have I been out?" I realized I had forgotten to ask.

"Two and a half days," he said as he gathered what I assumed was my chart under his arm and pulled up a chair. "You were in pretty bad shape. I'm Dr. Knight by the way."

"What..." I stumbled over my words. Everything seemed so quiet, I nearly felt like I was deaf. "What was wrong with me?"

Dr. Knight opened my chart and pulled a pair of glasses down to his nose from the top of his head. "This was kind of a strange case, Mrs. Wright. You contracted a case of malaria."

"Malaria?" I questioned. "Don't people usually get that from a mosquito bite in really hot, humid areas?"

"Yes," he answered, looking back up at me. "And you were recently in Costa Rica, your husband informed me."

I glanced over at Alex, catching that knowing look in his eyes as he nodded. I hadn't caught malaria in Costa Rica.

"But the really strange thing is that the string of malaria looks like it has been in your blood for a while. Your husband said you haven't been anywhere you would have contracted this in the last several years. Is that correct?"

"No," I said. "I haven't been anywhere other than Costa Rica in the last few years. England once, but nowhere warm enough for malaria."

The doctor's face was very serious looking. "Uh huh. Strange indeed. There are not many cases of malaria in Costa Rica."

"So that explains the chills, the fever? Why I couldn't keep anything down? Why I felt like my head was going to explode?" I asked. Alex squeezed my hand a little tighter.

Dr. Knight nodded, reading something in my chart. "Had you contracted malaria when you were a young child it would have been more difficult to diagnose. Those symptoms could be numerous childhood diseases from the flu to leukemia. As an adult this is a little easier to

298

pinpoint. All it takes is some blood work and a few other tests."

I glanced over at Alex, another knowing look passing between us.

"What is the treatment?" I asked, looking back.

"You're already on IV medication. You're receiving a drug called Quinidine. Normally this would be taken care of quickly but yours was a very advanced stage. You probably wouldn't have made it more than another day or two, at the most. But you'll be ready to go home with your medication in two days."

"Really?" I asked, my tone disbelieving. This was the third time I'd almost died from this thing, and now I was just ready to go home? *That was it?*

"Really," he said cheerily. "You still won't be feeling on the top of your game for a week or so but yes, you'll be fine. Though you might want to stay away from any tropical areas for a while."

"Oh my gosh," I breathed, tears starting to roll down my cheeks. "I'm going to be okay. It's... it's really over." I looked over at Alex, his own blue eyes filled with tears as well. "I'm going to be okay. I won't have to go back."

"Not for a long time," Alex said, squeezing my hand in his.

The nurse who had entered the room with Dr. Knight bustled about the room, changing my IV's, recording my blood pressure and oxygen levels.

"Things aren't going to be easy for the two of you when you get home but you're lucky to have such a strong support group behind you," he said, indicating the balloons and flowers. "You two are very loved."

Dr. Knight then excused himself, saying that he would be back in a few hours to check on us. The nurse finished up and left as well.

"Oh my gosh," I repeated, still not able to believe what I had been told. "I don't have to go back."

Alex leaned forward, pressing a kiss to my cheek. "It's all over."

"What…" I tried to make my thoughts coherent again. "What did you tell them happened to you?"

Alex chuckled, his eyes falling into his lap for a moment. "I told them that you had collapsed and I ran to get the phone to call 911 when I tripped and took a nasty tumble down the stairs. I told them I pulled myself back up and into the bedroom before I passed out. Then miraculously Emily and Austin showed up and called 911 for me."

I chuckled, shaking my head. "We're a couple of liars, you and me."

Alex chuckled too, shaking his head.

There was a light knock on the door before it was opened. In walked Emily, Austin, Amber, and Rod. Followed by my parents.

"Hi," I said, tears rolling down my cheeks again. My chest swelled at the sight of them. This time in a good way.

"You're awake!" Emily and Amber cheered at the same time. Mom started crying immediately and flung herself at me, covering me with her body, squeezing me in a slightly painful hug.

"I just had a feeling that you two going to South America was a bad idea," Mom choked on her words. "You almost *died*!"

"I know, Mom," I tried to reassure her, rolling my eyes at the ceiling. "I'm sorry."

"You're sorry," she chuckled as she sat up, wiping at her eyes. "You have nothing to be sorry about. What a crazy thing to pick up."

"Yeah," I chuckled again, reaching for Alex's hand again. "When did you guys get here?"

"Your sister called us the morning after you and Alex were admitted," Dad answered. "We flew out here that afternoon."

Everyone spent an entire hour gushing over the fact that the two of us were alive, how worried they had been, and how happy that we were going to be able to leave in just two days. I didn't miss the changed way Austin looked at me. I wondered how much Emily had told him.

And when everyone else was distracted, she whispered to me how she'd slept the night before. And hadn't had a nightmare.

But I knew Emily had redeemed herself. The afterlife wasn't going to risk a screw up like what happened to me again. Emily was free too.

My dad informed me that he, Rod, and Austin had been back at the house for the last four hours making it wheelchair accessible for Alex to use over the next few weeks until he could use crutches. Mom and Dad would be staying down in the guest apartment for a few days after we went home to help us get along.

I couldn't help but smile as I looked at everyone around me. I finally had what I wanted. A normal life. A family. People who didn't think I was crazy anymore.

"I have a weird question," I said as everyone settle down. "Did we ever go on any trips out of the country when I was really little?" I asked my parents. "Like before I was four?"

"My parents took us to Puerto Rico when you were about two," my mom answered. "Why do you ask?"

I smiled just a little bit and shook my head. "No reason. I just wondered."

And when I was two, while we were in Puerto Rico, I had been bitten by a mosquito, malaria had sat dormant in my blood for a few years. And when it nearly killed me, difficult to diagnose when I was so young, my father made a plea that had saved my life but put me through hell in exchange.

But it had all been worth it.

"Are you sure her eyes are so strange because of the malaria, Alex?" my mom asked suddenly, her eyes narrowing at me. "I've never heard of something like this happening."

"That's what the doctor said," Alex said. I detected another of his necessary lies.

"My eyes?" I questioned.

Alex looked at me, something in his eyes saddening, his entire countenance shifting. He looked over at the table next to his bed and pointed to something. "Would you hand that over, Rod?"

Rod picked up what I realized was a mirror and handed it to Alex, who extended it to me. Before looking into it, I looked at Alex for a long moment, my stomach filling with prickly butterflies. He just nodded.

Swallowing hard, I lifted the handheld mirror and looked at my own reflection.

My eyes had changed.

One was blacker than black. Just like Cole's. The other was bluer than Alex's.

A judged human. Split fifty-fifty.

"She's beautiful as ever," Alex said firmly, taking one of my hands in his and squeezing.

I swallowed again, and looked back at my reflection. I touched my fingers to the cool surface of the mirror. My mismatched eyes stared back at me, taking in every detail of my natural looking face. It felt just a little strange, not to see all the little things, every tiny hair that covered my body, every fleck of dust that clung to my clothes. But it was better this way. This was the way it was supposed to be.

I couldn't help but smile. I was human again. One hundred percent human.

I thought about all the times I had wanted to give up. It would have been so easy to let the angels win, to let the afterlife rule my life.

As I glanced back at all the people I loved that surrounded me, I knew I had finally won. Being there with all of them, my very being alive was proof that no matter how hard things might get, you must always fight.

Because in spite of everything that had happened, I was still there.

AFTERLIFE

THE NOVELETTE COMPANION TO

vindicated

FALL OF ANGELS

KEARY TAYLOR

COLE EMERSON never was and never will be a good man. He has his position for a reason. But there are consequences for returning to the world of the living. He is about to lose the one thing he still has, his leadership of the condemned. As if that wasn't enough, one of his brothers is hell bent on exposing what has happened to Jessica and Cole has no choice but to protect her. And he'll stop at nothing to do it. Even if it means ending a few lives.

Cole never was and never will be a good man.

AFTERLIFE

The Novelette Companion To

BY

KEARY TAYLOR

*"...new torments and new tormented souls
I see around me wherever I move,
and howsoever I turn, and wherever I gaze."*
- Canto IV, Inferno, Dante

They always screamed.

There was something satisfying about the intake of breath every single one of them would take, just before the scream came bellowing out. The way their eyes would widen. The way their chests would rise and fall rapidly, despite their need to breathe anymore.

There was just something satisfying about seeing another person writhe in misery.

"Down," Cole condemned the man before him. His followers around him heckled and cheered from the spiral staircase, sinfully delighted to be having another soul join them in their eternal wretchedness.

For that was what Cole was. Miserable. Damned. Forsaken.

He pressed the red-hot rod to the back of the man's neck, watching as his flesh gave way to the imprinted X. Moments later the man's own set of glorious wings burst from his back and Cole simply watched as the newly branded angel was dragged down into the fiery depths by his brothers.

Like it had been after almost every trial since he had been sucked back into the afterlife, shouts and brawls broke out around the cylinder. Some of the council left, mostly the do-gooders. They weren't ones to fight. Everything was peace and butterflies with them.

But those who served with him were built from contention and upheaval.

That was all the world of the dead felt like lately. Chaos.

Cole rubbed his chest absent mindedly as he zoned out the noise around him. He remembered the chaos that once filled him. He remembered the feeling of his entire being collapsing in on him. It had been a long time since he had felt pain. He barely even remembered what it felt like until he felt the pull from within. But even while he hid, licking his wounds in his crumbling family estate, he wouldn't return to his world. The pain made him feel... alive. Almost human again.

But a dead man can't fight the call of the dead any more than the tides could fight the pull of the moon.

Cole closed his eyes, drawing for a moment on his last few minutes in the human world. The feeling of Jessica's lips against his would be something he clung to for the rest of his never ending existence.

The shout and sound of flesh connecting with flesh brought Cole unwillingly back to the present. His black eyes flashed to the two brawling angels who occupied the catwalk with him. They threw fists, shouting words that were too horrendous to even have meaning in the world of the living.

"That's enough!" Cole bellowed as his hands curled into fists. The two men froze where they were, their own cold black eyes meeting Cole's.

"I expect more out of you, Duncan," Cole said quietly, his voice resonating who he was and just how much power he possessed. "You're a leader and you're acting like a freshly made angel. Whatever your quarrel with this man is, surely this is not the way a council member handles it."

Duncan's eyes grew hard as he looked back at Cole, the same way they probably had before he shot his mother and father-in-law at Christmas over one hundred and fifty years ago. Giving one last shove to the other lowly angel, enough to knock him into the abyss below, he turned to walk back to the staircase.

Cole tried to ignore his mutterings of "not under his leadership for much longer" as he watched Duncan retreat.

Letting his eyes search the stone walls, Cole looked for the cause of all this trouble.

As soon as Cole returned from the world of the living and reclaimed his position, Jeremiah had started the upheaval, hungry for the position of leader of the condemned back. He had so graciously pointed out Cole's grave betrayal in returning to the world of the living and abandoning his duties.

And now Cole might lose everything.

3

Unless Jeremiah was down below, spending time among their fellow men and women, Cole realized he wasn't in the cylinder. There was stone in the bottom of his stomach, giving him the sinking feeling that he knew where Jeremiah was.

Cole wouldn't pretend that he didn't hear the whispers. He sensed the doubt that others had in his ability to lead the condemned. Echoes about Cole losing it brushed the stone walls, each wondering how a woman could drive him to such madness as to return to the world of the living.

He had lost leagues of credibility.

Walking to the stairway, Cole stood in the shadows. He crossed his arms over his chest, his wings folding behind him.

He would wait for Jeremiah.

As much as he didn't like it, his follower's words affected him. They were right. He had lost it, in a way. Cole's love for Jane had tortured him for centuries but he'd dealt with it. But as soon as Jessica came along... She'd pulled out a whole new creature in him.

Time meant nothing in the afterlife, but *being* dragged on and on as he waited for Jeremiah to return.

And as simple as he might have felt a single drop of rain land on the back of his hand, he felt Jeremiah's presence again. Stepping out from the shadows, he watched as Jeremiah descended the stairs toward the heat of the below.

As soon as Jeremiah met Cole's eyes, a sly smile grew in the corners of his lips. The familiar beast of anger flared inside of Cole.

"Going missing in the afterlife is a dangerous thing," Cole said, managing to keep his voice even.

"As you would know best," Jeremiah tested. He stopped two stairs above Cole, meeting his eye, measure for measure. Jeremiah may have been young, but he didn't lack confidence because of it.

"Where have you been?" Cole asked.

The smile broadened on Jeremiah's face. He stepped down and passed Cole on the stairway. Stopping below Cole, Jeremiah half turned back. "She's a stunning creature. I see why you couldn't get her out of your head."

The beast inside of Cole snarled. "I don't know what you're referring to," he lied easy as he blinked.

"I wonder what her skin feels like, what those perfect lips taste like," Jeremiah said thoughtfully.

The crack of Jeremiah's head against the stone wall behind him echoed for all to hear as Cole's hand wrapped around his throat, pinning Jeremiah against the stones.

"You will stay away from her," Cole hissed.

Unharmed, and without the need to breathe, Jeremiah simply chuckled, his black eyes darkening in glee. "There's something peculiar about her. I can smell it. She's not fully one of them anymore, but not really one of us. Is she?"

"She's where she belongs," Cole growled. The knife that had been lodged in his chest for months now gave a little twist.

"I'm curious to see what she's capable of," Jeremiah said easily, despite Cole's tightening hand around his throat. "I think the others on the council might be curious as well."

Cole met Jeremiah's eyes, feeling the beast grow and shutter within him. But what could he say without giving himself, and Jessica away?

"Leave her alone," Cole said, releasing Jeremiah. Without waiting for a reply, Cole descended down the stairway.

"Thy soul is hurt by cowardice,
which oftentimes encumbereth a man
so that it turns him back from honorable enterprise."
- Canto II, Inferno, Dante

His eyes kept drifting to her serene looking face. The trials of the exalted were so boring, he couldn't seem to pay attention. So instead he watched her. Jane.

Cole recalled how infatuated he had been with her the first time he laid eyes on her. She was feisty, had a lust for life he had never seen in a woman in his era before. Their eyes had locked on each other, a terribly hot wave of connection fizzling between the two of them. Cole wanted her like he had wanted nothing else in his life.

Cole got what he wanted in life.

But to find that she had been promised to another man was a crushing blow to Cole's ego that he could not handle. He was Cole Emerson, women did not turn him down. Father's came to him, trying to strike bargains for him to take their daughters into marriage and into bed.

But Jane. Jane. She was destined for better. Given to the one man Cole would always be over-looked for.

Money did not equal love. Despite being given to another, one who was wealthier than even Cole was, she fell for Cole. Over the course of only a few short weeks, secret meetings were made, hesitant, forbidden touches began. The fire between them grew into a blazing torrent that threatened to destroy the both of them. And their families.

But despite everything Jane felt for Cole, despite everything that he *knew* she felt for him, she refused to break off her engagement.

Cole would never be quite good enough for Jane, or her power-hungry father.

Or their son.

Even creating a new life, a child together, was not enough to make Jane be a part of Cole's life.

As he watched Jane, now long dead and judged, he felt... distant. There was still that ache that was inside of him. There was a void that had slowly ate at everything else inside of him, that made him into the monster that he was. But it seemed to almost be a memory of what the past had been. Like he didn't feel the un-bearableness of everything. It was almost like he only remembered what he had felt, and like he had clung to it for so long that he didn't know how to let it go.

And every time he looked at Jane he saw Jessica.

Jane was a new kind of pain now. She was a constant reminder of the one thing in his life that he truly could never have.

Cole had money, he had houses and carriages. He had fine clothes and servants. Even though Jane would never marry him, he did have her.

But as much as Cole had wanted Jessica, as much as he did everything in his power to get her, Cole had, and never would have Jessica.

All because of a simple boy.

One boy was all it took to defeat the power that Cole had over women.

The trial ended with the man before them being escorted to the above, to a place Cole had never been allowed to see. The other residents of the afterlife set to whatever it was they did to serve out the rest of eternity.

But Jane stayed, staring emptily out into the vastness of the cylinder. Without thinking about it, Cole gave a powerful beat of his wings, carrying himself to the staircase just above her. She ignored his presence as he descended, her wings tucked comfortably behind her.

"I still don't understand it," Cole said, stopping a few stairs above her. "How did you manage to get into the above? After everything you did?"

"Of course you don't understand, Cole," she answered simply, shifting her weight back, propping herself up on her palms against the hot stone beneath her. "You have tunnel vision."

"What is that supposed to mean?" he asked, his voice harsh sounding.

"You fixate, Cole," Jane said, her blue eyes meeting his. "You see what you want to see and nothing else. You saw the sins I committed with you for those few years, and to you, I did nothing else with my entire life."

Cole stood there, anger at being made to look foolish by a nothing angel flaring within him.

"And you don't see what has changed within you," she said, a sly smile pulling at the corner of her lips. "You are not the man I fell in love with. Nor are you the man who has led the condemned for the last century and a half."

"I will always be Cole Emerson. I will always be a branded angel that those around him saw fit to lead them."

"Yes, you will always be those things. But you didn't used to be a man who would let a woman you care for go to another man. You didn't used to be a man who ached because he saw that woman hurting. You didn't used to be a man that was suffocating because of his own fear."

"What am I afraid of?" Cole scoffed. Fear was not a word anyone had applied to him since he was a human child.

"You're afraid of her being hurt," Jane said as she stood, standing just inches away from Cole. "You're afraid of Jeremiah bringing her back here and of what will happen to her once she joins our world."

Cole just held Jane's eyes, defeat sinking into his dead stomach.

"You know that once she joins our world she will truly be lost to you forever. You know where she will be placed. She's lead a good life."

He simply stood there, feeling a war raging in his body. Oh how he wanted to silence Jane, to make her stop speaking words he wouldn't admit were true. But this was Jane. He could never lay a finger upon her.

"This is the point where you have to decide what man you want to become," Jane said as she lifted her hand and traced a finger along Cole's jaw. "Are you going to be the man who sits back and lets Jeremiah have his way with her? Or are you going to be the man who will do anything for her, even if he can't have her?"

Everything felt very still inside of Cole as Jane dropped her hand from his face and stepped away. Holding his eyes for just a moment more, Jane stepped around Cole and started up the staircase.

He let his eyes slide closed, feeling as if he couldn't breathe. But no one would save the leader of the damned from suffocating.

Cole would ever be alone.

"O creatures foolish, how great is that ignorance that harms you."
- Canto VII, Inferno, Dante

Cole sat alone on the catwalk, waiting. Pondering.

He'd finally gone to her. He couldn't leave her unaware any longer.

Unable to take facing her in the real world, in seeing her face, in being so near her scent, Cole had gone to her in the only way he could.

In the In Between. The dream world, a state of passing. Limbo.

He'd told her that she was being watched. He had warned her to be careful.

Through the dark he could sense her. He could almost touch her, could almost smell her. But she wasn't in his world and he wasn't in hers.

And now here he sat, feeling shredded, ripped apart, like a wounded dog, beaten by his master, but still sitting at her feet, licking his wounds.

Yet again he had searched for Jeremiah, only to find him gone.

So he waited.

Only minutes later Cole heard the footsteps walking down the tunnel, out toward the cylinder. Cole continued to stare at the stone walls in front of him. His legs dangled above the abyss below.

"You've grown soft," Jeremiah said as he emerged from the tunnel. He stopped at the edge of the stone walkway.

"And you seem to think that your opinion matters," Cole said, not looking up.

"Look at all the talk I've created already," Jeremiah said. "Your reputation is failing. Just look at you."

"Careful," Cole said, his eyes feeling heavy. He wished he could remember what sleep felt like. "I have my position for a reason."

"You will not have it for much longer," Jeremiah said. Cole heard him turn to go.

"Jeremiah," Cole called. He heard him hesitate. "This is my final warning to you, to stay away from her."

"Or what?" Jeremiah scoffed.

"Or I will cause you to lose everything."

"Look around you my friend," Jeremiah laughed. "I have nothing to lose."

A smile cracked on Cole's face as he looked over at his subordinate. "You are so young. Remember that you still have people you care for in the world of the living. I am not above causing *them* to lose everything."

Jeremiah's face grew stony for a long moment. Cole saw the way he swallowed hard, the way his fingers twitched. "You dare not return to their world. You will lose everything should you return."

"Remember, I told you this was your final warning." Not waiting for a response, Cole spread his wings and pushed off from the walkway.

"Consider well the seed that gave you birth:
you were not made to live your lives as brutes,
but to be followers of virtue and knowledge."
- Canto XXVI, Inferno, Dante

The rain started to fall over the Rocky Mountains, the clouds thick and heavy. Cole could smell the earth as he walked swiftly down the sidewalk. He pulled his long, thick black coat tighter around his body as he turned right down another block.

The building that rose before him was simple to the extent of being sad. Wilting flowers hung from baskets that looked ready to fall apart next to the front doors. The gravel that formed the tiny parking lot had practically disappeared back into the Earth.

Letting the better part of him start slipping back into the afterlife, Cole let himself disappear from human eye and walked through the front door. A nurse sat behind the front desk, filling out a chart. She didn't even glance up as he walked behind her, sliding his thumb along the charts that sat on a rack behind her.

Lawrence Kepper, Room 207.

Silently opening a drawer of the nurse's cart, Cole reached inside and grabbed a syringe.

The smell of slow purification was almost overwhelming in the nursing home. Death hung in every corner here, lay on the floor, just waiting for someone to trip over it.

Finding the door Cole was looking for, he slowly opened it and stepped inside.

The old man was sleeping in his skeletal looking bed. He was old, but not old enough to be considered at the edge of death. He would still have several years. His scent wasn't strong.

Cole let himself wander the small room, observing the wall that was covered entirely with pictures. So many smiling faces, so many memories. All these happy people. How many of them would eventually end up under his reign?

He smiled as his eyes found a familiar face, staring back at him from a faded and slightly yellowed picture.

At least one of these faces already had.

Cole turned back to the sleeping man. Observing the tube that ran from the crease of his arm to a clear bag attached to a tall silver pole, Cole felt the itch of anticipation.

The contents of his deadly syringe didn't even discolor whatever it was in the old man's bag, slowly running into his withered body. They slipped un-alarmingly in, no one ever the wiser.

It would take some time, but eventually the old man's heart would stop prematurely.

He would stand before the council.   And hopefully, Cole's timing would be right.

Jeremiah should have headed Cole's warning.

"And just as he who, with exhausted breath,
having escaped from the sea to shore,
turns to the perilous waters and gazes."
- Canto I, Inferno, Dante

She just wouldn't leave.

First she had come back with Jeremiah. That time may not have been her fault but it did make Cole realize that Jane had been right. Jessica caused fear to course through his blood. He'd been terrified when she materialized in his world.

And then she came to him in the In Between again. Cole had told her to come, but a part of him had hoped that she wouldn't figure it out. Every second with her was another minute he couldn't breathe.

Finally she had put herself back in the afterlife and begged him not to take her precious Alex. He marveled at how he was able to sense her presence so strongly. She hadn't even called to him when she arrived, yet he felt her, sure as a lighthouse shines on danger in the water.

He just couldn't be rid of her.

Cole wouldn't admit that he didn't really want to be rid of Jessica.

He needed something to distract himself, before he went mad. And he had a score to settle.

Jeremiah was one visit to the world of the living ahead of him.

Checking to make sure no one was watching, Cole curled his wings around his body and leapt off the catwalk.

The wrench in his gut was enough to cripple Cole to his knees with a loud cry. Everything inside of him shredded and grated. Everything inside of him wanted to disappear.

Looking up, Cole tried to orient himself. He lay in a grass field, clothed in the same black clothes and trench coat he had stolen on his last visit. Forcing the pain into one of Cole's many dark corners, he pushed himself up onto his feet.

Windows glowed bright with soft yellow light not far from where he stood in the dark night. From the outside it looked like the perfectly charming farm house he'd seen on the covers of magazines at the grocery store.

But Cole could feel him inside, and in a few hours that perfect farm house would be thrown into chaos.

Cole moved soundlessly through the tall grass toward the house. The rise of anticipation and dark inside of him was more powerful than any modern drug.

There was something damningly exhilarating about ending a human life.

Disappearing from human eye, Cole silently let himself in through a side door.

The house inside did not match the house outside.

The kitchen Cole entered into was cluttered with dirty dishes and overflowing garbage. The floor was streaked with who knew what. Fruit flies clustered on some kind of unidentifiable food on the counter.

The entire space reeked of alcohol.

Stepping soundlessly through the kitchen, Cole wandered inside. Following his keen ears, he walked into an equally disgusting living room.

Among the filth sat an overweight, balding, dirty man. He stared emptily at the television, his eyes heavy and droopy. A brown glass bottle hung loosely in one of his pudgy hands. Cole could smell the alcohol already coming out of his very pores.

Almost disappointed at the lack of challenge, Cole walked back into the kitchen and opened the cupboard under the sink. Picking something that looked potent and colorful, he then went to the greasy-finger smudged refrigerator and pulled out another beer.

Twisting the top off, Cole poured a third of the contents into the sink, then topped the bottle off with his chosen poison. He dropped in a few pills he found in a cluttered cupboard for good measure.

Casually reentering the living room, Cole focused his thoughts. The man didn't even stir as Cole invaded his head.

"Have another, my friend," Cole said, extending the bottle to the man. He didn't even look up as he accepted and took a long swig.

He coughed violently as the toxins burned his esophagus but didn't tear his eyes from the screen.

Feeling the very skin he lived in tighten around him, Cole glanced down at his left hand. His veins were already straining out against his flesh. He watched the black of death slowly stain his skin.

Time was up.

"See you soon," Cole said, patting the fat man on the shoulder. He just grunted as Cole walked back toward the door.

Cole barely made it outside before he collapsed onto his hands and knees. The breath caught in his throat. Everything felt crushed inside of him. Cole eagerly gave into the pull of death.

"I came into a place void of all light,
which bellows like the sea in tempest,
when it is combated by warring winds."
- Canto V, Inferno, Dante

Skin had a beautiful way of yielding to Cole's branding iron. It softened, gave into the red-hot metal. Then it smoked. Cole left a lasting impression on a great number of the residents of the afterlife.

Closing his eyes and taking a deep breath, Cole inhaled the man's terror. It was an intoxicating thing. The man on his hands and knees before Cole whimpered, begging for forgiveness.

But there was no forgiveness for what this man had done.

The condemned sprung from the staircase as Cole stepped back. They heckled, screeched in glee as their hands wrapped around the man's wrists and ankles. The man thrashed and fought against them, but you can't fight where you belong.

With the masses disbursing, Cole prepared to join those he led.

"Brother," a kind voice said from behind Cole where he stood on the stone walkway. "May I borrow a moment of your time?"

"Of course, Richard," Cole said as he turned toward the blue-eyed, white bearded man. Even Cole, with all of his judgmental and pessimistic ways couldn't find fault with Richard, the leader of the exalted.

Richard folded his hands in front of him, his expression serious but ever kind. "Members of the council are concerned."

"I know what Jeremiah has been saying," Cole said, his voice cold as a block of ice. "You must also remember he is a branded man."

"I understand," Richard said, his blue eyes searching Cole's face. "That is not the cause of our concern however. You committed a very grievous sin when you abandoned your duties. You returned to the world of the living and failed to come back, for a very long time. Some have been saying they believe you have been returning again."

Cole didn't say anything as his eyes fell to the stones beneath his bare feet. He couldn't lie to such a pure man.

"You understand that you cannot stay there, don't you?"

"I know that," Cole said in a defeated, hard voice. "The pain does not let me forget."

Cole hadn't realized Richard had come closer until he felt his hand on Cole's shoulder. The fallen man inside of him wanted to jump away from his touch. He felt filthy next to Richard.

"Why do you cause yourself such torment?" Richard asked in a low voice.

Cole didn't answer right away. His eyes remained glued to the ground beneath him. "I don't know how to stay away."

"You must," Richard said, his voice kind but firm. "You are letting yourself waste away, chasing after unobtainable fool's gold."

"I know that," Cole said, his voice barely more than a whisper.

"Be careful, my brother," Richard said as he let his hand drop from Cole's shoulder. "I cannot guarantee you will keep your position if you continue on the path you are walking."

"I understand," Cole replied.

With a sad smile, Richard coiled his wings and lifted himself toward the blue skies above.

"These have no hope of death...
mercy and justice disdain them.
Let us not speak of them, but do thou look and pass on."
- Canto III, Inferno, Dante

Lying on his back, Cole stared up through the cylinder at the blue skies above. His head hung over the edge of the stair he rested on, his shadowed brand touching the hot stones underneath him. The air sweltered around him, rising in waves up to a place he could never go.

The sound of ruckus laughter disturbed Cole in his woeful self-pity. There was no peace and solitude in the land of the damned. Cole tensed as he recognized one of the voices.

"It won't be much longer," Jeremiah said to his companion.

"It will be a relief to finally have a worthy leader again," the other voice responded.

Suddenly their footsteps halted as they came into view of Cole where he lay. Cole didn't even lift his head to stare coldly at them. He wanted nothing more than to rip each of their un-beating hearts clean from their chests and watch the blood drip to the ground. But he was so tired. His entire being felt depleted.

"How was your last trip?" Cole asked Jeremiah, not even bothering to tear his eyes from the blue above him.

Jeremiah did not respond, Cole felt him tense, bracing himself to be attacked again.

"You were never the smartest man in your lifetime, where you Jeremiah?" Cole said evenly. "I would guess you had a tendency for getting yourself into trouble for making poor choices."

Still Jeremiah did not say anything. Cole heard him flex his fingers, balling them into fists.

"This is my final warning, brother," Cole said, the ice inside of him starting to frost into his voice. "Leave her alone. You will regret every time you looked upon her more than you can comprehend."

"And what are you going to do about it?" Jeremiah finally spoke. Even though he put malice in his voice, Cole detected the hints of uncertainty. "You've grown soft."

"Oh, I don't think so," Cole said, a smile curling on his lips. He felt that satisfied, wonderful feeling in his chest when he thought of the revenge he was about to have. "You have forgotten what the man who fought his own branding can do."

"Yet they still managed to sink the iron into the back of your neck," Jeremiah sneered.

"Which makes me a doubly branded man," Cole replied. "Stay away from her, brother."

"What a stiff you've gone after," Jeremiah said as he and his companion stepped over Cole on their way further down into the cylinder. "She doesn't even drink. What a bore. I don't see what your interest in her is."

Cole just closed his eyes as he listened to the two of them descend.

This had to end soon or Jeremiah was going to discover Jessica's little secret. And then even he couldn't help her anymore.

"...not without cause is this going to the abyss; it is willed on high..."
- Canto VII, Inferno, Dante

From a distance, with Jeremiah in his sights as well, Cole saw familiar races gather in an overflowing garden, each dressed color matching clothes. He could hear Jessica even from this far away. The family started to get frantic when she didn't walk out of the building on cue. He heard Jessica's cries, heard her tell everything to Alex. Cole couldn't hardly believe the boy was real. With everything Jessica had thrown at him, he was still by her side.

Then arm in arm, they walked down the aisle and said words that only the world cared about. They had been so unnecessary. Even with all Cole had seen, he'd never witnessed two people more committed to each other. Words repeating the commitment they had already made to each other seemed redundant.

The wedding was Cole's final defeat. He would never have Jessica.

But he didn't deserve her. Cole would never have sacrificed himself for love like Alex had for her. Like Jessica would for him.

As Jeremiah withdrew something metallic and cold looking from his pocket, Cole finally made his approach.

"I would highly advise you put that back where it came from," Cole said as he stopped at Jeremiah's side, watching as Alex and Jessica shared their first kiss as husband and wife.

Jeremiah started, turning wide eyes on Cole, then flashing to the shiny silver gun he held in his left hand.

"Blood is such a terrible way to ruin a wedding," Cole said, turning his flat back eyes on Jeremiah once again.

"What are you doing here?" Jeremiah hissed. Even still, he put the gun back in his pocket.

"I should be asking you the same question," Cole said, anger rising in his blood.

"You know why," Jeremiah said coldly. "She doesn't belong here yet she hasn't come to our world."

"You have no idea how much you're going to regret this day," Cole said, his voice becoming a demonic growl. Gripping Jeremiah by the back of the neck, Cole squeezed. Jeremiah buckled to his knees instantly, blackness spreading from his neck, up his face, staining all visible skin. Cole's own veins struggled to leap out of his skin.

"It's time to go home brother," Cole breathed.

Cole stole one more glance at Jessica in her white lace, smiling at all the people who mattered to her, again arm in arm with the man Cole hated almost as much as he hated Jeremiah. His chest gave a violent squeeze.

Before he could let the pain cripple him, Cole let him and Jeremiah slide back into the afterlife.

*"Without fame, he who spends his time on earth
leaves only such a mark upon the world
as smoke does on air or foam on water."
- Canto XXIV, Inferno, Dante*

The fire blaze through the blackened night. The contrast of the flames against the darkened trees was beautiful.

Cole had set the fire to the curtains in the ground floor living room first. It quickly spread throughout the room, moving on into the kitchen. From outside, he saw the glow as the fire spread to the second story. A moment later a maddening beeping sounded.

He pushed his hands into the pockets of his coat, hearing a woman cough. Only a few moments later he heard a scream.

Out here in these woods there would be no one to hear it.

A face appeared in the window. A woman not much older than Jessica stared directly at him with wide terrified eyes. She called to him, slapping her hand against the window, desperately calling to him for help.

Cole simply observed her as she lived the most terrifying time of her life. Her features were delicate, framed with long, blond, straight locks. She was thin but she looked fit, a woman able to handle herself.

But not a woman able to walk through fire.

As Cole simply stood there and watched, the woman looked back toward her only escape. Even from his position Cole could tell the flames were too great for her to exit without causing herself mortal danger.

That was exactly how Cole planned it.

The woman came back to the window, pleading to him to help her. Her cries became weaker as the smoke filling the house choked her. One of her hands came to her throat, her eyes closing as she coughed over and over again.

Her eyes met his one last time before she shrank out of view.

Love and lust made Cole do terrible things.

The little twist at the bottom of Cole's stomach was unexpected. Taking the old man and the drunk had been easy. But watching this woman burn all alone out here made him think twice.

But she was the ultimate payback.

The woman Cole was hearing scream as the flames consumed her was Jeremiah's own daughter.

Jeremiah was so young.

Her screams intensified, growing to the point of delirium. Cole shifted uncomfortably from one foot to the other. He didn't like this feeling of internal itching, like he needed to do something.

It wasn't until her screams stopped that Cole realized he wasn't as much of a monster as he thought he was.

The front door crumbled as Cole's foot collided with it. The torrent of flames raged about him as Cole walked calm as night through them. The hem of his long coat caught fire as he ascended the stairs. Locating the room he had been watching the woman from below, he opened the door. The skin on his hand burned away from the intense heat. And started healing instantly as he pushed the door open and let go.

The woman was collapsed beneath the window. Not moving and barely breathing, Cole took his burning coat off, put the flames out, and wrapped it around her. Lifting her body and holding it tightly against his, Cole grabbed the metal chair sitting at a desk. Giving it a small heave, it shattered the glass and flew out into the nighttime air.

Glancing once more down at the woman in his arms, Cole took two steps away from the window. Sprinting full speed forward, he leapt out the window.

His black shirt shredded as his glorious and powerful wings caught them as the sailed through the air. With a gentle beat, he set the two of them back safely on the ground.

The woman's eyes fluttered open, catching Cole's eyes. She didn't say anything, just stared at him.

As Cole let his eyes slide over her body, he knew she wouldn't make it long. Seeing her now, he questioned his actions. Such a beautiful woman, such a waste.

32

"I truly am sorry," he said quietly as he brushed her hair away from her burned flesh. "It's nothing personal."

She continued to stare at him, her eyes calm as they observed him. Cole felt his skin start to tighten, felt the familiar twist in his core.

"Are you real?" she asked in a raspy whisper.

"Not until you pass from this world," he said quietly. In the reflection of her eyes, he saw the blackness start spreading around his own.

Feeling around the woman's pockets, Cole found what he was searching for. He pulled out her cell phone and after a minute, figured out how to dial a number.

"911, what is your emergency?" a man asked on the other line.

"There's been a fire at 2119 County Road. Send an ambulance." And Cole hung up the phone.

"Thank you," the woman said, too eerily calm for what she had just gone through. Maybe it was the smoke inhalation.

"If only it was going to be enough," Cole whispered as he wrapped his coat tighter around her. "I will make sure your judgment is as easy as possible."

"What?" she started to ask before she started coughing violently. Her face scrunched up in pain and agony.

Cole straightened, his eyes never leaving her pained face. "I truly am sorry. Something that I am not very often."

Before he could let guilt fully form, Cole let himself be pulled to the world she would soon be joining.

*"Midway upon the journey of our life,
I found myself within a forest dark,
For the straight foreward pathway had been lost."
-Canto I, Inferno, Dante*

The score was even. In this game where the other team wasn't even aware it was playing, Cole had settled the score. The game was about to end and Jeremiah was going to learn just how many points Cole had beaten him by.

The final straw had been when Jeremiah dared try to murder Jessica at her own wedding.

Even with Cole's twisted side he knew Jessica deserved that day, after all he and his kind had put her through.

And so Cole had taken the one thing in this life Jeremiah still cared about.

Feeling the familiar pull within him, Cole knew it was almost time. The council was being called for trial.

Everyone's time had run out.

Settling into his seat, an evil smile curled on Cole's face. As Jeremiah settled next to him, Cole felt the stir of victory grow within his chest. A man was brought to stand before them, his name read.

Cole heard Jeremiah half gasp, half choke.

"Grandpa?" Jeremiah whispered so quietly only Cole could hear him.

The old man stood on the catwalk, his face covered, his hands bound. The old man from the rest home.

"Please," he started to cry. "It wasn't time. I told them there was something wrong with my medication. I didn't... I didn't get to say good-bye."

But it was too late for reasoning. The man was dead.

The leader of the exalted started the trial and soon the deeds of this man's life were being rattled off.

Jeremiah squirmed in his seat, his fingers threatening to crush the stones beneath his hands.

There was nothing quite like the satisfaction of revenge.

Grandpa was soon tried and unlike his posterity, was granted blue eyes and escorted to the above.

Jeremiah sat very still with two of his fingers pressed to his lips as they waited for the next poor soul to be brought before them.

The next man was brought before the council. Cole couldn't help the glee that shone in his eyes.

His timing had been perfect.

"Uncle Harold?" Jeremiah breathed, disbelief filling his voice.

Uncle Harold wasn't so lucky as Grandpa.

With Jeremiah still reeling in his seat, Cole leapt from his own and accepted the branding iron.

Never before had a branding felt so satisfying as he pressed the hot metal into Uncle Harold's neck. The man screamed, begging for mercy. His fingers clawed at the stones beneath him. As Cole pulled the iron away, the man collapsed onto the ground.

As his followers around him leapt to the catwalk to drag Harold to the below, Cole turned to Jeremiah, meeting his eyes.

The look of realization started growing in Jeremiah's face.

Once the walkway cleared, Cole returned the iron and flew back to his seat.

Jeremiah didn't say a word, just stared at the stones of the catwalk. Cole sat silently, relishing in the sweet feeling of justice.

Harold was followed by close friend Tom, followed by former co-worker Di. Followed by second-cousin Catherine.

"What have you done?" Jeremiah finally breathed, his voice sounding on the verge of cracking. Cole smiled when he observed Jeremiah's quaking hands.

"I warned you," Cole said calmly as he watched the next person being escorted to stand before the council. "You should have left her alone."

"And this is your revenge?" Jeremiah's voice did finally crack. A small whimper escaped his throat when he looked at the woman before them.

37

Even with her face covered, there was no mistaking this was the woman Cole had let burn for just a bit too long in the fire.

Jeremiah's daughter.

"You didn't," Jeremiah barely managed to make his voice work.

"I did," Cole said, swallowing the lump that formed in his throat.

"You've taken them all," he said. "Everyone I cared about."

"Do you understand what regret feels like now, my brother?" Cole said quietly. All of his insides felt very still as this woman's life started to be read.

Jeremiah didn't respond.

All the more regret filled Cole, accompanied by surprise, as this woman's deeds were read aloud.

He wasn't expecting to have to brand her.

Everything within him felt heavy as he gave a beat of his wings and landed on the walkway besides her. Accepting the branding iron, Cole turned toward the woman. As if on instinct, she shrank to her hands and knees, letting her blond hair fall from her neck.

He'd never felt anything but glee and satisfaction before when he branded someone. But then he felt only dead.

She screamed. They always screamed. Taking a quivering breath, Cole pulled the iron from her skin and threw it out into the air, where it turned over for just a moment, and then fell to the below.

Taking one of her hands in his, Cole helped her to her feet. Daring further wrath from those around him, he pinched the white fabric between two of his fingers and pulled the sack from her head.

"You," she breathed.

Cole stilled as his eyes met hers, green quickly fading to black.

"I didn't think you were real," she breathed. Her entire body shook from pain and fear.

"All too real now, I'm afraid," he said simply. He then turned and took his position again.

Cole didn't even care about all the hard and confused expressions his fellow leaders gave him when he returned. There was a pause for just a moment, everyone debating if this was the time to rebuke Cole for his continuing erratic behavior.

"Cambria Blake," the blue-eyed leader finally spoke, moving on. "Judgment has been placed."

Cole squeezed his eyes as the masses leapt at this woman. He tried not to wonder if, had he not taken her before it was her time, if she might have turned the scrolls of her life around.

Jeremiah sat very still next to Cole, as still as the stone he sat on.

"I won't bother her again," he finally said as the council started to leave. "It seems you deserve your position after all."

And then Jeremiah jumped into the below.

Cole closed his eyes again. He heard the whispers, felt the eyes flickering to his face. It was only guessing, but for the most part those guesses were correct.

And just like that, Cole had gained all respect back. He was a man to be feared again, a man none of them would challenge.

Cole was tempted to go below and seek out Cambria, thought about forming some kind of apology. But he would wait until she had reunited with her father.

Finally Cole thought about Jeremiah's promise. He no longer had to worry about his brother harming Jessica, about him exposing Jessica for what she had become. He didn't have to avenge her any longer.

But he knew he hadn't seen the last of her. Everything within him told him that somehow he was going to continue helping her.

Cole was not a good man, hadn't been in centuries. But there was something about Jessica. Something only she was able to dig out inside of him. Jessica… believed in him almost. But Cole was in his position for a reason. He wanted people to suffer generally. He enjoyed giving people what was coming to them.

But why did he want to help her? And help her to be with another man?

He resented her for making him question himself.
He hardly knew who he was anymore.

But here await me,
and comfort thy dejected spirit and feed on good hope,
for I will not leave thee in the nether world.
- Canto VIII, Inferno, Dante

Talk flew around the afterlife like gnats in the air. You couldn't move around without walking into some of it and breathing it in, causing you to choke.

Already a new exalted leader was being talked about. And Cole had heard the whispers about another.

Things were going to get complicated, very fast.

Cole was relieved when he felt the pull for a trial. He needed a distraction. He didn't want to be thinking about helping Jessica anymore right then.

Cole settled into his seat, only feeling slightly tense as Jeremiah settled into his. They hadn't uttered a single word to each other since Jeremiah found out Cole had eliminated much of his family from the world of the living.

"Sally Thomas," Cole's head jerked up as the trial started. "The deeds of your life have been accounted for and judgment will be passed. Your actions must be made known."

Had he been paying attention, Cole might have recognized the tiny frame, the tense shoulders. Even though her face was covered, he should have known her.

He had tried to convince her to kill herself once. And then tried to return and finish the job when she failed.

Sal stood there, her hands trembling where they were bound before her. She whimpered quietly, words sounding like "what's happening" stumbling out of her mouth.

Jessica was going to be devastated.

She didn't need one more horrible thing going on right now. She was already going to be losing the person who meant the most to her. She didn't need to be losing the person who meant second most.

Cole shook his head in frustration.

Why did he *care*?

Thousands of his brethren flooded the cylinder and Sal's cries increased.

"Sally Thomas, your deeds will now be revealed," Richard continued. Unraveling the scrolls of Sal's life, it was immediately obvious where she was going.

Mixes of boredom and interest piqued as the acts of her life were read. Every one of the condemned started zoning everything out, nothing of interest having taken place in her life. The list they got excited by was very short.

All the more whispers started going around the cylinder as Sal's good deeds were read. People who lead lives as good as Sal's didn't come around very often. Even if she hadn't really had any other choice when she was alive.

Judgment started being passed.

43

"Up," started the blue-eyed leader.

"Up," sentenced the next.

"Up," agreed the rest of their kind.

So did every one of the rest of them.

Richard smiled as he moved on. "Sally Thomas, judgment has been placed."

A scream ripped from her throat as a set of wings sprung from her back. She collapsed onto her hands and knees, the white sack sliding from her head as it hung between her shoulders.

A few exalted fluttered down to the walkway, lifting underneath Sal's arms, helping the woman to her feet. Their whispers of calm and assurance were enough to make Cole's stomach churn.

How could they stand being so… pure?

The cylinder started to buzz with talk again, excitement building in the tone of the masses.

"Sally Thomas," the exalted leader began again. "It seems you are being put up for election. The masses are being heard. Do you understand what has happened to you?"

Sal finally looked up again. Her eyes hesitated on Cole's face for a brief moment, her face blanching. But then her eyes slid to meet her leader. "I've died," she said, her voice shaking. "I understand that much."

"And you understand judgment?" he asked in a reassuring voice.

Sal nodded.

44

"Those around you are calling for a vote. The leadership here shifts, changes. People who lived a life like yours don't come around very often. Will you accept this position should the vote be granted?"

"I..." she stuttered, turning to look at these who surrounded her. "I don't know."

"You'll know soon enough," he said. "All those in favor of Sally Thomas joining the exalted council?"

The afterlife rumbled with replies of "I."

"All those opposed?"

A few replies fell flat against the hot stones.

"Just like that?" one of the exalted leaders hissed. Cole felt a twitch of a smile curl in the corner of his lips. "You would replace me just like that? When she isn't even sure if she wants this?"

"We will let her observe," the leader said, rubbing his hand over his bearded chin. "She can watch and learn what we do. Should she decide to decline, your position will be reconsidered."

Seeing that this council and voting was coming to an end, more of the blue-eyed's flocked around Sal, preparing to escort her to the above.

"Thank you," Sal managed to say. Once more her eyes flicked to Cole's face. He simply gave her a single nod before being taken to a place he could never go.

Being in the afterlife these days felt like standing on shifting sand.

"Necessity brings him here, not pleasure."
- Canto XII, Inferno, Dante

The seats of the changing council were all anyone could talk about. Deliberation seemed to be the only language the dead could use anymore. Sal's position on the council seemed more and more sure. Cole's remained to be seen.

But there was one person everyone in the afterlife seemed set on.

The one angel who wasn't there, yet was supposed to be.

Alex was all everyone could talk about. Most were anxious to have him pulled back, for him to return to their world and assume the position wanted of him. Yet Cole heard hushed whispers. Whispers about proxies and debts.

He didn't understand that part.

But he did understand one thing. Alex was going back to his world. Soon.

Cole felt the pull but didn't have to move. He was already seated. He wasn't the most active being those days.

It wasn't always easy to recognize a proxy. Most people who came into the cylinder were terrified. Most times the proxies were that way too. But there were times when one would seem just a tad too calm, knew just a little too well where exactly to stand.

And he recognized that curved form. He'd let his lips trail from that shoulder up to that hidden neck. He'd traced those legs with his fingertips, even if it wasn't the body he'd wanted, it was body he could still appreciate.

He'd invaded that head before.

But he also knew what Emily had done in her past, that she hadn't been allowed to return to his world because of it. Yet here she was again.

Interesting.

Seeing that none of the other council noticed anything different about "Morgan Denner" before them, Cole turned his eyes to the walls around them.

Cormack wasn't hard to spot among the masses. He sat with his legs hanging over the edge of the staircase, his head inclined forward, his burning blue eyes both sad and hopeful at the same time.

What a fool. Falling in love with a girl from the world of the living.

Cole chuckled at his hypocrisy silently. They were both fools.

The scrolls of Morgan's life were read, Cole didn't want to feel bad for what he knew was coming in a few moments.

"Down," the exalted sentenced.

"Down," his fellow men condemned.

Cole hesitated for a moment. Emily's head had turned in his direction. He sensed the fear she felt yet there was something bordering on confidence coming off of her.

"Down," he finally breathed.

The heckles and cries erupted throughout the cylinder. Trying not to feel anything, Cole joined Emily on the catwalk and accepted the branding iron. Emily dutifully fell to her hands and knees, exposing the back of her neck.

"Welcome back," Cole whispered so quietly only Emily could hear.

Her screams echoed off the walls as he sank the red hot iron into the back of her neck.

"...Let us descend into the blind world."
- Canto IV, Inferno, Dante

"You're different than I thought you would be."

Cole turned where he was seated along the walkway and saw Cambria ascending toward him, her glorious wings trailing behind her. He didn't say anything as he watched her sit just two stairs below him.

"I expected you to be more... bad," she said as she stared down into the flames with him.

Cole gave an empty chuckle, his eyes never lifting. "Apparently you've forgotten what I did to you."

"Trust me, I haven't forgotten," she said with a laugh. It reminded him of the bells his mother put out on Christmas. "There's no way of forgetting death in this place."

"So you still don't t think I'm bad?" Cole asked hollowly. Honestly he didn't really care.

"You seem to deserve your position," she said as she rested her elbows on her knees. "But I almost don't believe you want this position."

"I haven't the faintest idea what I want anymore," he replied honestly.

"Yes you do," she said quietly. "You just can't have it. And you don't know how to deal with that."

49

Cole glanced over at Cambria, his eyes studying her strong features, her sunlit hair. "Some of us aren't meant to ever have what we want in life," he said.

"And sometimes we need to learn to let go of the things we want but can't have," her black eyes seemed to dance as she looked into Cole's.

Cole reached up and traced his fingertips along her cheek bone, letting his eyes trace her glowing skin unabashedly. He let his fingers fall to her lips, his eyes lingering there for a long moment. For a moment, he wondered what they might feel like against his.

He suddenly sat back up, his hand falling from her face.

"Thank you," he said, his voice a little firmer than he had meant it to be.

"For what?" she asked, her face slightly dazed looking at his sudden change of mood.

"For making me forget for a moment."

"A moment is better than never at all," Cambria said as she stood. Without another word, she turned and descended into the heat below.

*"Here one must leave behind all hesitation;
here every cowardice must meet its death."*
- Canto III, Inferno, Dante

Things had gotten so totally and completely out of control.

He'd seen Jessica, twice, among those along the wall. What she was doing, he had no idea. But being there, she was in more danger than she could possibly imagine.

Time had run out. The entire afterlife knew it. There were only moments left.

All had gathered, the staircase crowded with his brethren. They waited anxiously for Alex's return, for him to finally meet his fate.

Cole's stomach felt hollow. He'd always believed Jessica would figure out a way to save him, to somehow beat the afterlife.

But yet again the afterlife was going to win.

The air shifted and grew colder. Everyone shifted where they sat or stood, leaning forward in anticipation.

A cry echoed throughout the stones, barely audible at first, growing in volume quickly. It seemed to fill the air between and around each of them. And just when Cole thought the sound would drive him mad, Alex suddenly appeared before them and instantly collapsed onto his hands and knees.

All fell silent in that instant, as if this moment weren't quite real, as if Alex himself were an apparition that might vanish at any moment.

Suddenly, Alex's head snapped up, his gray eyes falling on the council.

"No," he breathed, his eyes hardening. "I won't stay here."

The afterlife suddenly erupted, some cheering, some hissing and calling words that helped earn them the brands on the backs of their necks.

"It is your time," the exalted leader started.

"I cannot stay," Alex said as he slowly rose to his feet. "Not when Jessica is still there unprotected from him." Alex's hand rose to point directly at Jeremiah.

"Explain yourself," the leader said, his eyes narrowing, growing stormy.

Alex's eyes shifted from Jeremiah's face, to the leaders, and then to Cole's. They stared at each other for a long moment, a million unconnected words passing between them. Cole gave the smallest of nods.

"He's been back in the world of the living, trying to bring death to the woman I saved," Alex condemned.

"Liar!" Jeremiah shouted, pounding his fist on his stone armrest. Small cracks formed on its surface.

"You had better have some explanation for us brother," Richard said, turning hard eyes on Jeremiah. "You understand it is forbidden to return to their world, to cause harm to any of them."

"He lies!" Jeremiah bellowed. "The man simply wishes to fight his fate."

"No," Cole interrupted, his insides turning hard. "What the boy says is the truth. Our brother has been back, has tried to take the woman's life."

"As has our leader!" Jeremiah accused, turning burning eyes on Cole. "As punishment he eradicated my entire living family!"

Shouts broke out, among those around them, and those on the council. The accusations a few exalted made from the walls around them were enough to drive Jeremiah at their throats. Literally.

With madness and death in their eyes, a few of his kind dove at Alex, determined to drag him below without a trial even. The blue eyed's dove as well, fighting and clawing at each other in the air as they collided with the walkway. The new conveyor who had replaced Cormack sprinted out from the tunnel, his fist instantly colliding with the jaw of one trying to get to Alex.

A circle formed around Alex, determined to protect their new leader from the vengefulness of the condemned.

A smile curled in the corner of Cole's mouth. He had to give it to Alex. It took a lot to cause a war like this in the afterlife.

The black-eyed council member to his right leaned toward Cole. "It's been nice serving with you, brother," he hissed.

"Oh, this isn't over yet," Cole said in a low voice.

"Enough!" Cole and the blue eyed leader bellowed at the same time.

The entire afterlife fell silent. Finally.

"That is enough," Richard repeated. "You will all calm yourselves and let the proceedings go as usual. I will not have a war starting under my watch."

Roughly shoving another man away, Jeremiah finally returned to his seat. Cole felt his entire frame tense as they sat side by side. Cole felt on edge. Something big was about to happen and he didn't need Jeremiah making things crash and burn.

"You, my boy, have caused a great deal of stir around here," Richard said in a voice filled with authority. "The voices of most have been heard. Can you tell what is happening here lately?"

Cole did feel a little satisfied snake curl up in him as things were explained to Alex, what was wanted of him, that he couldn't go back. The chaos around them attempted to pick back up and died again and Cole knew it was coming before Richard even spoke.

"Alex Wright," he began. "The deeds of your life have been accounted for and judgment will be passed. Your actions must be made known."

"No!" Cole heard the scream from the masses around him. Prickles flashed along his skin. He knew that voice all too well.

And then she landed on the catwalk, looking fierce and ready to fight with every living cell of her body.

"No," Jessica breathed again, her eyes burning. "You cannot take him."

Cole couldn't help the grin that spread on his face.

This was nowhere near over yet.

"...and when he had moved on, I entered along the deep
and savage road."
- Canto II, Inferno, Dante

Cole closed his eyes for a moment, simply breathing in and out. He could feel her, with everything in him, he could still feel her.

Jessica.

So close yet so far away from him now.

She wouldn't be coming back to his world for a long while now. She'd finally escaped them, for a full human lifetime. She'd gotten the help she needed and she'd been cured of the disease that infected her body.

He'd watched her. A part of him needed proof that she wasn't coming back, that she truly was gone for good. He had to finally admit that she was when he saw that she was again aging.

There would be no more chasing Jessica, no more holding out hope that someday, maybe someday...

Cole opened his eyes when he heard the rustling of feathers. Thousands upon thousands of beings flooded the cylinder, every pair of eyes resting upon him where he stood there on the stone walkway.

Not a word was spoken as they watched him. Today Cole would finally learn his fate.

It was his election date.

The council drifted into their seats, some new faces, some he had served with for over a century.

Cole couldn't help feeling smug that Jeremiah's face was not among them.

He turned to meet their eyes, resting on the blue-eyed leader's face. They stared at each other for a long moment, memories becoming a blur of time that was endless. They'd served with each other for a long time, they knew each other like brother's.

"The fate of our brother rests in your hands," he finally began, tearing his eyes from Cole to search the masses. "You all know what he's done, how he's broken our laws. You've all see how he's lead the condemned. You must all decide now if he is to continue his leadership."

Cole's eyes fell to the ground for a moment. The last year had filled him full of so much doubt and fear and a million other things he didn't think he was capable of feeling any longer. Somewhere along the way he had forgotten who he was.

His eyes lifted to those along the wall, instantly meeting a familiar face. Cambria met his eyes strong, her chin lifting just slightly.

Something stirred in Cole's stomach. Something felt hungry and greedy.

Cole may not have been able to pursue Jessica any longer. But he finally realized he no longer wanted to chase after a ghost.

Jessica was not the end of all things.

There was something sitting right in front of him that maybe Cole did want. There was a position that proved Cole was not worthless and was not soft and weak and a sad broken being.

He stood a little straighter, his eyes focused on Cambria's for another moment, before looking at his brethren and sisters. They each studied him in the quiet that filled the cylinder.

"All those in favor of Cole Emerson continuing his leadership of the condemned and the condemned council?" the re-elected, blue-eyed leader finally spoke in a voice filled with power.

There was a fraction of a moment where the afterlife's residents hesitated, considering where they wished to pledge their allegiance to.

"I," the echoes finally boomed, loud enough to make the stones beneath his feet quake.

Cole felt his insides re-harden in a familiar way and the corner of his mouth twitched.

"All those opposed?"

Only a few scattered, weak sounding voices fell flat in the air.

Cole met Cambria's black eyes again, his eyes smoldering as he looked up at her from under his black lashes. A twisted smile curled on each of their faces.

"Welcome back to the council, brother," Richard said.

This was who Cole was. He was not a good man, never had been and never would be. He'd changed this last year, but he would always be the selfish man who did what he wanted, who valued his non-life over everyone else's. Cole was the man who had fought his own branding and then branded thousands of others throughout the centuries.

Being the leader of the damned was who he was.

And it felt so satisfying to be at it again.

"It's good to be back."

ACKNOWLEDGEMENTS

Wow, this is it, the Fall of Angels is really over! This has been an incredible journey, these last two and a half years. And I really couldn't have done it without the incredible support I've received. I first have to thank my husband Justin for his never ending support, for always listening to my endless talk about writing stuff. Next I have to thank Jenni Merritt, for her unending support and encouragement. Thank you to my editor, Steven. And thank you to every one of my readers, you really do mean so much to me, there are just too many people to thank to begin to list. Thank you all for allowing me to live my dream!

KEARY TAYLOR is the independent author of BRANDED, FORSAKEN, VINDICATED, AFTERLIFE (*Fall of Angels* series), and EDEN. She lives on a tiny island in the Pacific Northwest with her husband and their two young children. To learn more about Keary and her writing process, please visit
www.KearyTaylor.com
or
http://KearyTaylor.blogspot.com

Don't miss the action packed post-apocalyptic novel by
Keary Taylor

Available Now!

*Eve knew the stories of the Fall, of a time before she wandered into the
colony of Eden, unable to recall anything but her name. She's seen the
aftermath of the technology that infused human DNA with cybernetic
matter, able to grow new organs and limbs, how it evolved out of
control. The machine took over and the soul vanished. A world quickly
losing its humanity isn't just a story to her though. At eighteen, this
world is Eve's reality.*

*In their Fallen world, love feels like a selfish luxury, but not
understanding what it is makes it difficult to choose between West, who
makes her feel alive but keeps too many secrets, and Avian, who has
always been there for her, but is seven years her senior.*

*The technology wants to spread and it won't stop until there is no new
flesh to assimilate. With only two percent of the human population left,
mankind is on the brink of extinction. While fighting to keep Eden alive,
Eve will discover that being human is about what you will do for those
you love, not what your insides may be made of. And even if it gets you
killed, love is always what separates them from the Fallen.*

Taylor, Keary.
Vindicated

MAY   2013

22321727R00221

Made in the USA
Lexington, KY
24 April 2013